HAROLD'S WILL

—————— GREG ROYER ——————

 FriesenPress

One Printers Way
Altona, MB R0G 0B0
Canada

www.friesenpress.com

ISBN
978-1-03-918382-7 (Hardcover)
978-1-03-918381-0 (Paperback)
978-1-03-918383-4 (eBook)

1. FICTION, FAMILY LIFE

Distributed to the trade by The Ingram Book Company

Dedicated to those like me
who wonder

"The only source of knowledge is experience."

Albert Einstein

CHAPTER ONE

There was nothing about this man, lying face down in the dirt, that would give anyone the slightest hint of who he was, of the things that he had accomplished. The expensive winter clothes were dirty, tattered, and torn from the abuse they had recently suffered because of the devastatingly stupid decisions of the man who wore them. The man and his clothes had acquired the pungent smell of ammonia that comes with the accumulation of urine, feces, and sweat. He was unshaven and unwashed. The simple act of standing under a shower was hard for him to recall and something, he acknowledged, he might never experience again.

In his present state, the mere act of standing, of which he had done little in recent days, was something that he wasn't sure he could sustain for any significant length of time. Walking seemed completely out of reach. The blood from his injuries had mixed with the dirt that surrounded him, caking in his hair, on his skin, and his torn and tattered clothes. His broken bones had made life tedious, but had not yet killed him. At this point, they still might.

In what now felt like a different lifetime, he had built a thriving business, raised a family, and distinguished himself as a philanthropist who cared deeply for his community. His wife and children loved and respected him, his staff looked up to him, and the community revered him.

Now, in what should be the best years of his life, he was alone, lying in the filth and dirt that had become his home. He wondered how, after decades of being the man he aspired to be, he had so easily lost his way. Was the fear of death that compelling? Was fifty years not enough to remove the shame and guilt of his childhood?

On this day, he would have one chance at redemption, one opportunity to fix what he had broken. The word "impossible" had been uttered by many, but not yet by his family, and not yet by him.

Suddenly, he was fully awake, completely aware of every feeling that he was experiencing. The grinding in his stomach, driven by the fear that he won't make it, overrode all other feelings. The physical and emotional pain, the anxiety about the trials that he would face today, and even the guilt from his past were all subservient to the overwhelming fear of not making it home.

The sun had not yet risen; he did not take the time or energy to check what the clock said. It was not important. He painfully pulled himself into a sitting position and began what could prove to be an impossible journey home.

CHAPTER TWO

Nine Days Earlier

It was Monday morning at 5:00 a.m. Harold was sitting in the leather chair in his study, wearing the dark blue dress pants, light blue dress shirt, and blue tweed sports jacket that had been his workday attire for most of his adult life, reading through his last will and testament. He was proud of the document; and he had convinced himself that upon his death, it would provide a carefree transition and long-term security for his family. This, he believed, was a document that would convey what he felt was important in life and would make certain future generations of his family would enjoy the fruits of his hard work and good fortune, without having to go through tough times themselves. This would ensure that his family would not have to make the tough decisions that could drive a wedge into otherwise strong relationships.

Harold had not taken the time to talk with his family about the will. They had never experienced what he had, and they would not understand. It would be better to let them take the time after his death to recognize the value that this document would provide for their future without him.

The driving force behind this will was Harold's upcoming sixty-fourth birthday, which was only nine days away. Harold had always been and was still the picture of health. He was on no medications, didn't suffer from high blood pressure, drank moderately, ate healthy food, exercised regularly, and had the heart of a forty-five-year-old man. His only medical issue was a higher-than-normal cholesterol level, which the doctors had failed to control due to his lack of tolerance for statins.

Harold's interest in his upcoming birthday was fuelled by his father, who had dropped dead from a massive heart attack one week after his sixty-fourth birthday. His father had also suffered from high levels of cholesterol. However, he had also been a heavy drinker and smoker, had been badly overweight, and had apparently been allergic to any form of exercise. It could be argued that he had driven himself to an early grave. So, it was reasonable that Harold's doctors were only mildly concerned about the fact Harold had inherited his father's high cholesterol.

Harold's lifestyle gave his doctors the luxury of partially ignoring his family history. But ignoring it was not so easy for Harold, who, with his mother and brother, had watched his father drop dead at the dinner table from a heart attack commonly known as a widowmaker, the sudden nearly complete blockage of the left ventricle artery. Watching your father drop dead in the middle of a meal has a way of sticking with you, no matter what the doctors say.

While Harold acknowledged that his lifestyle reduced his chances of experiencing a widowmaker, it certainly did not eliminate them. And it wasn't just the heart issue. Harold knew neither he nor the doctors could control when he was going to die. Hell, he could get hit by a truck walking out of the doctor's office.

The will wasn't going to stop him from dying, but it would stop him from dying unprepared and leaving behind a family and loved ones who were ill-prepared to deal with the many issues that Harold, in the last few weeks, had decided were his responsibility to handle for them. Another discussion that he had not bothered to have with his wife or family.

When his father had died, the family was left in shambles. His father's lack of planning and foresight had created massive and ongoing problems for the loved ones he had left behind. Harold's mother had always trusted his father to take care of all their financial issues and was completely unaware of the three mortgages on their house, the mountain of unpaid bills, and the money he had borrowed from their friends and family. Of course, she had signed off on the mortgages, but she had never read them and had not realized there were three completely *different* mortgages that added up to more than the value of the house. She had been told by her husband they were simply renewals, and she had chosen not to check.

Harold's mother lost her home, had no job skills, and had no way to get out from under the debt Harold's father had left for her to deal with other than to declare personal bankruptcy, which she could not bring herself to do. Because of his father, Harold, his mother, and his younger brother spent the next five years paying off the debts, repairing relationships with friends and family who felt that they had been lied to and swindled, and getting his mother financially re-established so she could enjoy her retirement years.

Harold, in contrast, had no debt, had made no promises he could not keep, and would leave his family with significant financial resources. He would ensure that when he was gone, everything would be taken care of through the appropriate use of these resources. His loved ones could live in comfort without the concern for financial security. There would be no complications, no unpayable taxes, and no need to sell the family home or live with relatives who never missed an opportunity to point out their generosity. Businesses would not be destroyed; jobs would not be lost. Harold's loved ones, he would make sure, could go on living life as if nothing had changed.

As Harold sat there patting himself on the back for his efforts in creating what he now considered a wonderful document, his mind wandered off to his childhood friend, Mark.

Harold's brow furrowed at the thought of Mark, who had lived a troubled life filled with a variety of addictions and personal turmoil that repeated visits to rehabilitation centres had not helped. In the end, only weeks ago, Mark had taken his own life at sixty-three. Harold had tried to help, quietly paying for many of Mark's reoccurring visits to rehab. He had once even tried to rekindle the relationship they had shared as young teens, but Mark's inability to deal with his past caused Harold to fear being dragged into Mark's world of self-degradation and self-hatred.

Shifting his mind back to the present, Harold decided his lawyer should complete the will and prepare it for execution. But Harold never took the time to fully consider what was driving this dramatic change in direction, or why he was in such a hurry, or why talking to his wife about the will was completely out of the question. He had convinced himself that the contents of this will were exactly what was needed for everyone involved.

CHAPTER THREE

Three hours later, Harold was sitting in his five-year-old silver-grey BMW in the underground parking structure below his brother Jerry's office in downtown Calgary. He was already late for their meeting, but the presence he felt in the car with him was overwhelming. A presence so powerful Harold felt that if he spoke, he could expect an answer. It was not something that frightened Harold; he was certain it was not real, but the perceived reality of it intrigued him. He shook off the feeling and headed upstairs.

Harold was incredibly close to Jerry, even though Jerry was six years younger. Jerry was successful in his own right. He had translated an architectural degree into a significant design company that had designed commercial and office buildings across Canada, including several of Harold's buildings. Thanks to their individual success in business, Harold and Jerry had put together a charitable foundation focused on the youth of what people liked to call "underserved" communities.

They had named the foundation after their mother, Margaret Mary Bower, partly in honour of what she had gone through when their father died and partly to have a good excuse to spend some time with her. Although, in the last few years, their mom's dementia had made it impossible to include her in the foundation's business. The foundation was not large, but it was growing, and it had done some good things for some good people who had not caught a lot of breaks in their lives.

Jerry's office was on the thirtieth floor, and Harold reflected on the presence as he went up. He had first noticed the presence shortly

7

after he had heard the news about Mark and about the same time that he had started working with Shane, his lawyer and friend, on his new last will and testament.

This was also not the first time he had felt an odd presence in his life. It had been an almost constant companion during the months that surrounded Mark and his family moving out of town when Harold was fourteen. During that time, Harold's emotions, especially the negative ones, had often overwhelmed him. He had spent a lot of time in his room alone, and his mom had spent a lot of time apologizing for him. Harold's mom had been certain that losing such a close friend had been the cause of Harold's behaviour and moods. She had been convinced that when Harold found a new friend, everything would get back to normal, but Harold had never found another friend, at least not a friend like Mark. The feeling of a presence had happened less and less and had eventually stopped entirely, but it would be well over a decade before he let himself get close to anyone.

When his father had died, Harold had got worse. He had treated the friends and family that were owed money like they were strangers. He had committed to repaying them and set about doing exactly that and no more. Even the people who had insisted they did not need to be repaid received their money. Harold and his mother had insisted on it. He had not wanted him or his family to owe anything to anyone. His actions had been kind and considerate, but he had been cold and calculating.

He had finally begun to change when he had gone to work for Fred Bannister, which, through an unusual set of circumstances, had led to his courtship and marriage to Nancy. Fred, a kind and generous man who everyone loved, had helped Harold understand that he needed to make the decision to either change or accept that Nancy, or someone like her, was never going to be a part of his life.

Recognizing the pain that he was going to experience if he lost Nancy, he had decided to do everything he could to be the man he assumed she expected him to be, the man he believed she deserved. He had been determined to be a good husband, a good father, a good friend, and a trusted employee. And through daily effort and commitment, Harold changed.

He decided that smiles were like underwear—you shouldn't go walking around without them. The more he smiled, the better other people seemed to feel, and he liked that. He practised listening, really listening to the people around him, which, to his surprise, made people around him feel valued. Finally, he decided to talk. It didn't have to be much. He responded to questions, he started conversations, and he asked people to tell him about their life. He smiled, he listened, and he talked.

For over thirty years, Harold had been pretty comfortable with this version of who he was. It worked for him, and it had worked for the people that he loved. Anger, frustration, and moodiness were simply no longer tolerated in his life. Harold saw them as signs of weakness, and so did Nancy. They were a perfect match.

Now, as he rode up thirty floors in the elevator, he wondered why the presence was back, why the mood swings had started again, and why he suddenly found it difficult to control his emotions. All of it was unacceptable, and he needed to get it all under control, and soon. These were not the feelings and actions of the man Harold expected himself to be.

CHAPTER FOUR

"Christ, you look older every time I see you," was the greeting Harold received from his smiling brother as he walked into the office. That and a big bear hug.

"Fuck you! You wish you looked as young as I do," Harold replied with a correspondingly big smile.

"I don't know, old man, just about sixty-four. And you know sixty-four is not a great age for the men in our family," Jerry shot back, having absolutely no idea of Harold's sensitivity to the subject.

"Now that's low, comparing me to a man who ate, smoked, and drank himself to death." Harold could not bring himself to share his paranoia with Jerry or anyone else. "The only exercise our father ever got was walking to the fridge for another beer. And looking at you makes me think that the next time you get up to grab a beer, you should walk right past the fridge and head for that fancy gym you put in your house instead. I would be happy to come over and show you where it is."

Jerry, who was definitely a little thicker around the mid-section than Harold but was easily in at least as good physical condition, put his hands on the side of his stomach, laughed, and said, "All muscle, my friend. All muscle. And I wasn't referring to your heart. As old and decrepit as you are, your heart is probably still in pretty good shape, with all the boring wholesome living that you insist on. I was referring to the chances of you dying in an industrial accident. You're pretty fucking accident-prone."

"Oh, my God, what a dick! A guy has a little run-in with a forklift thirty years ago, and you have to hear bad jokes about it for the rest of your life. It wasn't even my fault. The forklift driver took a sudden unexpected turn. You should talk. You're probably going to die of lead poisoning from continually stabbing yourself with pencils."

Jerry laughed and responded, "Christ, Harold! I was six. You were thirty. You can't compare the two."

Harold laughed. "I can, and I did," he said as he sat down in the chair across from Jerry's desk, signalling the end of the chit-chat. "So, what are we talking about today? Is this a chew-the fat, tell-me-about-your-latest-escapades meeting, or is there something impor- tant that we need to discuss?"

"What the fuck? Are you suggesting my adventures aren't impor- tant? Harold, these 'escapades,' as you call them, are what life's all about. You would do well to find some time in your schedule to join me. A couple of us are heading to Vegas to see Celine Dion and have a little fun. Nothing Nancy would disapprove of. Why don't you join us?" The last part Jerry meant.

"Hmm, let me think. Go to Vegas, eat too much, drink too much, throw away some money at the blackjack table, and fight my way through a crowd to listen to someone I don't even listen to on the radio. Sounds less like fun and more like torture. I think I'll pass," Harold responded.

"Christ, man, you are way too young to be this set in your ways. You really need to chill out and learn to enjoy the finer things in life," Jerry responded in that joking-but-not-joking voice we all have.

"Wow, I don't think that I've ever heard anyone refer to Vegas as one of the finer things in life. But I'll tell you what, if you cut back on the trips to the beer fridge, I'll have more fun."

"Sounds like a deal to me. I prefer wine and rum and Coke anyway," responded Jerry with a giant grin.

"Fuck you," laughed Harold. "So, what did you drag me over here for?"

"Oh yeah, sorry," Jerry said as he grabbed a file and pushed it across the desk toward Harold. "The foundation. I wanted to talk with you about some ideas that I had for the foundation and how we could go about funding them."

The Margaret Mary Bower Foundation had been around for about ten years, and every year, both Harold and Jerry would put more money in. They had agreed on the amount that each would put in this year, but as Harold looked at the numbers in the plan Jerry had handed him, it appeared Jerry wanted the number to be a lot bigger.

"Those are some pretty big numbers. How are you expecting to fund all that?" Harold asked.

"I've spoken with a couple of other people with small foundations and they're interested in covering some of it, but the majority would have to come from you and me. It's not a small amount of money, but unless you've recently developed a cocaine or gambling problem, I know you can afford it. Please don't tell me that your youthful figure comes from the excessive use of cocaine. That's really going to put a dent in my admiration for you."

Harold looked at his young brother, thought for a moment about how much Jerry loved to talk, and then responded, "I think I mentioned it before, but fuck you." He paused for effect. "And it's not a matter of what *we*, remember it's Nancy's money too, can or cannot afford—it's about whether this is a good way to approach supporting the work the foundation pays for. We want to make damn sure that it's not a one-and-done thing. We want it to be sustainable."

Harold had no intention of telling his brother the real reason for his reluctance. One of the key items in the new will that Harold was having written was a very large one-time donation to the foundation. Given his concern that the will might very well come into effect in the near future, he did not want to double down on the donation and significantly reduce the amount left for his family.

Exactly how would that conversation go? I'm planning to die in the next few months. Yes, I understand I'm being totally illogical, but it's my paranoia and my money, so let me deal with it as I choose.

The answer, for right now at least, was quite easy. Harold really believed it was Nancy's money just as much as it was his, and he would never make this big of a decision without discussing it at length with her. "Let me go over this with Nancy and see what she thinks."

"Of course, but what do you think of the proposal in principle?" Jerry asked.

Harold smiled. "Come on, Jerry. You know me better than that. I'm not going to tell you what I think and then discuss it with Nancy. What I think isn't relevant. What *we* think is what we'll do. I'll let you know when Nancy and I have had a chance to talk and agree on how we'd like to proceed."

Jerry laughed. "Fuck, Harold. You're the only guy I know that can say, 'I have to ask my wife,' and still sound tough. Of course, I'll wait for you and Nancy to discuss how you'd like to proceed. You're right. It's not a small amount of money."

"Jerry, thanks for putting the proposal together. No matter what we decide, Nancy and I really appreciate all the effort you put into the foundation. Unless there's something else, I should get going. I have another meeting I need to get to."

"There's one other thing. I was up visiting Mom the other day, and she really wants someone to take her to church."

"Don't they have services every Sunday at the senior's home that she lives in?" Harold asked.

"They do, but they aren't Catholic services and she really wants to go to the church that she attended for thirty-some years."

"So, take her when you get back from Vegas. I'm sure they'll still let you in," Harold said, slapping Jerry lightly on the shoulder.

Jerry paused for a moment, knowing that the next part of this discussion was unlikely to go well.

"She'd really like you to take her. I don't know why, but it's really important to her."

Harold took a deep breath; he had dealt with this issue calmly for years, but at this moment, for reasons he did not understand, he found himself desperately trying to control his temper. He really did not need this shit at this moment in time. "Jerry, we've discussed this over and over. I don't know how I can make it any clearer to you and Mom, and anyone else who cares to listen. With the one and only exception of Mom's funeral, there is absolutely no way I will ever

13

step foot into a Catholic church again in my life. Not for you, and not for Mom."

"Come on, Harold. She's ninety-two years old. Grant her a dying wish—go to church with her. You don't have to embrace the church; just spend an hour in it for your mom."

"Sorry, Jerry, not going to happen," Harold replied, really hoping Jerry would drop it.

"For fuck's sake, Harold. Why do you have to be so fucking absolute about everything? Take the old lady to church. It won't kill you."

Harold stiffened. "You have no fucking idea what will or will not kill me, and I will not discuss this anymore, with you or anyone else. I have told you both that I'll go to her fucking funeral and if you keep pushing, I won't go to that either. For the last time, drop it. You want to go to that fucking church with Mom, you go right ahead, but I won't, and stop making her think I might."

Both Harold and Jerry were now standing, and the position that each was taking was viewed as completely unreasonable by the other.

"What is it with you? What happened to you? What could possibly make you hate the church so damn much that you won't even go there for the woman who raised you?"

"I've told you before that what happened is none of your damn business, and even if it were, it's not my story to tell. The only thing you need to know is you should keep your nose out of things that don't have anything to do with you."

"Well, this does affect me. Mom is constantly asking why you won't go to church and I don't know what to say."

"For Christ's sake, Jerry. You're a fucking grown-up. Tell her you don't know, or tell her whatever you want. Christ, her dementia is so bad you could tell her I'm an atheist and she wouldn't remember it twenty seconds later."

"Is that it? Are you an atheist now?"

"It's none of your fucking business what I am."

Harold turned and walked out of the office without saying goodbye. He hated acting this way in front of anyone, especially his brother, whom he loved unconditionally. Harold really was unhappy about the dementia comment. That was completely out of line. But, after all this time, Jerry should know better than to push Harold about the church. He knew how Harold felt and he knew that there were things that Harold wouldn't or couldn't talk about. Still, that was no excuse for his behaviour, and he knew it.

He silently admonished himself. *Pull yourself together. You can't let how you're feeling change who you are, not again, not now.*

He drove to his next meeting, forcing himself to calm down and promising himself to never repeat that behaviour. Not with Jerry, not with anyone. Some promises are easier to keep than others.

CHAPTER FIVE

Scientists say that the amygdala, the walnut-shaped part of our brain located in the temporal lobe, can give us the capacity to perform some pretty significant actions without focusing on them. This apparently includes driving a well-known route and having no memory of any part of the trip.

Harold's amygdala must have been hard at work on the drive back to his office because the rest of his brain was fully engaged in a daydream about the time when Mark and his family were about to move away.

"Well, I can't say that I'm sorry to see them go," Harold's father, Ted, said as he sat at the kitchen table, drinking his regular 5:00 p.m. beer. "Suddenly, there seems to be nothing but drama over there. Someone is always screaming at someone."

Harold's mom, Margaret, standing over the kitchen sink and peeling carrots for tonight's dinner, responded, "They've certainly had a difficult time in the last few months, but they've always been such nice people and they've always treated Harold like he was part of their family."

"Harold, what's going on with young Mark? The two of you used to be inseparable. Now I can't remember the last time I saw the two of you together," Ted remarked as he finished his beer and asked his wife to bring him another.

"I don't know. Why are you asking me? It's not my job to know what Mark is up to every minute of the day," Harold responded with a tone of voice that had recently become far too common as far as his dad and mom were concerned.

"Watch your mouth, young man. First of all, you don't talk to me in that manner, and second, I asked you a reasonable question. You can provide me with a reasonable response."

Harold did not lift his eyes from the paper he was looking at and responded in a tone only moderately less offensive. "I don't know what's going on with Mark. He hardly talks to me; he hardly talks to anyone. I think he just hates everybody and everything and can't wait to get out of this town. They don't even leave for another week, and today was his last day of school."

His dad pondered the information for a moment. "Pretty strange. I heard his dad doesn't even have a job to go to, and it doesn't appear that they've sold their house, at least not yet. It almost seems like they're skipping town, maybe a debt problem."

"Maybe, but I heard that Mark's dad was down at the church a lot a few weeks ago, shouting and carrying on about something. They even had a meeting with the bishop at one point. That seemed to settle things down for a while, but the next thing we hear is that they're moving to a different town almost immediately," Margaret remarked while continuing to prepare dinner.

"Christ, you gotta feel for these priests. Everyone bringing them their problems. I'm sure they do their best to help, but some people are just too proud or too stupid to accept help," Ted responded.

As these words were coming out of Harold's dad's mouth, Harold's face was turning red with anger. He stood up, slammed his textbook down on the table, then packed up his things and stormed out of the room. "Maybe they weren't lookin' for help. Maybe it wasn't help they wanted." Harold spat these words out like they were pieces of rotten food as he ran up the stairs, slamming his bedroom door behind him.

"What was that all about?" Ted asked as he finished his second beer.

"I don't know. Maybe he has whatever Mark has. He seems angry all the time but refuses to talk about it."

"Don't know why you bother to try. It's puberty. God damn teenage boys seem to all get crazy when they're going through puberty," Ted mused as he opened his third beer, which was delivered to him without him having to ask.

Puberty! thought Harold, overhearing his parents through the all-too-thin walls.

Years later, as the stories came out in dribs and drabs, and even after charges were filed, Mark and his family remained silent and so did Harold.

As Harold drove into the parking lot at his office, he was more than a little concerned that he remembered nothing about the drive from Jerry's office. What concerned him more was that he had originally had no intention of driving back to his office. He had a meeting with his lawyer and had intended to go there from Jerry's. Harold drove into the parking lot and right back out, feeling more than a little sheepish and hoping no one noticed him.

CHAPTER SIX

Shane Richards was one of Harold's oldest friends. They had known each other for close to thirty years, had gone on family vacations together, raised their children together, and the two couples had even gone to Europe together twice for bicycle and wine tours.

You simply could not ask for a better friend, and Harold thought the world of Shane. But, as close as the two of them were and as close as the families were, Shane was his lawyer first and his friend second. Harold treated Shane that way, and he expected Shane to treat him in the same manner. Shane was a total professional, and if there was ever a moment when he felt that his friendship with Harold interfered with his advice as a lawyer, he would have sent Harold to someone else immediately. So far, it had not come to that.

Today's meeting, which was taking place in the law firm's overly posh offices on the forty-fifth floor of the city's tallest office tower, was about business. Harold and Shane would start the meeting with casual conversation, and they would take the time to check on the health and well-being of each other's families. However, once they moved on to business, that was where it would stay and where both of them would expect it to stay.

"Hey, Harold. Always a pleasure to see you," Shane said as he ushered Harold into the office. "How are Nancy and the kids? Hopefully, dinner is still on next weekend. We've hardly seen you guys in the past year."

"It's been a little crazy, and there never seems to be enough time, but yes, dinner is still on, and we're all looking forward to it," Harold remarked as he walked into the office and sat down. "And Nancy and the kids are great. How about your family?"

"Everyone is great. Thanks for asking."

Having wasted time earlier driving around in a dream, Harold was pressing himself to catch up, so he sat down, opened his brief-case, and pulled out his laptop. Shane assumed Harold wanted to move on to the business at hand.

Shane sat down at his desk, turned to his computer, and opened a file. "I assume that you've read the will that we prepared for you as per your instructions. Before we get into the details, let's talk about whether it clearly represents what you want to happen with your wealth upon your death."

Harold was looking at his computer screen and did not look up at Shane as he spoke. "Most of it is exactly what I want, but I'm not sure that we've covered the multi-generational nature of the trust suffi-ciently. It specifically talks about the children of my grandchildren, but it seems to stop there. I want it to be clear that once my wealth goes into a trust for the benefit of Nancy and all our offspring, it never leaves that trust and that a professional trustee manages the trust in the manner that I've set out in the will."

Shane checked something on the computer screen, and then said, "Harold, the multi-generational issue is clearly specified in clause 12.01a."

Shane paused while Harold turned to the clause and carefully reviewed it, then looked up at Shane and said, "Yeah, okay, sorry, I missed that."

Pausing for a moment, Shane wondered if he should say what he was about to say. This will was not something that he would ever recommend to a client, and he was desperately trying to understand Harold's motivation. "I just want to say again that testamentary trusts are very tricky when they span multiple generations and deal with the type of detail that you have asked us to include in yours. They can be and often are challenged, but even if the trust isn't chal-lenged, you are making the decision to put your trust in a profes-sional manager rather than your family. Is that really what you want to do? Are you not concerned about how Nancy and the kids are going to take this?"

Harold could feel himself getting angry again. He wanted to remind Shane that he was Harold's lawyer, not the family's lawyer and that it was his wishes that he needed to focus on, not the family's needs or their feelings. But Harold knew that was unfair, and he did not want this conversation to deteriorate like the one that he had just had with Jerry.

"Shane, we went through all this weeks ago. I understand that creating a testamentary trust with this many specific instructions may appear like I don't trust my family, but you know that's not the case. I simply want to make sure that I take the steps necessary to ensure I leave my family with as few problems and concerns as I can, so they can focus on enjoying life."

"Harold, your will requires your grandchildren's children to maintain a 3.5 GPA to get money to fund their education. Isn't that going a little too far?"

"I don't think that setting reasonable standards is going too far. And clauses like that one will make it much easier for my children to set standards."

"And you don't think that having a trustee from some bank checking up on your great-grandchildren's grades is going too far?"

Harold, in an effort to stay calm, chose not to respond.

Realizing that he might have said too much, Shane backed off, deciding on a different tack. "Have you spoken with Nancy and your children about this will? You always say that it is not your money, it's the family's money, but this will clearly states it's your money and it will always be your money. Is that the message that you want to send?"

"Shane, I don't know why we need to keep rehashing this. It's not about trust or even me controlling what happens to the money. It's about not leaving the burden of the money and all the assets and their use for Nancy and my children to worry about. I don't want Nancy to have to worry about who gets what and under what conditions. I don't want my children having to worry about Nancy getting remarried to someone who throws away their inheritance, and if Nancy wants to get remarried, I don't want her to worry about what that new man may do with our children's inheritance. I just want my family to enjoy life and not have to worry about these types of decisions. Is that too much to ask?"

"I just don't want you signing something that you will regret a year from now. Talk to Nancy. Your intentions may not translate to your family if the first time they see this document is after your death. They may see it as a clear lack of trust in their ability to make decisions. Please show it to Nancy, at least, and explain your intent before you sign anything."

Harold understood that this was Shane, his lawyer, talking. Any lawyer worth their salt would advise their client to talk with their spouse about their will. But Harold really didn't want to talk with Nancy about the will, about his dad's untimely death at sixty-four, or about Mark. What he wanted to do was get the will completed, to stop thinking about things he could not control, like the timing of his death and what happened to Mark. He needed to complete the will so he could continue taking care of his family, even after he was gone. Nancy would understand that, but talking about it now would only focus everyone's attention on his health. Not what he wanted at all.

"Okay, Shane, I get your point. The rest of the changes are minor typos. I will send you a list. When you send me a final draft, I'll sit down with Nancy and walk her through the whole thing," Harold said, knowing full well that the conversation with Nancy was simply not going to happen.

"I'm glad to hear that. As soon as we get your changes, I will send you a new draft. I should remind you, as I do at every one of these sessions, you have an existing will that leaves half of your estate to Nancy and 25 percent to each of your children. It is not the most tax-effective way to handle your estate, but as long as there is a reasonable amount of liquid assets to pay the taxes, it shouldn't be a problem. So, to the best of my knowledge, there is no rush to sign this new will," Shane said as they both stood, signalling the end of the meeting.

As they shook hands and Harold made his way to the door, Shane said, "Let me know when you and Nancy have talked."

"Sure," Harold responded, hating that he was lying to his lawyer and his friend and happy that he would not be there when Shane found out.

CHAPTER SEVEN

Harold and Nancy absolutely loved their tradition of Sunday night dinners with the family. When the kids were growing up, everyone was so busy and Sunday was the only day when they would all be together. Nancy and Harold had insisted that no matter what, everyone had to be there, and the kids had almost always found a way to make it work.

Now that Jessie, their thirty-three-year-old son, and Megan, their thirty-year-old daughter, had families of their own, it was more difficult to maintain the tradition. But everyone did their best, and most Sundays, everyone was there.

But this week they had postponed the Sunday night dinner until Monday. Both Jessie's two-year-old son Brennen and Megan's eighteen-month-old daughter Layla were not feeling well, and with what was apparently the worst flu season in decades constantly in the news, everyone agreed it would be better if Phillip, Jessie's partner, and Edwin, Megan's husband, stayed home with the kids. So, it was Monday, and it was just the four of them, which was nice but very unusual.

"How many times have the kids been sick this year?" Harold asked.

"Since they started going to the day home, it seems like they simply go from one cold to the next. I don't remember it being that bad with you kids," Nancy responded.

"Edwin and I talked about the same thing last night. It does seem like a lot of colds, but Edwin keeps track of them in his calendar and it was a lot less than we had thought. Though, like you said, Mom, it's still more than I remember being sick as a kid," Megan added between bites of salad. Nancy made the best salads, and they were always the best part of the Sunday meal. "Damn, Mom, how do you decide what to put into a salad? They're always so good."

"I don't know. I just throw in whatever I have in the fridge. I don't put a lot of thought into it," Nancy replied.

"I love this song," Harold interrupted, suddenly singing along with a popular song from the sixties that was playing on the radio.

No one wasted their time telling Harold to not sing at the dinner table and Megan and Jessie chimed right in.

"Frankie Valli, he was amazing," Harold declared as the song ended.

"That wasn't Frankie Valli," Jessie said casually, without looking up from his food.

"Of course it was Frankie Valli. Nancy, back me up on this. You love Frankie Valli," Harold retorted.

"Don't look at me. I didn't even know that I loved Frankie Valli. I have no idea who that was," Nancy responded with a laugh. "You two can fight it out between you."

Harold laughed, "Go ahead and google it. No one believes me. I grew up on these songs."

"Grew up on them?" Jessie said as he pulled out his phone. "You were what, six?" There was a short pause as Jessie found the facts. "Okay, according to Google, *that particular song* was performed by Mel Carter in 1965, so as I said, you would have been six, right in the prime of your life."

"Yeah, yeah, yeah, but who wrote it?" Harold replied, still convinced that he was somehow right.

"Google thinks that Harry Noble wrote it, and Karen Chandler, whoever that is, recorded it back in 1952. Definitely not a Frankie Valli song. Sorry, Pops," Jessie said with a big smile.

"Are you sure? That can't possibly be right. Frankie Valli must've recorded it later and turned it into a big hit." Harold smiled, pleading for some proof that he knew his music.

"Nope, Google says the most notable covers of the song were Mel Carter and Gloria Estefan. If Frankie Valli recorded it, he kept it quiet because Google doesn't know about it."

"Harold, it always amazes me how certain you can sound when you're totally wrong," Nancy said with a laugh.

Harold smiled. "Before Google, I could convince the three of you about almost anything. I hate Google."

They all laughed and went back to enjoying the meal. Nancy would never call herself a great cook, or even a good one, but when pressed, she would call herself a practical cook. She put out nutritious meals that people enjoyed, were easy to make, and were easy to clean up after. Harold, on the other hand, could not cook at all—not even barbeque—and when he helped out in the kitchen, Nancy would tell you that other than washing dishes, any help Harold provided was more harm than help.

"Megan, you've been awfully quiet. Is something wrong?" Nancy asked between mouthfuls of an incredibly tender pork tenderloin that Harold had managed to not destroy on the barbeque. The mustard sauce she had prepared from a new recipe had turned out quite nice.

"No, nothing's wrong," replied Megan. "In fact, just the opposite. I may have this wonderful opportunity, and Edwin and I have been talking about what we would have to change to allow me to pursue it."

Megan was an incredibly bright and capable engineer whose career had really taken off over the last couple of years, especially in the last six months since she had returned from maternity leave.

Harold knew the CEO of the firm where Megan worked, and who had shared with Harold, in confidence, that Megan was going to be offered a very significant promotion with a big increase in compensation. Harold assumed this was what Megan was going to tell them. Smiling knowingly, he asked, "So, what's this big opportunity?" believing he was setting Megan up to tell them something he already knew.

"You guys remember Gary Sing?"

Everyone nodded in recognition.

"He and I have been working on a project together for the last three or four years, and I think we're really close to a prototype."

Harold was confused. He could not see what this had to do with the promotion. "I didn't know you and Gary worked for the same company."

"We don't. This is something we've been working on outside of work, mostly in Gary's garage."

Nancy piped in, "What type of project is it?"

"It's an extremely thin solar panel that has incredibly high solar capture and conversion rates. The panel's so thin and so efficient that, theoretically, you could put it on the hood, roof, and trunk of an electric car, and it would more than double the distance the car could go on a single charge."

"That sounds amazing, sis."

"But that isn't the truly exciting part. If it works how we think it can, it'll make long-haul shipping with electric trucks viable. You'd cover the cab and the trailer with the panels, and it'd allow the truck to have a third of the batteries they would presently require. The global reduction in greenhouse gases would be astronomical."

"If it works, that'd certainly change a lot of lives," Nancy exclaimed. "But, specifically, how does all this create such a big change in your and Edwin's lives?"

"To make it happen, Gary and I feel we both have to commit full time to the project, which means quitting jobs we enjoy and, for me, less time with Layla, at least for a while. Between not having jobs and having to buy equipment and materials, we'd likely eat through our savings and maybe even have to increase the mortgages on our homes. It'd be easier for Edwin and me than it'd be for Gary. We'd still have Edwin's income."

"How does Edwin feel about all of this?" Jessie asked.

"He's 100 percent on board. He wants me to go in tomorrow and hand in my resignation," Megan said with a big smile.

Harold had stopped eating and was staring at Megan. None of this made any sense. Megan and Edwin had a great life. What about the promotion? Why would she want to screw it all up? Did she even know about the promotion? Why take on all this risk, especially right now, especially just before his sixty-fourth birthday?

"Does this thing even work?" Harold asked in a fashion that was more aggressive than he had meant it to be.

"We won't know for sure until we build a prototype, but theoretically, it should be a no-brainer," Megan replied, either not noticing the aggression in her dad's question, or choosing to ignore it.

"Are you going to theoretically pay your mortgage and raise your kid? Jesus, Megan, you guys have a great life, and you're just starting a family. Why would you piss it all away for something that theoretically might work? It's like you're back in college, changing majors every semester. Why can't you just focus on what you have and make the best of that? Is sticking to one thing that difficult?" Harold blurted out.

Nancy, Jessie, and Megan were more than a little surprised at Harold's reaction.

"I think you're overreacting, Harold," Nancy responded, a little cross with Harold's level of emotion. She always preferred reason to hysterics, especially at the dinner table, and especially from her husband. "I'm sure that Edwin and Megan have talked this through carefully and have a plan. After all, they're grown-ups, and it's their life."

Harold was beginning to perspire. This was not the plan. Why was Megan doing this to him?

"If they're grown-ups, they should act like it. You don't give up everything to chase some pipe dream." Harold's emotions were now in complete control.

"They aren't giving up everything. Edwin has a great job. Who cares about having a higher mortgage? And if it is a complete failure, Megan can get another job anytime she wants," Jessie responded, trying to defend his sister.

"Dad, I don't know what's bothering you," Megan said with an exaggerated calm, "but I want to be clear. I wasn't asking you; I was simply informing you. If what Edwin and I plan to do with our lives doesn't meet with your approval, I'm sorry, but they're our lives."

"Do whatever you want, but don't expect to come running to me when the whole thing falls apart. I can't just change everything because you don't like your job," Harold huffed, thinking only of how this decision could affect his carefully planned will. What if he did not have time to make changes? What would those changes look like?

Before Nancy had a chance to shut down what she felt was a totally inappropriate and dysfunctional discussion, Jessie spoke up, "Jesus, Dad. You're way out of line. No one's asking you for anything."

"Out of line? Out of line? Who do you think you are, telling me I'm out of line? This is still my goddamn house, and I can say whatever I feel like saying. If you and your sister don't like it, too bad," Harold responded.

"*Our* house," Nancy corrected Harold. "And I think that this discussion needs to stop before someone says something truly stupid."

Hearing that, Harold stood up, threw his napkin on the table, and stormed off toward his den.

Looking from one to the other, Nancy, Megan, and Jessie were all wondering who the hell had just taken over Harold's body. This simply was not how they spoke to each other, ever. They quietly waited for Harold to go into his den and close the door, which he did, with door-slamming aggression.

"What the hell was that about?" Megan asked, more puzzled than hurt and not really expecting an answer. "I don't think that I've ever seen Dad storm out of a room before. What's he so upset about? Edwin and I haven't even made a final decision yet."

"I'm not sure, but whatever it is, I'm sure it's not you, dear," Nancy responded. "Regardless, knowing your father, he's probably sitting in his office right now, regretting the outburst."

"Were there other outbursts?" Megan wondered out loud.

"No, not that I'm aware of. In fact, he's been quieter than usual—you know how much your dad likes to talk—but no other outbursts," she said, having no idea about what had happened in Jerry's office. "And this really wasn't all that bad. You kids should see what goes on in my office," said Nancy, wanting to take the conversation in another direction. "Some of my clients go absolutely bonkers. I can never understand why they think throwing tantrums is ever going to be helpful." In her work as a family law lawyer, Nancy had seen some truly bizarre behaviour.

"God, Mom, I don't know how you do it," Jessie offered. "Some of the stories we hear about the cases you've been involved with are heartbreaking. How are you not in tears all the time?"

" 'Cause your mom is a heartless bitch," Nancy laughed.

"You always say that, but that's just deflection," Megan butted in. "Seriously, how do you deal with it?"

"Really, I don't get emotionally involved. These aren't my friends and family. They're clients."

"Come on, Mom. I've seen you hugging and consoling your clients. There's no way that you're not emotionally involved," Megan said as she got up to clear the dinner dishes.

"Ha, you amateurs! All that stuff is important in developing a relationship with a client. It's good practice, but it's not emotion. I hug the people that need to be hugged to get them to be honest with me, or to get them to calm down before we go into court. I yell at people that need to be yelled at for the same reason."

"You never just hug them because they need a hug?" Megan asked.

"Oh sure, when they win or lose, but I give them a hug because they need a hug, not because I need one."

"Jesus, Mom, you are heartless," Jessie said while laughing. "And what's your professional opinion about what we should do about Dad?"

"In my professional opinion, I think that we should let your dad figure it out for himself. Whatever it is that's bothering him, I think he can handle it without our help. But for now, we should call it a night. I'm sure we all have busy days tomorrow. I know I do."

It took five minutes to complete the cleanup, and then Jessie and Megan were on their way.

Harold sat at the desk in his study with his head in his hands, wondering what the hell was wrong with him. Dealing with worry and change was something that he had handled his entire adult life, and he had never allowed it to affect him like this. He knew he wasn't completely wrong. But why was he acting so irrationally. He could not even remember what exactly had set him off.

Sure, the idea that Megan and Edwin would take this type of risk on something that did not even have a prototype, something that might not even work, seemed like a questionable decision to Harold. But this was not the first hair-brained idea that his children or wife had come up with. Harold would often disagree with them and even encourage them to reconsider, but not like this, not with this type of anger.

He wanted to go out and apologize, but what would he say? "Hey, your plans are screwing up my will, and given that I could die in the next few weeks, I really don't have time to change it." He knew he was being irrational, and it was clear that he was being selfish. But he could not seem to stop himself. For the second time in a day, the suggestion of change had sent him into a childish tantrum. He knew the will was the right thing to do. Why couldn't he just explain it to them?

When Harold finally left his study to go to bed, his conversation with Nancy was short and direct.

As Nancy climbed into bed, without looking at Harold, she said, "I'm not sure what that was all about, but hopefully it isn't something we're going to have to get used to."

Without turning to face Nancy, Harold responded, "Megan just caught me off-guard, an isolated situation. I'm sure I'll be back to my calm, cool, and predictable self tomorrow."

Nancy smiled.

Lying in bed, they both reached to turn off their bedside lamps, said "goodnight" and "I love you," turned their backs to each other, and settled in for a good night's sleep, as they did most nights.

CHAPTER EIGHT

Harold always wondered why people hated mornings. He thought mornings were great. They were a fresh start, the opportunity to get busy dealing with something you had been thinking about all night. Of course, Harold had no way of knowing that most people did not think of things all night with the regularity that he did. Today, it was all about completing something Harold had been working on in conjunction with his will. He looked over at his alarm clock. It was 4:00 a.m. He knew he was not going back to sleep, which was fine with him. There were lots of things to do, and he might as well get at it.

When the children had moved out of the house, Harold had moved all his clothes to Jessie's old room and started using the children's bathroom to get ready in the morning. He knew Nancy was a light sleeper, and even though she never complained, he was certain that his habit of getting up and going to work at crazy hours had disturbed her sleep far too often.

This morning he got up as quietly as he could, closed the door to the bedroom behind him, and went down the hall to get ready to go to the office.

The office of Bannister Management Services was about a fifteen-minute drive from their house, and Harold seldom ate breakfast, other than a cup of herbal tea and a banana or apple, which was typically consumed around 10:00 a.m. This allowed him to be sitting at his desk only thirty-five minutes after he got out of bed. He could not imagine what it was like for people with forty-five-minute commutes. He completely understood why they would probably want to work remotely.

This morning was all about putting the final touches on Bannister Management's ten-year plan. It had been specifically designed to tie in nicely with his will, but in contrast with his will, he was planning to share the plan with Ramesh Kumar, the company's CFO, and Alison Baxter, the COO and CMO. Normally, he would have brought them into the planning process much earlier, but he knew this plan would be controversial, and he preferred having only one argument about it. He hoped he could persuade Ramesh and Alison to come around to his way of thinking, but because of the plan's relationship with his will, he was unwilling to make many changes. Especially on the big issues like the level of debt or the disposition or acquisition of assets. The goal of this ten-year plan was stability, protecting the cash flow and the value of the existing buildings, and avoiding any unnecessary risks.

His biggest concern was that the company be able to provide a comfortable living for his family and the staff for many generations to come. In his mind, any possibility that an overly aggressive growth plan or a series of poor management decisions could hurt the company's cash flow had to be eliminated. He was certain this would be accomplished with the combination of the ten-year plan and his will.

The difficulty Harold had faced while creating the ten-year plan, and the difficulty he would face when explaining it to Ramesh and Alison, was that he did not want to tell them anything about his will or why this approach was so important to him. Especially the part about them reporting to a bank-appointed trustee, who would have very limited authority to consider change, being almost completely constrained by the terms of the will.

As Harold completed the final changes to the ten-year plan's PowerPoint presentation, he noticed it was just about 8:00 a.m. The team would arrive any minute, and as he did most mornings, he wanted to make the rounds. Fred Bannister had taught Harold how to treat people and how to trust people. As much as Nancy was a positive force in Harold's life, Nancy probably would not be a part of his life if it had not been for Fred. Bannister Management was a family business, and Fred considered every member of their staff to be part of the family. When Harold had taken over the company, he had maintained that attitude. Harold went out of his way to make the staff feel like work was a second home, just as Fred had before him. Morning rounds were a big part of that.

The first stop was always Gail, the receptionist. She did not formally start work until 8:30 a.m., but she was always there early, making coffee and greeting the rest of the team.

"Good morning, Gail, and how are you this fine winter morning?" Harold asked with a big smile. It was his opinion that a big smile and a friendly greeting were part of the job requirements for the boss. Fred Bannister had taught him that on his first day of work at Bannister.

"Good morning to you, Harold. I'm great, but I'm done with winter. The older I get, the harder it is to deal with bundling up in parkas and shovelling snow. I think shovelling snow is probably the only thing that I truly dislike." Gail said all of this while cleaning up the lunchroom behind the reception desk, making morning coffee, and saying hello to other staff members as they filed into the lunch-room to drop their lunches in the fridge.

Harold laughed. "Nobody enjoys shovelling, but most of us don't have sixty-foot-long driveways. Have you considered moving?"

"Harold, I love my house and my neighbours. The only way that I'm leaving that house is in a pine box. I'll just have to learn to accept shovelling or spend the winter in Palm Springs."

"Well, I vote for accepting shovelling. We couldn't get by without you for a whole winter."

They both laughed. Harold wished Gail a great day and moved on to the next person on his morning rounds. The conversations with the rest of the staff varied, as they did every morning. Some were a quick "Hello, how are you today?" Some were longer if Harold or the staff member had something specific to discuss. What they discussed also varied dramatically, from business issues to personal issues. Kids going off to school, sick family members, last night's game (usually the Calgary Flames, their local NHL team), the new car they were buying, and much more were all subjects covered during Harold's morning rounds, which took anywhere from forty-five minutes to an hour pretty much every day.

When Harold finally got back to his office, Ramesh and Alison were waiting for him. This was their regular Tuesday morning meeting, where they would normally discuss the issues arising from the previous week and the plans for the upcoming week. Today Harold planned to use the meeting to discuss the ten-year plan at length. The only information that Ramesh and Alison had was that the meeting was going to be three hours long instead of the normal half-hour. It was unusual for Harold to call a three-hour meeting without an agenda, but he was the boss, and Ramesh and Alison did not think to question him about his lack of an agenda.

"Good morning. How are you two today?" Harold asked as he entered the office and walked to his desk to grab his computer.

"A little curious about this morning's meeting," Ramesh responded. "It's not like you to call a three-hour meeting without giving us a heads-up about what we're going to discuss."

"I assumed that after all these years of working together, you just wanted to spend some time reminiscing. I know how much you love to reminisce," Alison chimed in, knowing that Harold hated wasting time talking about the past during working hours.

"I wanted to talk about the future of the company and I wanted to present my entire plan to the two of you before you make any judgments or form any opinions on the individual pieces of the plan," Harold stated as he sat down with Ramesh and Alison at the large board table and plugged his computer into the thirty-six-inch screen that sat at the far end of the table so that all three of them could look at the screen at the same time.

Harold's office was large by today's standards but was pretty average for an industrial space built in the 1990s. He had ample room for his desk, which was exactly the same as every other desk in every other office at Bannister, and a six-foot-long board table with ergonomic chairs similar to all the desk chairs at Bannister. A service credenza contained glasses, cups, water pitchers, and a coffeemaker, all of which had seemed like a good idea when they were purchased but had seldom been used. There were two plants, both about four feet high. One was called elephant ear and had massive leaves that, as you would suspect, looked a lot like elephant ears. The other was a hibiscus that, every year, produced beautiful pink flowers Harold barely noticed. Thanks to Gail, these two plants thrived in the confines of his office.

The screen lit up at the end of the board table, and the PowerPoint title page appeared. "The Future of Bannister Management Services" was the main title, accompanied by a subtitle that read, "Creating Security for Decades to Come."

Harold spent the next ninety minutes painstakingly walking Ramesh and Alison through the deck of slides. He was more than happy to answer any of their questions, but not willing to discuss any objections until they had been through the entire presentation, which caused both Ramesh and Alison to take copious notes during the presentation.

When Harold completed the presentation, Ramesh and Alison were momentarily speechless. The plan was so detailed and so much in contrast to every discussion that the three of them had shared over the last five years about the future of the company. They simply did not know what to say.

"So, what do you think?" Harold asked, fully expecting that they would have some concerns, but that they would like the overall concept of the plan because it so clearly assured the security of their futures.

"Harold, that's a lot of detail, and it's a lot longer than ten years. The way that you have set this plan up, it'll outlast all of us. It specifies maintenance and renovation cycles and dictates sale and replacement plans for every one of our buildings, and it even talks about cycling tenants so that we don't get caught with dying organizations," Ramesh said to open the conversation.

"I certainly wouldn't want our tenants to see this document. We've always treated them like family. This document suggests we should start treating them like a commodity," Alison joined in. "And the debt provisions will make it almost impossible for us to grow, which is a very important issue for the senior management team."

"I think that you guys are missing the point of the plan. This will create incredible security for everyone involved, through every type of economic environment short of a complete meltdown," Harold offered.

"That's true," Ramesh said, "though I'm with Alison about not wanting our tenants or even our staff to see the comments about churning the tenants. What I'm struggling with is why we would want to go in this direction. It's almost the opposite direction we discussed when you so kindly restructured the company three years ago. It appears to undo, or at least nullify, the effect of the restructuring. What's changed?"

Harold was getting a little frustrated. Why was Ramesh bringing up the restructuring? This had nothing to do with the restructuring. "Senior management will retain the shares they were given three years ago. This doesn't affect that at all."

Ramesh and Alison looked at each other, knowing that they were thinking the same thing. How could they point out to someone, who had given them a gift out of the kindness of his heart, that he was now dramatically reducing the value of that gift? It was still a gift. He had been under no obligation to give it to them. They would sound ungrateful if they complained, but they also knew the devastating effect this plan would have on the morale of the team.

Alison carefully ventured into the subject, trying her best to not sound ungrateful for what she had received. "Harold, it was incredibly generous of you and your family to give shares in the company to the entire senior management team, but you understand that without growth, those shares have very little value. The way the new ownership structure works, we only share in the growth after inflation."

"Sure, the plan reduces the chance of the senior management's shares experiencing a dramatic escalation in value, but it practically guarantees their salaries, pension contributions, and profit sharing for as long as they wish to work here," Harold said, certain that the issue was that Ramesh and Alison had missed this important detail.

"Yes, we see that, Harold," Ramesh piped in, "but our best people don't work here for security. They work here for the opportunity. They want to grow, both financially and intellectually. As you always tell them, 'As good as we are today, we must be better tomorrow.' They believe in that and want to be a part of it. This plan changes it to 'We're good enough. Let's stay where we are.' "

Their inability to see the value of a secure future, free of concern, frustrated Harold, but he was doing his best to not show it. What he could not tell them was that this plan was not a discussion. It was all but set in stone. The will Harold was about to sign laid out all the provisions of this plan in detail. He had to stay calm and sell them on security over growth.

"I realize this will limit the growth of Bannister, but I'm not concerned with the growth. I'm concerned with security. This plan assures everyone the ability to maintain their lifestyles, to move ahead with their plans, without fear of economic cycles," Harold offered.

Both Ramesh and Alison were struggling to respond. Harold had given them both so much. How did they tell him it was not enough? If he had not restructured the company's shares, if he had not given senior management the shares, and if he had not created expectations, this would be a much easier conversation, but the restructuring was a huge part of the reason they were both still there to have this conversation.

"Harold." Alison was aware of how often they were saying Harold's name, but it seemed necessary. "When you worked for Fred Bannister, he did the same thing for you as you have done for us. He gave you shares that only had value if the company grew. Then he let you grow the company, which not only created great value for you but also put you in a position to buy Fred out when he asked you to. We don't want to buy you or your family out, ever, but we all have ambitions that growth would fund. Sure, some of us want bigger houses and nicer cars, but we also want to emulate your generosity with charities. We would like the opportunity to support our children's dreams. Harold, you didn't put together a team of people who'll be happy with security. They all want more and are willing to work for it."

They were clearly at an impasse. Harold had told no one about his obsession with his father's untimely death because of the widowmaker and his concern that he was going to follow in his footsteps. Without that information, this total change in the plan seemed to be coming out of nowhere.

"Okay, I hear what the two of you are saying. Let me consider it for a few weeks and get back to you." Harold knew the plan was only a plan, and regardless of what they agreed to put into it, if he died, his will would dictate the future of Bannister. He thought he could maybe agree to some limited growth, as long as he was alive. He, of course, would not describe it that way, nor would he tell them about the provisions of the will, which he was unwilling to discuss or change.

The three of them dealt with a few immediate business issues, and talked a little about their activities from the previous weekend and the news from the team, which Harold had gathered on his morning walkabout. Harold never formally adjourned the meetings. He would say something like "Anything else?" and if no one had anything, he would follow that up with "Great, thank you both. Have a great day," and Ramesh and Alison would leave.

The moment that they left his office, his cell phone rang. As he pulled the phone out of the pocket of his sports jacket, he reflected on how seldom his desk phone rang, which was almost never. If it did ring, it was usually a salesperson making a cold call. Harold tried to be courteous when answering these calls—they were just trying to make a living—but more and more, he simply let the phone ring.

It was Jerry. Damn it, he really did not want to talk to Jerry right now. He had not spoken with Nancy about the foundation and did not know when he would or what he was going to say.

Why was everyone making it so difficult?

CHAPTER NINE

"Hey Jerry, what's up?" Harold said as he put the cell phone to his ear.

"Good morning, Harold. How was your dinner with the kids?"

"How was dinner with the kids? Jerry, I'm pretty sure that you have never once phoned me to ask me how my dinner with my children was. It was fine. How was your dinner?" Harold replied somewhat sarcastically.

"Mine was terrific, which is the real reason that I called. I had dinner last night with a couple of the guys with smaller foundations and we got talking about what you and I might want to do with the Margaret Mary Bower Foundation." Jerry emphasized the word "might."

Having had no idea that Jerry had dinner with anyone, Harold was caught off guard by the response. "Sorry, who did you say these guys were, and what exactly is their interest in the work our foundation does?"

"Bill and I had dinner with Dan Jeans and Will Maki, friends of mine who both have small but growing foundations that also focus on underserved community youth. We had a great chat about the plan I showed you yesterday."

Bill Tessler had been the executive director of the Margaret Mary Bower Foundation for three years. Harold really appreciated what he had accomplished with the foundation and especially appreciated his attention to detail. Too often, charities and their executives had disappointed Harold by the significant difference between what they said they would do and what they actually did. Too often, their inability to deliver was accompanied by a request for additional funds to complete the project that Harold had been a part of funding. Bill was not like that. If he said he could complete a project for a specific amount of money, he made sure it happened. Harold attributed the difference to Bill's ability and willingness to properly plan a project, which seemed in short supply in other charities.

"How is Bill? I haven't spoken with him in weeks. I understand his wife had a particularly tough battle with the flu." Harold hoped he could divert Jerry's attention and that he could avoid the conversation on the foundation.

"Bill's great, and his wife, Theresa, is finally symptom-free, but I was really phoning about the foundation and the proposal I gave you yesterday. I hoped that you'd have talked with Nancy and that you'd have an answer for me about moving forward. Everyone's pretty eager to get going."

Wow, Harold thought, *it hasn't been much more than twenty-four hours. This must be really important to Jerry.*

"Jerry, what's the rush? I've not even shown Nancy the proposal, let alone had a discussion with her about it." Harold was not eager to show the proposal to Nancy for fear that she would like it. But he was not about to share that information with Jerry.

"Harold, you know what the rush is as well as I do. These kids are making decisions about their futures every day, without a complete view of the possibilities. This program will not only open their eyes to futures that most would not even consider, but it'll also help fund many of those futures. This could be the difference between dozens of kids quitting school or continuing their education."

Harold had no question that the work was worthwhile, and he did not want to stand in the way of getting it going, but he couldn't show it to Nancy and get her all excited about it until he had figured out how to integrate it with his new will. This was a significant commitment, something that Harold definitely did not want to see get started and then cancelled because of his poor planning. A cancellation like that could easily end up hurting the kids more than not doing anything at all. He needed a little time.

"Yes, Jerry, I know how important it is, but this is not a brand-new problem, and a day or a month to give you an answer will not have a significant effect on the outcomes."

"Jesus, Harold, why would it take a month? There's not that much to consider. If it's the money, just say so. We can lower your commitment. I'm sure I can find someone to pick up the difference. Hell, I can increase my commitment, if that's what's needed."

Harold hated when Jerry did this. Whenever Harold wanted to think things through thoughtfully and Jerry wanted to rush right in, Jerry would pull the "I'll cover the difference" card. He even did it back when they were trying to clean up the mess that their father had left behind, except back then, it was simply an empty promise. Jerry barely had the ability to cover his own commitments, let alone anyone else's. But it never stopped him from making the offer, or threat, depending on how you interpreted it.

"Jerry, if you want a quick answer, I can easily give you one," Harold said emphatically. This was one of Harold's often-used negotiating tools when people were pushing him for an answer that he was not ready to give. The quick answer, of course, would be "no," which Jerry knew. Jerry also knew that a "no" from Harold was far more problematic than Harold not putting his additional funds into the program. It meant the foundation could not participate at all. They had agreed when they created the foundation that all decisions that expanded the work of the foundation had to be signed off by both Harold and Jerry, or they could not proceed.

"Don't get your panties in a knot. I'm not asking for a quick answer. I simply want you to know that everyone is ready to move, and the sooner you can give us an answer, the sooner we can start making a difference," Jerry responded in an effort to calm down the rhetoric.

"You mean start making a bigger difference?"

"What?"

"You said that we could start making a difference. Hopefully, we're already making a difference."

"Yes, of course. We can start making a bigger difference."

Harold was now purposely being annoying so he could get out of having the conversation and buy some time.

"Jerry, when do you really need an answer? I don't want to rush Nancy, and as important as the foundation is to you and me, it isn't the only charitable program that Nancy supports. I'm just not sure what her expectations or commitments are to the other charities." This was not a complete lie. Harold did not know for sure what Nancy had committed to with other charities, but he knew that her primary focus was the foundation, and he had very little question that she would agree to this proposal almost immediately, once he showed it to her.

Jerry did not have to question Harold's desire to slow down. It would not even cross his mind as unusual. Sometimes it was hard to believe that they were brothers. They were so different in so many ways. They didn't even look alike. Some people said there was a family resemblance, but neither of them could see it. What was so interesting about the brothers was that their differences never drove them apart. No matter how hard Jerry pushed or how hard Harold pushed back, and even if they could not find common ground, they never let it interfere with their relationship. If they agreed to disagree, they would simply move on to the next thing, never letting the disagreement or even the strong language cause anything more than a momentary annoyance for either.

"There really is no absolute drop-dead date for any of this. The sooner that you let us know, the sooner we can take action. What timeline are you comfortable with?"

"I'll give the proposal to Nancy tonight, but she's going to the cabin at the end of the week, so we may not have an opportunity to talk about it until she gets back Sunday afternoon. Unless she has some significant concerns, we should be able to give you an answer Monday morning." Harold was certain this would allow him the time to make the necessary changes to his will to accommodate the changes in the donation plan. Not a perfect solution, but a lot better than trying to explain that every decision he was making was based on the possibility that he would soon be dead.

"That's great. Sorry I'm being such a pest." Jerry wasn't at all sorry. It was who he was, but it sounded like the right thing to say. "If you or Nancy have questions or concerns about the proposal, please call me at any time. I'll be more than happy to provide you with answers." In contrast to others who made this statement, Jerry actually meant any time.

"Thanks, Jerry, I'll call you Monday."

"Looking forward to it. Have a great week."

They each said goodbye and then hung up.

Harold really only had three days to deal with the change in the will. He made a note to call Shane and discuss possible changes today, in case it was more complicated than he expected it to be. Shane would probably ask if he had spoken with Nancy, a question he was not looking forward to answering. He was never comfortable about bending the truth. Outright lying, especially to a friend, was particularly distasteful. Mark and the incident that happened so many years ago popped into his head. He hadn't lied; he hadn't said anything.

He had told himself that lie so many times over the years that even he had started to believe it.

CHAPTER TEN

It was just about 7:00 p.m., and Harold was sitting in his study, waiting for Jessie and Phillip to show up. Jessie had called earlier that day and said they had something they wanted to discuss with him and wondered if he would be available that evening. Harold had not bothered to ask what it was about. He enjoyed their company and was more than happy to meet with them, regardless of what it was.

Harold and Nancy loved both of their children, and relative to some of the stories they had heard from friends and family, neither of their children had caused them any real problems and had pretty much been drama-free while they were growing up. Each of the kids had their own unique proclivities, some wonderful and some a bit of a challenge. Megan struggled with curfews, seldom calling when things changed, and had a definite issue with authority. Of course, she only had problems with authority when she felt they were wrong, which was surprisingly often.

Jessie was prone to exaggeration, especially when talking about something that was done to him, and especially if Megan was the person that did it. Of the two, Jessie was much better at keeping his parents informed about what he was doing—often too well informed, as he described in detail every aspect of some marginally important aspect of his life. When it came to helping around the house, Megan was terrific and Jessie was practically useless. Like his father, Jessie seemed incapable of understanding the role that a hanger played in the care of clothing.

Jessie and Phillip had met at university, and according to them, it was love at first sight, a concept that Harold completely believed in. It was how he had always felt about Nancy. However, he had struggled at first to understand the concept of an immediate attraction between Jessie and Phillip. They were nothing at all alike. Jessie was tall, thin, and athletic; Phillip was of average height, and while he was athletic, he was also more than a little dumpy. But in fairness, Harold could never understand what Nancy saw in him, either.

Jessie and Phillip had met on the basketball court. The two of them had gone for a beer after and had been almost inseparable ever since. There was an almost immediate physical and intellectual connection between them. They looked directly at each other when they spoke, and they touched frequently, even while doing something as mundane as washing dishes. Harold had no trouble understanding why they stayed together. It took no effort whatsoever to see how much they loved and respected each other. They shared an unusually strong bond, one that even Nancy and Harold were a little envious of.

Both were bright and capable, and both had landed great jobs, but Phillip was the ambitious extrovert and Jessie was more of a homebody. When they told Harold and Nancy that they were going to have a baby, no one had to ask who the primary caregiver would be or who would leave work if there was a problem. It was not that Phillip would not participate in raising the child—he absolutely would—it was just that Phillip was much more focused on his career than Jessie was. A fact that Harold struggled with just a little. It was great that neither of them had to make a compromise in order to have a family. Both were getting exactly what they wanted, but Harold often thought it would be nice if Jessie was a little more like Megan when it came to ambition. A thought that he made a point of keeping to himself.

A few minutes later, when Harold watched the two of them walking up the driveway, swinging two-year-old Brennen between them, it crossed his mind that the three of them looked like the perfect family without a care in the world.

Harold did not bother to greet them at the front door. He assumed it was unlocked, as it normally was during the day. But if it wasn't, Jessie and Phillip knew the code, and they knew where they would find him. As they walked into the den, Harold got up to give them both a hug, something that had been foreign to him as a child, but Nancy and the children had taught him to appreciate as an adult.

"What happened to Brennen?" Harold asked, already knowing the answer. "I saw him walking up the driveway with the two of you."

"He saw Grandma as we walked through the door and, suddenly, his dads no longer mattered," Phillip said with a smile. "Every time he comes over here, he never wants to leave."

"Yes, Nancy has that effect on children, and I'm sure that she appreciates Brennen giving her a break from work as well," Harold responded. "Grab a seat and tell me what this visit's all about."

Phillip and Jessie sat down in the comfortable leather chairs on the other side of Harold's desk from where Harold sat in his large leather desk chair. The setup was a throwback to the more formal days of business meetings, and although Harold acknowledged it was more than a little outdated, he could not be bothered to change it.

"You know, we could be just coming over to visit because we enjoy your company. There doesn't always have to be a reason," Jessie joked.

"No, you're absolutely right. There doesn't have to be a reason, but I'm betting there is."

Jessie and Phillip laughed and Jessie said, "Well, this time you're right, there is a specific reason for this visit. Phillip and I are thinking of having another child."

"That's fantastic. Does your mother know? She'll be thrilled."

"No," Phillip responded, "you're the first person we've talked to."

This really surprised Harold. This was the type of information he would normally receive last. Suddenly, he found himself waiting for the next shoe to drop, which it did.

"We're not planning to use a surrogate, as we did with Brennen. This time we're thinking that we would adopt," Phillip continued, with more caution in his voice than seemed appropriate.

Harold recognized immediately that he had to be thoughtful in his response. These were two intelligent and accomplished adults who must have a good reason to want to go the adoption route despite its increased risks. "The surrogacy path went so well with Brennen. Why wouldn't you want to repeat it? I remember how much the two of you enjoyed going through the pregnancy with the surrogate. Sorry, I can't remember her name."

"Cara," Jessie said, "and you're right, experiencing the pregnancy with Cara was amazing, and being in the delivery room when Brennen was born was magical. Something that we'll never forget. But there are children around the world who desperately need a home, and we have the ability to provide one."

"What do you mean around the world? Where are you thinking of adopting a baby from?" Harold asked, alarm bells suddenly going off in his head. Adopting a Canadian child was risky enough. There were genetic concerns and worries about how the mother behaved before and after the birth. Knowing the laws around adoption was tough enough in Canada, but understanding the laws of other countries and how they might affect you and your child was significantly tougher. The other unknown about adoption was the extended family. There was a father, grandparents, and maybe aunts and uncles. What rights did these people have in other countries?

"There are some places that really need help, like the Ukraine, India, or Nigeria. If we're going to have a little brother or sister for Brennen, we want to create an opportunity the child would never have without us. There's no shortage of Canadians wanting to adopt Canadian babies. There is a shortage in these other countries," Jessie responded, obviously having done the research.

"India? Will they even allow you to adopt an Indian child?" Harold did not consider the need to explain his question further.

"Technically, India doesn't allow same-sex couples to adopt, but we've spoken with an adoption lawyer, and he assures us that there are ways around that restriction," Jessie said, but before he had a chance to explain the statement, Harold interrupted.

" 'There are ways around the restriction.' Jesus, guys, that statement alone should send you running in the opposite direction," Harold was already developing scenarios in his mind that he did not like, and hoping that Jessie and Phillip would not get involved in any of them.

"Well," started Jessie, "India is only one of the places that we're considering, but if it was India, the mother and child could come to Canada and then proceed with the adoption when they're here."

The first thing that crossed Harold's mind was, why was he perspiring? The second thought was that Jessie and Phillip had to be smart enough not to get involved in some legally questionable adoption.

Unfortunately, he chose to say the third thing that crossed his mind. "You do know that you're parents now, don't you? If this thing gets screwed up, if you get a child with real issues, it not only affects you, but it could also put Brennen in harm's way. It's bad enough that the two of you want to take this type of risk. Or do I need to list all the very significant risks involved in adopting a child from any of these countries?" This last comment was particularly insulting to Jessie and Phillip. If Harold had been thinking clearly—which he definitely was not—he would have known that they would have completely researched the issue and gained all the advice needed to make an informed decision.

"Why are you even telling me? You must have known that I wouldn't agree with a hair-brained idea like this."

Jessie was not at all surprised by his father's concern. This was an enormous decision that they were making and, as his dad had pointed out, it came with a lot of risks. He was, however, surprised by the emotion in his dad's response, the perspiration on his forehead, and the pain that appeared on his face. Was this turning into a repeat of last night's discussion about Megan's business opportunity? Jessie was no longer concerned about the adoption. He was concerned about his dad. This was not him. This was not how he dealt with difficult subjects. Something else was going on.

"We brought it to you because we thought that you would help us think it through. We understand that there are risks involved with adopting a baby and that they increase dramatically by adopting a child from someplace like India, but Phillip and I have carefully weighed those risks and taken the time to determine how to mitigate them. If you don't wish to be involved, we understand."

Harold was again on a roll. He was not thinking about the wonderful life these fine young men could give a child. He was thinking only about all the bad things that could happen. The problems that an unknown child with unknown origins could bring to a family. How this could screw up the plans he had created for their future. Harold had always considered what could go wrong, but then he would think about how to avoid it or how to fix it. In that moment, all he could think about was what could go wrong and the fact that he may not be there to fix it.

"What do you mean if I don't wish to be involved? Do you think you can raise a child and your mother and I could not be involved? Of course we would be involved, but that isn't the point. It's about you guys making decisions that have the potential to screw up multiple lives and help no one. You don't need to be bringing children in from places like India. For God's sake, there are more than enough options right here in Canada." Then Harold, feeling a growing numbness in his left arm and a growing sense of disorientation, went somewhere where he had never gone before, not even when Jessie and Megan were children. "This is crazy, and I won't allow it."

It was fortunate Harold had made this absurd statement to Jessie, his calm child, and not Megan, from whom he would have received an earful.

Jessie, noting Phillips's growing annoyance and recognizing that any further conversation was likely to cause his dad to make even wilder declarations, decided to put an end to the conversation. However, he felt that he had to, at least, ask about his father's obvious increasing physical discomfort, "Christ, Dad. Are you okay?"

"I'm fine. This isn't about me," Harold responded, even though the physical discomfort he was experiencing made it difficult for him to think about anything else but himself.

"Well, Dad, you don't seem okay. Phillip, let's get Brennen. I think it's time to get him home to bed. Get some rest, Dad. I don't know what's going on with you lately, but you definitely aren't yourself."

Harold was in too much physical discomfort to argue, so he said nothing.

Despite Harold's behaviour, both Phillip and Jessie gave him a hug, said goodbye, and told him they loved him before leaving him alone in his den.

Harold sat in his desk chair, and the discomfort he had been feeling disappeared as quickly as it had appeared. He listened to the laughter and conversation outside his door as Jessie, Phillip, Nancy, and Brennen said their goodbyes. Nancy would be furious when she found out about Harold's "I won't allow it" comment, but he was more concerned about what had caused him to say it.

Two nights in a row, he had lost it. He didn't like Megan's idea of going into business and he liked Jessie's idea for adoption even less, but this was not the way he handled things. He kept saying that he was not expecting to die, that he was merely preparing in case he did. Was that still true? And what the hell were these symptoms all about? Harold knew all about heart attack symptoms, and what he was experiencing shared some similarities, but he was pretty sure that heart attack symptoms didn't instantly disappear as soon as you were alone.

CHAPTER ELEVEN

When Harold finally emerged from his den, he found Nancy in the family room, watching television. While the den reflected Harold's tastes, the family room was much more of a reflection of Nancy and the things that she felt were important for a family. A large flat-screen television hung on the far wall, with a seating area directly in front of it that would comfortably seat six people, eight if you sat close, and maybe on top of each other, which the Bower family had often done when the children were young. Directly behind the seating area was the adult sports area, which included a Ping-Pong table that could be converted into a pool table by removing the boards that were placed on top. There had once been a dartboard on the wall at the far end of the pool table, but after a few near misses when Jessie and Megan were teenagers, Nancy had relegated the board and the darts to the storeroom.

To the left of the pool table was the children's play area, which they had converted to a seating area when Jessie and Megan had become teenagers, but had restored as a play area when the grandchildren had arrived. One wall contained bookshelves, only three feet high, which were filled with books, most of which Nancy had purchased for her children, and more recently for the grandchildren. The other wall had built-in bench seating that did double duty as toy storage. When the children lifted the seat of the bench, they would find a wonderland of toys, some brand new and some so old that they had served to amuse Nancy's mother when she had been a child. In the middle of this area was a brand-new children's table and chair set.

The remnants of Brennen's effort at colouring sat in the middle of the table, where he had left them only a few hours earlier.

"Hey, what are you watching?" Harold asked as he entered the room and sat down in the chair next to Nancy.

"I'm not really watching anything. I'm reading through a case file. The TV's just on for background noise," Nancy replied without taking her eyes from the papers in front of her.

Harold stared at the screen for a few minutes, not really focusing on what he was watching or listening to. "How was your day? Anything unusual?"

Nancy patiently closed the file that she was looking at and turned to face Harold.

"It was great. I had lunch with Dawn and Sandra at Dawn and Rick's new house." Nancy continued, "They finally moved in last week."

Dawn and Rick, two of their closest friends, had been building their dream home for well over a year, which to Harold seemed like an unnecessarily long time. Harold had walked through the house half a dozen times with Rick while the house was in construction, but had not yet seen the finished product.

"How did it turn out?" Harold asked, not showing a lot of interest. "The layout was certainly impressive, and the finishings were first class. Knowing Dawn and Rick's flair for design, I imagine it's beautiful."

"Yes, it certainly is beautiful, and I would agree with your comments about Dawn and Rick's flair for design, but I would say the beauty and functionality of this house have more to do with their pocketbook."

Harold, not really knowing anything about the design and construction of this specific house, was a little surprised to hear this statement, especially from Nancy, who was not much of a gossip.

"Dawn told us at lunch today that they had decided they wanted a house that was design-magazine worthy, so they hired a team, including an interior designer from New York, who have all had homes presented in at least one of the top designer magazines, and told them to go to it. Money was not an object." Nancy had a smile on her face and lightheartedness in her voice that surprised Harold. This type of over-the-top display of money was not something that would normally impress her.

"The result is incredible. Everything you could want is in the house. The interior designer even picked out all the small appliances, which are all built into the cupboards and counters. They considered the relationship between every detail of how they will use their kitchen in the design. Apparently, the designer gave Dawn a two-hour walkthrough of the kitchen and explained how to maximize its efficiency. Dawn gave us a condensed version. The way they've thought through simple everyday tasks to make them easier and more efficient is truly amazing. It certainly opened my eyes to how inefficient our kitchen is."

"Isn't this house something like eight thousand square feet?" Harold asked, pretty sure he knew the answer.

"Something like that," Nancy responded.

"And their kids are all grown up and on their own, so it's just the two of them living in this massive designer home?"

Nancy responded with a sarcastic smile and comment. "They do need room for the grandchildren when they come to visit."

"Okay, so Rick is what, sixty-eight years old? Dawn's about the same. Both of their kids are in their midthirties, and neither is married. I'm not saying they'll never have grandchildren, but realistically, how many do you think they'll have? Christ, with the size of this house, they could lose a grandchild in it," Harold joked as he picked up the paper, wondering why they still had the damn thing delivered.

"Well, it's their money, and if that's how they want to spend it, I guess that's their business. It's a beautiful home," Nancy responded.

Excessive spending had never impressed Harold, but Nancy was right, of course. It was their money, and Harold really didn't care what they did with it. What he really wanted was to talk with his wife about something that was totally unimportant, and this seemed to fit the bill. "Sure, it's their money, but it doesn't mean they have to throw it around like a couple of drunken sailors. I mean, did they really have to waste it on hiding their toaster? Does an appliance, especially a minor appliance, really need its own home?"

Nancy gave Harold a wry smile. "Yes, all appliances need a home, and you know that Dawn and Rick are extremely generous with all kinds of important causes. Has either of them ever said no to one of your pet causes?"

"Totally fair and accurate, but not really the point of the discussion. A house that comes with separate houses for items within the house is way over the top. Now, if these were homeless appliances that would be something totally different. But I'm guessing these are affluent appliances that are used to the lap of luxury."

Nancy laughed. "Hey, that's not fair. Even high-quality appliances need to know that someone loves them."

"Okay, okay, enough about the new house. How's work going? Any new cases that are driving you crazy?" He was always interested in talking about Nancy's cases. There was something about talking to Nancy, especially about her work, that calmed Harold, and although he was not totally sure why, he badly needed calming tonight.

"Nothing new in my world. Same old families in trouble and the same line-up of abusive fathers, just different names and faces," Nancy replied.

"Hey, cheap shot. It's not always the father."

"That's fair. It's only almost always the father. Sometimes it's an abusive brother or uncle," Nancy responded, thinking it was a little sad that they could joke about these terrible situations she had worked with for over thirty years. "What's going on with you? Anything unusual in your life?"

"No, nothing. Same old, same old."

"Have you heard anything more about the death of your friend? Sorry, can't remember his name."

"Mark. No, nothing new, just that it was suicide. Not even sure how he did it. I have to admit, it's having a bit more of an effect on me than I expected it would."

"Yeah, I noticed that. When was the last time you saw Mark?"

"When his family moved away when we were fourteen. I didn't see him or even hear from him for maybe eight years, then out of the blue, he called me up to have lunch. We kept in touch for a while after that, but between the three divorces, the amount he drank, and his constant financial problems, he was pretty hard to be around." Harold had never told Nancy about Mark's three stints in rehab, all of which Harold had paid for.

"Have I ever met him? I can barely remember you even talking about him."

"I think that by the time we met, Mark and I had pretty much given up on each other, so it's been at least thirty-eight years since I last saw him."

"How did you find out about his death?"

"A mutual friend sent me the obituary and told me to call him. He wanted to let me know that Mark had died by suicide. Although I'm not sure why he thought it was important that I was aware of that specific piece of information."

"And that's all that's been bugging you?" Nancy asked.

"Actually," Harold said, wanting to change the subject, "the other thing is that Jerry came to see me with a new proposal for the foundation, and he wants us to put a lot more money into it." He had thought for a second about bringing up the will and decided instead to talk about the foundation.

"Is it more than we can afford?" asked Nancy.

"I don't think so, but I have the proposal in my briefcase. I'll leave it on the kitchen table. You can look at it in the morning and let me know what you think."

"What do you think? I assume that you've read it."

"Yeah, I've gone through it pretty thoroughly, but I'd prefer not to say anything until you've formed your own opinion. I want to make sure that we're both happy with the direction they want to take the foundation."

Now, this sounds a lot more like the Harold that I know and love, Nancy thought. "Okay, I'll read it tomorrow morning, and we can talk about it tomorrow night, unless you have something else on."

"I told Jerry that we'd give him an answer on Monday, so we can talk about it tomorrow over dinner, or we can talk when you get back from the cabin on Sunday evening."

"I'll probably be tired on Sunday, so let's talk tomorrow."

"Sounds good. I'm going to go upstairs and read, and you can get back to your file," Harold said as he got up and kissed his wife on the forehead, which he often did when she was sitting down and he was standing.

As Harold was about to step away from Nancy, she reached out and took his hand in hers, gave him a knowing smile, and said, "I could go to bed right now, if that would interest you."

Harold smiled back at Nancy, squeezed her hand, and responded, "That would be great."

Letting go of Harold's hand as she stood up, Nancy said, "You go on up. I'll be there in a moment. I just want to put this file away."

Harold changed, brushed his teeth, and took a pill. He had no problem getting an erection, but had recently experienced a little problem maintaining it. Nancy had not been impressed and seemed to take it personally, so rather than allow it to become an issue, Harold simply took the pill. If Nancy had noticed, she hadn't said anything.

CHAPTER TWELVE

Harold was standing in front of a church. It was early morning, the air was fresh and clean, and the sun was only starting to rise. He was drawn to the church by the massive doors, open and welcoming, encouraging its parishioners to bring their worries and uncertainties and leave them on the steps of the church.

He was surrounded by boys of all races, sizes, and descriptions. They bore neither smiles nor frowns. Their faces, other than a thin hint of sorrow, seemed lifeless. The small mass began to move slowly toward the doors, their movement carrying him along even as he did nothing to move himself. He looked across the faces, trying to find some hint of recognition. Why was he here? Who were these boys? Where were they going, and why?

Then, at the back of the pack, he saw Mark—young, quiet, and gentle Mark—moving forward with the group but seemingly unaware of why. As he looked from Mark back to the gaping opening created by the massive doors, he realized that he had to close the doors. He had to stop the boys from entering.

He desperately tried to push through the crowd that surrounded him, seeming to hold him in his place, never pressing ahead, never falling behind. Simply holding his place in the constant flow. By the time he finally reached the doors, dozens of boys had already entered ahead of him. He didn't know whether to close the doors, locking them in, or leave them open, allowing more to enter. So, he did nothing. The crowd continued to move, but it lost interest in him as he was left at the door, never entering, never walking away.

Finally, Mark passed by him, not stopping to acknowledge him, simply following the flow through the doors.

It was over. He was alone, standing on the steps of the church, having no idea what to do next. He called out, looking for direction, someone to guide him, but no one responded.

The alarm went off and Harold rolled over to silence it. Sleeping until the alarm went off was unusual for him, and he always worried that he would wake Nancy when it happened. He swung his head around to see if Nancy was awake, but she appeared still sound asleep.

Harold seldom remembered dreaming, let alone the details of what he dreamt about. This morning was only modestly different, a sense of discomfort, a flash here and there of faces and doors, but nothing specific. He got up to have a shower and quickly forgot the tiny bit that he had momentarily remembered.

CHAPTER THIRTEEN

At 11:00 a.m. that morning, Nancy received a surprise visit from Jessie and Brennen. Nancy was reading through Jerry's proposal for the foundation when she heard an easily recognizable voice calling for Nana.

"Nana is in the kitchen, Brennen," Nancy called out.

Brennen came running into the kitchen and, with his arms high in the air, ready for a hug, he made a beeline to Nancy, throwing himself into her arms as he arrived. Nancy swept him up into her arms and gave him a big nana hug, which, according to the hug authority, Brennen, is much nicer than a bear hug.

"Hi, Jessie. To what do I owe this unexpected surprise?" Nancy asked as she parked Brennen on her lap.

Jessie came over and gave his mom what turned into an awkward hug because of Brennen's presence on her knee. "Hi, Mom. A little surprised that we caught you at home, but I had the day off and Brennen always wants to visit Nana, so I thought I'd stop by and say hi. I thought maybe we could talk about Dad. He's been acting kind of weird lately."

"Weird? I'm not sure that weird is a word that could ever be used to describe your father."

Jessie chuckled. "Totally fair, so not weird, but definitely not Dad-like. His reaction to Megan's comments about quitting her job and focusing on the solar film was shocking. Megan and I have had a lot crazier ideas than that one, and you could always depend on Dad to talk with you like you had not lost touch with reality. Remember when Phillip and I were going to get married at university in a mass cult ceremony to protest the government not allowing same-sex marriages? To this day, I don't know if Dad thought it was a good or bad idea. He asked us a bunch of questions on every side of the issue, and then said, 'Whatever you two decide to do, you know I will support you.' and left it at that."

Nancy had also been surprised and a little annoyed by Harold's response to Megan. There was definitely something going on, which was not unusual. What was unusual was that Harold had not talked with her about it. No matter how tough things had got throughout their marriage, Nancy thought that Harold would talk it over with her. There were times, back when they had first met, when Harold would bottle things up, like the mess that his father had left behind. But that was a long time ago, well before they were married.

"Yeah, it's unusual for him to express such a one-sided opinion about a decision that isn't his to make. I was just reading through a proposal for the foundation from Uncle Jerry, and your dad wouldn't even make a comment on it for fear that anything he said might subvert my opinion before I had a chance to form it on my own. Even at work, your dad is big about making sure that the right people are making the decisions, and that they receive input, not direction, from others. Megan probably just caught him at the wrong moment. I'm sure that it's nothing."

Nancy was not at all sure that it was nothing. Outbursts driven by emotion were definitely not what she had come to expect from Harold, and given what she had to deal with at work, not something that she appreciated at home.

"As unusual as it was, I thought the same thing on Monday. I even talked with Megan the next day and told her not to worry. She knew Dad would support her in whatever decision she made."

"Good advice. I'm sure that you're right."

"I thought I was too until the incident last night."

"What happened last night?" Nancy asked, completely unaware of the incident between Harold, Jessie, and Phillip.

"Dad didn't tell you?"

"No, he didn't say a word."

"Phillip and I told Dad we wanted to adopt a baby, and he responded about the same way as he had to Megan. He completely blew a gasket, yelling and slamming his fist. He was sweating, his face turned red, and his eyes looked like they were going to pop out of his head. And then he topped it all off by saying that he 'would not allow it.' Christ, Phillip was furious on the way home. Good thing Brennen was with us, or I'm sure Phillip would have had some choice words about his opinion of Dad's reaction."

Nancy knew Jessie could be a little prone to exaggeration or telling a story in a fashion that created the strongest response, so she calmly asked a few questions before overreacting. "That doesn't sound like your father. I know it would thrill him to hear that you and Phillip were having another baby. Was there something about the adoption that was unusual?"

"In fairness, we did say we were thinking of adopting from another country," Jessie explained as if this was unneeded information that in no way better informed the story.

"Which countries?"

"The Ukraine, India, and Nigeria were the ones that came up."

By raising a single eyebrow, Nancy let Jessie know what she thought of the facts he had left out. However, as much as these added pieces of information might have changed the nature of the story, they did not change the fact that this was just not how Harold would normally react to a situation where someone he loved was trying to make a tough decision.

"Jessie, you know I appreciate your concern for your father, but until he's willing to share with us exactly what's bothering him, there isn't much that we can do. As far as adoption is concerned, I will give you the same advice that you gave your sister. You know your father will support you and Phillip in whatever you decide. And I will give you a little advice from someone who deals daily with families in crisis. No matter where the child comes from, find out as much as you possibly can about them and their circumstances. If something goes wrong, you won't be able to stop it from affecting your entire family, especially Brennen."

"We get that, and we appreciate that type of advice," Jessie responded. "Unfortunately, the conversation didn't get close to having that discussion. 'I won't allow it!' kind of killed the momentum. I thought that at that point, the best strategy was simply to leave before the conversation got any more heated."

Jessie picked up Brennen and said, "You know, Mom, through the years, Dad and I have had some pretty heated debates about a lot of things, including, at times, my behaviour. But I have never seen him get as visibly angry as he has been the last couple of nights. And it wasn't just that he was angry. He was perspiring and appeared to be in significant physical discomfort. There's definitely something wrong. I just hope that it doesn't take Dad too long to figure out what it is."

"How physically distressed?" Nancy asked with a furrowed brow.

"I'm not sure. But he sure didn't look good. I mean, it could have just been that he was really angry, but I don't understand why this is happening all of a sudden. It's just not like him."

With that said, Jessie and Brennen gave Nancy hugs, said goodbye, and headed back out the door.

As Nancy watched them drive away, she really didn't know what to think. If something was troubling Harold, she would expect him to tell her. He always seemed so good about letting people know how he felt. Harold would spew his positive emotions at every opportunity, telling his family and close friends how he felt about them. He was always at the front of the line praising her, his children, and even his employees. And no one was more appreciative of the amazing life they had acquired than Harold. He also didn't struggle to let someone know, in a kind and constructive way, if something they were doing was a problem. Surely if something was bothering Harold, he would simply tell her, though for the life of her, she could not remember the last time that anything was bothering Harold.

Harold's childhood friend Mark crossed Nancy's mind. *Why, after not seeing someone for decades, would his death bother someone as much as Mark's death seemed to be bothering Harold? It was not like it was the first time someone close to Harold had died. Was it because Mark had died from suicide? That was certainly sad, but why would that make the death any worse for Harold?*

"Well, I guess the best thing is to just ask," Nancy said to herself.

CHAPTER FOURTEEN

Harold glanced at his watch and realized that it was already past five. It had been a delightfully uneventful day, with no tough discussions with people who wanted to change their lives, and no frustrating conversations on where to take the company. It had been a great day, but he had promised Nancy that he would be home early, and he really needed to call Shane before he left. It never crossed his mind that Shane might not be in the office, so he dialled Shane's direct office line instead of his cell phone. He picked up after the first ring.

"Shane here." Very few people had the number to Shane's direct line, so he was comfortable that it would be someone he knew well.

"Shane, Harold here. How are you?"

"Good, Harold. What's up?"

"Shane, I want to stop by and sign my will on Thursday, but there are a couple of changes that I want you to make first."

There was a brief pause before Shane responded. "You've spoken with Nancy, and she's okay with the will?" There was a perceptible amount of surprise in Shane's voice that Harold ignored.

"We are planning to talk more tonight," Harold said, knowing that they were discussing Jerry's proposal for the foundation and not the will, a fact that he chose not to share with Shane.

"Okay, what are the changes?"

"Jerry has proposed a significant increase in Nancy's and my annual contribution to the foundation for this year. I'm not sure that we will make it, but if we do, I would like to have the amount given through my estate reduced by the amount of this year's extra donation, and then I want the amount given to the foundation spread over twenty years instead of a lump sum as we previously discussed."

Shane, who did not like almost every part of Harold's will, disliked this part even more. "Listen, Harold, I understand you're trying to control the use of money after your death, but are you sure you want to drag out contributions to a private foundation for that long? It could easily be thirty years before your will comes into effect, and then you're going to spread contributions into it for twenty more years. That's a long time. What if the foundation no longer exists?"

Harold completely ignored the point that Shane was obviously trying to make. "Good point. You should add a provision that if the foundation no longer exists, the funds should go to a minimum of five registered charities whose work focuses on the needs of youth in underserved communities."

"And who would make the determination?" Shane asked, fearing that he knew the costly response.

"The trustee will determine which charities will receive the funds."

"Why would you not have Nancy and your children determine who receives the funds? It makes no sense to pay a trustee to do the research and make the decision when your family would do it for nothing and probably enjoy the process." Shane could not understand the lengths that Harold was going to ensure that Nancy and the children had nothing to concern themselves with. Especially something like this, where they got to provide money to young people that really need it.

"As I've said throughout the drafting of this will, Shane, I do not want to leave burdensome work or opportunities for bickering behind for my family to deal with. If you want to put something in there that the family can submit recommendations, go ahead, but I want the trustee to make the decisions."

Shane started explaining the limitations of a trustee, especially one who would barely know the family, and the problems with trying to control his family's behaviour from the grave. Harold was not listening. He was thinking about how much easier this would be if he could simply explain to Shane why this was so important and why it was so immediate, but how could you tell someone that you think that there was a real possibility that you didn't have much time left in your life? How could you explain you were trying to take care of things while you still could?

"Look, Shane, we've been over and over these points. I get it. You think I'm putting too many restrictions in the will. However, clarity is extremely important to me. I don't want my family fighting over unimportant issues. I don't want them burdened with a bunch of paperwork, and I don't want my family to have to figure out a lot of issues that I can address before I die. Could you please just add the clauses that I asked for and get the will ready for my signature on Thursday?"

"Is there any chance that there may be some additional changes based on your conversation with Nancy tonight?"

Based on how Shane asked, Harold was certain that either Shane suspected that the conversation would not actually happen, or that Harold would not consider changes regardless of the conversation. He was certain that Shane was right. He truly believed he was doing what was best for his family, but it was quite likely they would not immediately recognize the value. Sure, Nancy would be annoyed when she first read the document, but once she saw it working for a couple of years, he was certain she would thank him. So why have the argument now? She could be pissed at him after he was dead.

"If there are any, I'll email you the information tonight or first thing tomorrow morning."

"Okay. Is 10:00 a.m. on Thursday okay for you to come over and sign the will?"

"Sure, that'd be great. See you then."

Shane said goodbye, and Harold shut down his computer and headed home. In Harold's mind, everything he was doing was going to make his family's and his employees' lives so much easier. He wouldn't leave a legacy of problems as his father had. Why was he the only one who could see the logic in his plan? Why did Shane continue to fight it?

CHAPTER FIFTEEN

"You can let the rest of the dishes air dry," Nancy remarked after Harold had dried and put away the pots and pans he had just washed.

"Thanks, but it's just as easy to dry them and put them away now," Harold replied. "What are you working on?"

"Just reviewing some notes from a case that I'm in the middle of, nothing urgent. Can I ask you a question about Mark?" Nancy ventured.

"Sure."

"Why do you think Mark's death is bothering you so much, and do you think it has anything to do with your recent anger issues?"

"Wow, that's a pretty big question. I don't know. I guess because it was suicide."

"I don't want to be callous, but as sad as that is, why would it affect you when you haven't seen Mark in decades?"

"Christ, Nancy. I don't know," Harold responded, really not wanting to have this discussion.

"Were the two of you close throughout school?"

"No. As I told you last night, after Mark and his family moved away when we were about fourteen. I didn't see or hear from him for years. There was no internet or Facebook back then. And teenagers didn't write letters, or at least not this teenager."

The more information Nancy got, the less sense it all made. Your best friend at the age of fourteen moved away. You had no contact with him for years, yet the news of his death fifty years later hit you hard. This was definitely a puzzle with more than a few missing pieces.

"And you never saw or heard of him again until you heard about his death?"

"No, I told you, we reconnected when we were in our early twenties. Mark had just gone through his first divorce, he was broke, and he was drinking heavily. I guess he thought reconnecting with his past might help."

"And did it?"

"It seemed to help a little. I got him into a rehab facility, and he was in pretty good shape for about a year. He even remarried, which was probably a mistake because that marriage didn't last much longer than the first, and he went right back to drinking."

"So that's when you lost track of him?"

"No, at that point, I wouldn't hear from him for months at a time, and then he'd show up on my doorstep sober and fully committed to staying that way. He'd ask me to help get him back into rehab, which I would, and he'd be good for six months to a year. Then one day, he'd fall off the wagon and disappear again."

"Did you go and look for him when he disappeared?"

"No, I never had any idea where to even start. The last time he disappeared was a couple of years before we met."

"How many times did he go into rehab?"

"Three that I know about. He might have gone more often, for all I know."

"Harold, rehab isn't cheap. How could he afford to keep going back if he couldn't keep a job?"

"Look, Nancy, I'm not sure how you would expect me to know all of this. He was a guy I knew as a kid who was in trouble. I tried to help him out, it didn't work, he disappeared. Not much more to the story."

Nancy was silent for quite a while as she tried to understand this relationship and the effect that this Mark had on Harold. "Harold, I could understand you trying to help the guy out once or twice, but after that, why would you keep taking him in? Whatever you were doing was clearly not working."

"You're probably right, but not much that I can do about that now."

Harold suddenly stood and started looking around for something, finally settling on the kitchen clock as the thing he was looking for. Once he had taken a good look at the clock, he turned to Nancy and said, "Christ, it's almost ten o'clock. I need to get to bed. I have a busy day tomorrow."

Nancy, recognizing immediately that Harold was trying to change the subject, asked again, "Harold, I'm just trying to understand why you would've done so much for someone you hadn't seen in years."

"I guess I was just a sucker who got conned by a sad story. I don't know, and what does it matter now? Can we just drop it?"

Harold was now busy getting ready to head for bed and was clearly trying to avoid making eye contact with Nancy. He just wanted the conversation to end. It was not going anywhere and would not change anything.

"Look, I don't know what you want me to say. I'm not sure why I tried to help Mark, and even less sure why he showed up on my doorstep after all those years. I guess I just wanted to try and make a difference. Finding out that he died by suicide just reminded me that I didn't. Can we stop talking about it?"

Nancy did not respond. There was no reason to, since Harold was already halfway down the hall, heading for their bedroom.

CHAPTER SIXTEEN

When Harold came through the back door, seeing his father, Ted Bower, sitting at the kitchen table with another man surprised him. His immediate reaction was to look around for his mother. She was not in the kitchen, which was also unusual, especially at this time of day. The other man had his back to Harold, so he was uncertain who it was, but the broad, slightly rounded shoulders, greying hair, black shirt, pants, socks, and shoes made Harold pretty certain it was Father Brown. Neither the priest nor Harold's father acknowledged his presence. They were deeply immersed in what appeared to be an intense game of cards.

There were three piles of money on the table, one in front of each of the men and the largest one centred between them. The two ashtrays were full, and the whisky glasses were nearly empty. It appeared the game had been going on for a while, which was no surprise to Harold.

Walking farther into the kitchen, Harold called out, "Mom. Hey, Mom? Mom, where are you?"

"Stop making so much noise. We're trying to talk over here. Your mom went to the store," Harold's father responded without looking over at Harold, maintaining his focus on whatever was happening at the table between him and Father Brown.

"Well, Father, it's up to you. Lay down another fiver and you get to see the cards that will beat you, or you can hold on to the parishioners' money for a few more minutes. One way or the other, you're going to lose it to me. You always do."

The look on his father's face, the smoke hanging in the air, and the sweat visible on the back of Father Brown's neck seemed even more sinister than usual. It seemed more like a melodrama than real life. A young boy walked into the room carrying a bottle of whisky. His hair and his clothes were a mess, as if he had slept in a haystack or a dirty old barn and not bothered to clean up. As he solemnly turned his head, Harold recognized the face. It was Mark. He did not acknowledge Harold. Mark appeared completely devoid of any emotion, like all the life had been squeezed out of him.

Mark poured whisky into Harold's father's glass and then approached the priest. The priest told Mark to genuflect before he poured whisky into his glass. He claimed it was a sign of respect, and all children should show respect to priests. Mark genuflected, then poured whisky into the priest's glass. As he was pouring, the priest reached around behind Mark and grabbed Mark's ass with a hand so large that it nearly covered it completely. Mark visibly cringed but said nothing.

"Get your hands off of him," Harold said in a voice barely loud enough to be heard.

The priest swung his head around, and for the first time, Harold could see his face. It was ugly, twisted, and mean. His nose and cheeks showed the signs of excessive alcohol consumption. A cigarette dangled from his overly large lips, his eyebrows were thin, long, and completely out of control, and his dirty hair was plastered to his head.

"What did you say, boy?" the priest asked. There was no anger in his voice, only a challenge, curious to see if the child had the nerve to repeat his comment when he knew it would be heard.

Harold desperately wanted to stand up tall and repeat his demand. But it was all that he could do to whisper, "I told you to leave him alone."

"Perhaps I should leave him alone. Maybe it is time that I focus my attention on you. What do you think, Ted? Do you think it is about time that I taught your mouthy son a thing or two?"

Harold's father said nothing. He didn't even look up from the cards in his hand.

"Come here, boy. Let's you and I have a little talk. I'm kind of tired of talking to Mark. It would be nice to have someone new to talk with." The priest pushed Mark away and turned his chair around so that his entire body was facing Harold. "Come on over here, boy. We can have a nice conversation."

The priest was hideous. His eyes were bloodshot and even at that distance, Harold could smell the body odour and the bad breath. He desperately wanted to grab Mark and run from the room, but he could not move. He wanted to scream at his father or yell for his mother, but he could do neither. He simply stood there, staring at the leering priest.

Suddenly, the priest stood and walked toward Harold. He moved slowly, giving Harold lots of time to run, but as much as Harold wanted and tried to, he could not make himself move. He looked at his father, whose eyes were still on his cards, seeming to be completely oblivious to what was happening between Harold and Father Brown.

As the priest got closer, he smiled a smile so evil it turned Harold's stomach. He could feel himself retching. Harold leaned his shoulder against the wall for an anchor as the priest walked into range and reached out to grab him. Harold kicked his foot out in a sideways karate kick that he had never done before. The kick landed on the priest's chest, knocking him back momentarily. The priest's smile became even larger, and he laughed as he reached out again to grab Harold. Harold kicked again, this time hitting the priest in the face, but the priest kept coming. Harold kicked again and again, hitting the priest repeatedly but barely slowing him down. Harold was terrified. In a fit of desperation, he summoned all his strength and kicked his leg out once again, letting out a blood-curdling scream as his foot landed squarely on the priest's face.

Suddenly, from the darkness, Harold could hear a woman's voice screaming his name over and over. There was genuine terror in the voice. Whoever she was, she was clearly terrified by what was happening. But it wasn't his mother's voice.

"Harold, Harold, Harold?" Nancy screamed as she watched him violently kick the blankets off the bed while screaming something that was completely incomprehensible.

On the last kick, Harold woke up. He instantly knew Nancy's voice and recognized that it was a dream. Nancy was standing at the end of the bed and visibly shaking from what she had just witnessed. Harold's first concern, despite being drenched in sweat, was Nancy.

"It's okay. It was just a dream," Harold said as he jumped out of the bed and rushed over to hug Nancy.

She stepped back as he approached with open arms. "Don't hug me. You're covered with sweat." He couldn't tell if the quiver in her voice was because she was angry or frightened.

"You're going to have to change the sheets before you can go back to bed. What on earth is wrong with you? You were scream- ing and then suddenly you started kicking, over and over." As she hugged herself and maintained her distance from Harold.

"It was just a bad dream," Harold said, honestly not knowing how to explain it.

"What the fuck were you dreaming about?" Nancy responded as she grabbed a blanket from the chair beside the bed and wrapped it around herself.

"I'm not sure. I don't know, maybe, well, probably. I don't know. It's all pretty much a blur."

"Well, you scared the shit out of me. Harold, I don't know what is going on, but you need to get control of yourself."

As they stripped the bed and Harold changed into a dry T-shirt and boxers, Nancy, slowly calming down, asked for more details about the dream. The little that Harold could remember, he was not willing to share. Fortunately, Harold seldom remembered anything about his dreams, so Nancy reluctantly accepted his lack of explanation, but she was clearly not at all happy.

Harold lay awake in the clean bed linens and thought about the parts of the dream he could remember. It was clear what it was about, but why now? Why, after all these years? The feelings of guilt and shame had never gone away completely, but they had never caused him to have nightmares. Laying there, he could again feel the presence. It was going from annoying to disturbing. Harold, for the first time, was concerned about his personal state of mind.

CHAPTER SEVENTEEN

Harold was already sitting at the kitchen table, drinking his morning coffee, when Nancy came out of their room.

"Well, you certainly gave me a fright last night," Nancy said as she poured herself a cup of coffee.

"Yeah, that certainly was odd."

"Can you remember any more about the dream?"

"All that I can remember is kicking at someone, but I don't remember who or why," Harold said, knowing that an honest answer would take them down a rabbit hole that he had neither the time nor the interest to pursue.

"Did it have anything to do with the stuff Megan and Jessie shared with you?"

"Wow, that's pretty arbitrary. What made you think of that?"

"Your behaviour, I'm trying to figure out where all this is coming from. Aren't you?"

"What do you mean by 'all of this'? I had a nightmare. Haven't you ever had a nightmare?"

"Not one that involves shouting and kicking. And it's not just the nightmare. It's the outbursts. You're not yourself, and I'd think that you would want to know why. I know I would if it were me."

Harold got a big smile on his face. "That was pretty crazy last night, wasn't it? But I really do think that you're blowing things out of proportion. I'm sure it's just a lot of things hitting me at the same time, nothing to be concerned about. And no, I don't think the dream had anything to do with Megan and Jessie's stuff."

"Okay. If you say so." Nancy had to remind herself that Harold was not one of her clients. It wasn't her job to figure out what was happening with Harold—he could do that on his own. At least, she thought that he could.

"Do you want to talk about Jerry's proposal before you leave for work? I've reviewed it and really like what they have in mind." Nancy opened the file and continued, "How do you feel about giving them that much money? It's more than I expected."

"My concern is the sustainability of the program if something unusual happens. Things are great right now, but shit has a way of happening when you least expect it. I'd hate to make a commitment like this and then have to rethink it a year or two from now," Harold responded, thankful to talk about anything other than his recent behaviour.

"There was nothing in the proposal that suggested that we had an option for a similar but smaller program. Do you think that's possible?" asked Nancy.

"I think we should tell Jerry what we think is reasonable for us, and then let Jerry and the foundation figure out how they can get there. They may want to find alternate sources of money rather than reducing the size of the program."

"Are you okay with that?" Nancy mused. "Would you let someone other than you and Jerry put money into the foundation? Wouldn't they want some say in how the money is used?"

"There are already other people putting smaller amounts of money into the foundation for specific projects, and I'm okay with it as long as the control of the foundation and the work it does remains with Jerry and our family."

"The amount of money Jerry is committing to this program is also surprising. I know he's very committed to these kids, but that's a pretty big number."

Harold smiled. He was very proud of his younger brother and his commitment to this work. "It isn't just the money for Jerry. He spends a lot of personal time with these kids. This is his family; these are his children. It's very important to him that they get a chance in life."

"Do you think Jerry will ever get married and have a family of his own?"

"Anything is possible, but it becomes less probable every year. He may get married; he has had a couple of semi-serious relationships, but I don't see him having kids of his own. He's fifty-seven. I can't imagine him changing diapers at this point."

"Well, in my opinion, the foundation and the kids that it helps are the benefactors of Jerry's decision to not have a family."

"I couldn't agree more. So, what should I tell Jerry? We support the proposal as-is; we support it, but you need to find an alternate source of some of the funding; or we support it, but we want you to reduce the size of the program?" Harold asked, knowing that he was not providing Nancy with all the information she might need to make the decision.

"I know the amount they are asking for this year is not a problem for us, but saying yes means years of similar contributions. Are you okay with that?" Nancy asked, truly unsure of how Harold may respond.

Harold, just for a second, wanted to tell Nancy about his new will, and how he had set it up to ensure that they could continue to make this level of contribution for the next twenty years. But he realized that this information would lead to a whole series of questions about why he was changing his will, and what other changes he was making. Should she be changing her will as well? All questions Harold did not want to deal with at the moment. "Yes, I'm confident we can afford it. If you want us to."

Nancy got a big smile on her face. Making this decision made her feel good. It was one of those moments where having a husband who seemed to be constantly working was worth it. "If you are okay with it, yes, I would like to make the commitment."

"Okay, it's a done deal. I'll let Jerry know. I'm sure both Jerry and Bill Tessler from the foundation will call you to thank you. This is an enormous deal for all of us." Harold got up and gave his wife a big hug and kiss. He was always proud of his wife, and proud of himself for being smart enough to ask her to marry him, but moments like this were especially gratifying. She was a truly wonderful woman, and he was thrilled to be a part of her life.

CHAPTER EIGHTEEN

Dr. Jeff Wang had been Harold's doctor for most of Harold's adult life. He was the only person aware of Harold's obsession with the timing and nature of his father's death.

The room looked like a thousand other examination rooms, though Harold could not recall being in any other examination rooms other than the four in Dr. Wang's office, and they were definitely all the same. They were the same size, Harold guessed eight feet by ten feet, and the walls were all painted a boring off-white. There was a small set of shelves on part of one wall and an examination table on the opposite wall. The ceiling was off-white acoustic tile to match the walls, with fluorescent lighting to maximize the sterility of the room. Harold had never taken the time to inventory the room, but he was pretty sure that every one of Dr. Wang's examination rooms had exactly the same equipment and supplies, right down to the same number of cotton balls and tongue depressors.

Dr. Wang entered the room and said hello to Harold while he was reading Harold's file. It was never clear if he had not previously read the file, or if he was simply refreshing his memory before talking to Harold about the contents.

"Good morning, Jeff," Harold said in response. "So, am I going to live?"

Harold had started getting a battery of tests every year about three years ago. The tests were more than the health system would pay for, and more than Jeff felt were necessary, but Harold insisted and paid to have them completed.

"Before we get into the test results, I have a couple of questions," Jeff said as he sat down on the chair beside Harold.

"The usual?"

"Yes, the usual: any cold sweats, chest pain, light-headedness—"

Harold smiled as he interrupted Jeff. "No, I have not experienced any symptoms. How about the test results?"

"Nothing much different from last year's tests. Your LDL continues to be considerably higher than I'm comfortable with, but that is mostly offset by your high HDL. It is unfortunate that you have such a poor reaction to statins. I assume you continue to get lots of exercise and take it easy with the wine."

Jeff did not wait for an answer. Based on the test results, he had no doubt that Harold was on top of both. "The CT scan of your heart and the CT coronary angiogram both look acceptable. All the other numbers look good, as they did last year. According to the tests, your arteries continue to narrow, and sometime in the next few years, we'll want you to see a cardiologist about a possible angioplasty. But so far, the diet and exercise seem to be keeping you in good health."

"No open-heart surgery?"

"No, not yet. But, Harold, you have to remember that despite your hard work, you have inherited a problem that'll be more and more unpredictable as you get older."

"But for now, I'm in good shape and shouldn't worry," Harold said as more of a statement than a question.

"Harold, dealing with conditions like yours can be tricky. On the one hand, it's very serious and you have to be diligent about maintaining your healthy lifestyle and sticking to the practice of regular checkups. And, of course, it's important that you let me know of any changes in your health, especially if you're experiencing any of the symptoms." Jeff paused, wanting to make sure that Harold had absorbed this information. "On the other hand, you can't live your life constantly worried that you're going to have a heart attack."

"I don't worry about it. I'm just aware of it." Harold responded as he always did to this comment from Jeff.

After reviewing the results of the raft of tests Harold had insisted on having, Jeff was a little skeptical about that response. "You don't worry about it? Do you think about it often? Does it affect your decisions? Does it affect your moods or behaviour? Harold, you're incredibly healthy, and you can take most of the credit for that, but you have to put your father's heart attack in proper perspective. Absolutely maintain the healthy decisions. That's great. Be prepared if something happens. Also great. But other than that, focus on enjoying life. Thinking about it all the time is simply not a healthy way to live."

This was a great opening for Harold to talk about what he was going through, his obsession with preparing for his death, his mood swings, and his inability to talk to anyone, even Nancy, about it. Jeff was not only his doctor; he was a friend. He was someone Harold could trust; and he was someone who would get Harold some help without judgment.

Instead, Harold responded, "I don't think about it all the time. In fact, you're the only person I even talk to about it."

"Harold, going to the other extreme also isn't healthy. Tell your family, especially Nancy, about your condition. Give them an opportunity to understand what you're dealing with and exactly what to do if something did happen. With a widowmaker, an immediate response is critical."

"Jeff, you worry too much. I'm fine."

Jeff contemplated that comment, wondering if Harold was really fine, physically or emotionally. He wondered how society had come to this—individuals taking all the steps necessary to care for themselves, while ignoring or denying the critical role of community.

"Harold, I still think that it'd be helpful if you brought Nancy to an appointment. The more that she knows about your condition, the better for everyone."

Jeff had made this suggestion many times before, to no avail. Unfortunately, only Harold could make the decision to inform Nancy. Jeff was obliged to follow his patient's wishes.

Harold's response, as it had been on this subject in the past, was surprisingly quick and excessively blunt. "No, Nancy doesn't need to be worrying about this. I'm doing everything that needs to be done."

"Harold, you are doing a great job, but you have to understand, this type of thing is incredibly unpredictable. You could be as healthy as a horse one day and dead the next."

"I said that I have it."

"Harold, if you won't talk to Nancy, I would be happy to refer you to someone who specializes in this area."

There was a look of surprise on Harold's face. Jeff had never gone down this road before. Where was this coming from? More importantly, where was it going? "Someone who specializes in what area?"

"Someone who deals with our inability to admit that we are mortal."

"That's not something I struggle with."

"Then tell Nancy."

"I will when I'm ready."

"Hopefully, that won't be too late."

"Didn't you just tell me that everything looks great and that I'm doing all the right things?" Harold questioned, though the tone of his voice suggested more of an accusation than a question.

Jeff's response was direct and to the point. "That doesn't mean you absolutely won't have a heart attack. It just means that it's unlikely. There are so many uncontrollable factors. Why not take as much risk out of the situation as you can? Tell people and let them prepare themselves to help if it's ever needed. Why is that so hard?"

"Look, Jeff, if I tell people, they're just going to worry and then start treating me differently. I don't want to be treated differently. When the time comes, I will tell them. But now is not the time."

"Your call, of course," Jeff responded reluctantly. "Before I let you go, do you have any questions or concerns we haven't covered in this session?"

"No. I'm good," Harold responded, not comprehending how Jeff could not understand how he felt. Harold didn't want people looking after him. Looking after people was his job.

As Jeff opened the door to leave, he turned back to Harold. In a voice of friendship that revealed his personal concern for his friend, he said, "Harold, you have my cell phone and home phone numbers. If anything changes, please call me immediately. No matter what time of day it is."

Harold smiled. "You worry too much, but thank you. And yes, I'll call if anything changes."

Once Jeff left the examination room, Harold took a moment to consider what had just happened. He had no intention of letting people baby him. Jeff had said himself that Harold was in great health; telling Jeff about the mild little symptoms he had experienced recently would not have changed the test results. He was fine. It was way too early to tell anyone.

CHAPTER NINETEEN

When Harold arrived at the office, Gail let him know that Ramesh and Alison were in their offices and that they hoped they could meet with him for a few minutes as soon as he came in. This was not an unusual request, so as soon as he arrived in his office, he sent them both a text, letting them know he was in and would be happy to talk as soon as they were free. Alison responded immediately, saying they would be right down.

"Hey, Harold, thanks for seeing us so quickly. We've taken a more in-depth look at your proposed ten-year plan and have some suggested changes that may get the plan to accomplish both of our goals," Ramesh said as he walked into the office directly behind Alison.

"Good morning," Harold responded.

"Sorry, good morning," Ramesh said with a smile. "How's your day been so far?"

"So far, so good. How about the two of you?"

"It has been a little busy. Lots of opportunities out there, which is why we're so eager to talk about the company's future," Alison piped in.

"I don't believe I've ever seen the industry so buoyant. Everyone wants industrial and warehouse space. If we build it, Alison can lease it, and with our reputation as landlords, she can get a premium," Ramesh said enthusiastically.

"That's great," Harold responded. "Just keep in mind that we built that reputation on providing a premium experience for a premium price."

"Of course, that's a given. We'll check competitors' lease rates and the terms of their leases before we even consider setting ours," Alison offered.

"And if you agree with our suggested modifications to the plan, we'll make sure that our new buildings offer the premium amenities our customers want, not the cool ones that no one knows how to use," Ramesh piped in.

"Okay, so let's look at what you're suggesting." Harold thought he might be able to get his head around a little well-considered and conservatively financed growth that would protect the family's wealth and provide some upside for the management team.

What Ramesh and Alison showed him over the next twenty minutes did not even come close to meeting his expectations. There was far more growth and far higher risk than he had expected. If he was going to be there to manage the risk, it was a well-thought-through, risk-mitigated plan. If he was not going to be there, the plan was full of unnecessary and indeterminable risks. He could feel the immediate change in his mood. This plan did not in any way meet his need to take care of his family before he was gone.

"Guys, I thought we talked about a small growth program that would create some upside for the management team. This is 15 percent growth per year for the next six years. That is way more risk than we talked about," Harold said, trying his best to maintain a calm and businesslike manner, despite the feeling that he was already perspiring.

"It is a lot of growth, but the financing is still very conservative. We wouldn't even be close to the debt-to-equity ratios that the bank would be comfortable providing," Ramesh offered.

Debt-to-equity ratios? What the fuck? This is my family's future you are playing with . . . hammered across Harold's brain. Instead, he said, "Keep in mind the bank's job is to lend us as much money as they are confident we can pay back, even if we don't need it. Our job is to make sure this company is around for a very long time by not taking unnecessary risks."

"But Harold, these risks are much smaller than we've taken in the past, in much less appealing economic conditions," Alison offered, anticipating that Harold, as he always had been, would be open to listening to a completely different point of view. She continued, "I don't think any of our bankers or advisers would classify these as unnecessarily significant risks. In fact, just the opposite. I would suggest that they'd call these well-considered risks that would keep the company up to date for years to come."

The bankers and advisers aren't running this fucking company, was what he wanted to say. Struggling to keep it civil, Harold said, "Yes, you're probably right. But it's not their risk, so I'm not inclined to put too much credence in what they think."

"But don't you agree that a reasonable amount of growth would be good for the organization?" Alison asked.

The feeling that he was losing control made it difficult to think clearly. Their arguments were sound; his emotions were not. He could feel his internal temperature rising. He could feel the sweat and desperately wanted to wipe his forehead, but mostly he wanted to stand and walk out of the room without saying a word.

He looked down at the papers in front of him but had no ability to focus on anything that was written on them. No one said anything. Ramesh and Alison looked at each other, neither knowing what to say or do next. They had never seen their boss like this. He was always in complete control. Harold kept his eyes on the paperwork, not saying a word. Finally, after what seemed like an eternity, he lifted his head and looked first at Alison and then at Ramesh. They could see the sweat on his face. His eyes lacked any expression, as if he were alone, staring at a blank wall. His face was pale and lifeless.

"Harold, are you okay?" Ramesh asked.

It took Harold a moment to respond as he tried desperately to gather control of his emotions. "I'm fine, just a little distracted by some other issues that I'm dealing with." He could feel the anxiety diminishing. "Sorry, where were we? Alison, you were saying something about a reasonable amount of growth being good for the organization. Do you want to explain that comment?"

Alison looked again at Ramesh, not sure that she should continue.

"Are you sure that you're all right, Harold?" Ramesh asked. "We don't need to do this today. We can talk about it next week if you'd like."

What Harold would like would be for the two of them to accept his plan as-is and let him get on with taking care of everyone's future while he still could. Instead, he said, "Actually, that's a good idea. I'm a little distracted, and this really needs my full attention. Leave your proposed changes with me to mull over for a few days, and then we can sit down and have a more fulsome discussion."

"We don't have a formal presentation. We only have our notes, but we could have something for you by the end of the day," Alison offered.

"Sure, that'd be great."

There was one significant problem he did not want to share: the will he was determined to sign tomorrow would not allow for this or any other change of plan. The will would instruct the trustee to follow Harold's plan, and they would not have an option. Harold was truly tired of explaining things.

CHAPTER TWENTY

"I'm glad you caught me before I left work. I was just walking out the door." Jessie had called just before Harold left his office to see if Harold could give him a lift home.

"Sorry for the inconvenience. My car was supposed to be ready, but the shop phoned and said that the parts didn't arrive so it won't be ready until tomorrow. I could have taken an Uber," Jessie responded.

"No, I'm glad you called. It'll give me an opportunity to apologize for my behaviour," Harold continued, not giving Jessie an opportunity to accept the apology. "I don't think what you and Phillip are considering is a good idea, but that doesn't make my response acceptable or appropriate."

"Dad, just a suggestion, but you may want to work on your apologies," Jessie said with a smile that blunted the comment. "So, what is it about the idea that you don't like?"

Harold thought for a moment, wanting to provide his son with some good advice without sounding like he was telling him how to live.

"I think it's great that you and Phillip want another child. You're fantastic parents, but I'm very concerned about the level of risk involved with bringing a child in from some of the countries that you mentioned."

Jessie was not at all surprised that his dad would take this position. "You don't think that a child from one of those countries is in far more need than either a child that we create with a surrogate or a Canadian child looking for adoption?"

"Oh no, I agree that this specific child has a greater need and is less likely to have it filled than either of the other children you described, but that's not my point."

"So, what is your point?" Jessie said with a genuine sense of interest.

"The risk is that the problems created by the baggage that comes with that child could negatively affect a lot of other people's lives."

"How?" Jessie asked, not completely disagreeing but curious about the risks that his dad would focus on.

"In innumerable ways," Harold said and then started to list them. "The government could take the child away, which would be crushing for everyone; there may be serious genetic problems that may make the child a threat to Brennen or Layla; the family may show up and make threats, or worse, do something terrible like kidnap the child because they believe it is truly theirs."

"Wow, Dad. I think you're going off the deep end of paranoia."

"You might be right. But when you consider that there are some very different and, in some cases, archaic cultures in this world, are you really sure you know what to expect from some of these countries? I mean, look at what the Catholic Church and the Canadian government did to children," Harold said as he stopped the car to let a pedestrian cross the street.

The car had just started to move again, and Jessie was just about to respond by asking what the Catholic Church had to do with the situation, when the strangest thing that Jessie had ever experienced unfolded, without any explanation.

Suddenly, in what appeared like a single motion that was far beyond the normal abilities of a sixty-three-year-old man, Harold slammed on the brakes, put the car in park, unbuckled his seatbelt, opened his car door, and sprang out of the car, yelling, "You dumb piece of shit! Fuck you! Try saying that to my face."

Harold, at six foot two and two hundred pounds, was not a small man, but fortunately for everyone involved, Jessie was bigger, faster, and a lot more agile. So, before Harold could make physical contact with the target of his ongoing verbal abuse, Jessie had placed himself between the two men.

"Dad, take it easy. Calm down," Jessie said as he tried to redirect his dad back to the car.

"You stick that finger up at me again, and I'll break it off and shove it up your ass," Harold screamed at the much smaller man, who was now visibly shaken and apparently very happy with Jessie's intrusion into the situation.

"Dad, just get back in the car. It's not worth it," Jessie said, trying to calm his dad even though Jessie had absolutely no idea what had caused this response.

Harold offered no real resistance to Jessie, turning back to the car and saying no more after the instructional comment about the man's finger.

"Are you okay, Dad?" Jessie asked once they were both back in the car.

"Yeah, I'm fine. I don't know why that self-righteous little prick set me off," Harold said as he put the car in gear and drove away.

"Do you know him?" Jessie asked.

"Yeah, he's an obnoxious prick from the club who's always shooting his mouth off about how the church is being unfairly condemned because of the actions of a few rotten apples." Harold's heart was pounding, his chest hurt like hell, he was sweating, and he knew he had made a complete fool of himself in front of his son.

"He actually says that?" Jessie asks, more than a little surprised.

"Not in those exact words."

"That's what set you off?" Jessie asked, still shocked by what he had just experienced.

"No. After I stopped to let him cross the street, he was barking something at me as he walked in front of the car. I couldn't tell what it was, but I could tell by the expression on his face that it wasn't pleasant. Then, as we were driving by him, he turned and gave me the middle finger. I know it was a stupid way for me to respond. I shouldn't have responded at all, and normally wouldn't. But today, it was just too much."

"Why today, Dad? What happened today?"

"Oh, nothing specific."

Harold was really not at all sure what it was in the last couple of days that would cause him to get this angry over something that he would normally have laughed at.

"It has been a tough couple of days, and I guess I just snapped. Sorry about that, and thanks for getting in my way."

"Dad, I'm really worried about you. There has to be something happening that is causing this behaviour. It's not at all like you."

"Jessie, I appreciate your concern, but it really is nothing specific, just a few things mounting up at the same time. Please don't worry, I just need a little time to get through a few issues."

"You should talk about it with someone. This is not healthy."

"There is really nothing to talk about. I really am fine," Harold responded, noting to himself that this was the second person, on the same day, who had made this suggestion.

As they drove up to his house, Jessie tried to extend the conversation, desperately wanting to help his dad. But Harold told Jessie that Nancy was waiting for him and that he really needed to get going. Jessie knew that he had no choice. If Harold did not want to talk about it, there was nothing he could do to force the conversation. As Jessie walked to his front door, he took his phone from his pocket and made the only call he thought might help.

CHAPTER TWENTY-ONE

Nancy decided that if Harold would not open up on his own, it was time to push him for a more open conversation about his recent behaviour. If Nancy was uncertain before, Jessie's call confirmed it. Something was seriously bothering Harold. At this point, she could only guess what it might be.

When they had first met, Harold had been prone to mood swings. And Harold's mother often told stories about his mood swings as a teenager, and how many problems they caused for her and him. But it had been years, decades, since she had seen anything like what she was seeing now. Harold was notorious for his smile, his optimism, and his ability to deal calmly and thoughtfully with adversity. This recent behaviour was bizarre.

He would be home for dinner soon, and Nancy decided that tonight had to be the night. Whatever was bothering Harold, they had to deal with it. The sooner, the better, as far as Nancy was concerned.

The garage door opened; Harold was home. Dinner was almost ready, and Nancy decided to broach the subject while they were eating. She hoped he would be less emotional with his mouth full of broccoli, his favourite vegetable.

The moment Harold walked in the door, Nancy knew that this was going to be even more difficult than she had anticipated. Harold, who almost always gave Nancy a hug when he came home, walked right by her on his way to the closet to hang up his coat. A barely audible grunt was his only acknowledgement of Nancy's existence.

"Tough day?" Nancy asked in what could not be described as a kind voice.

"You heard?" Harold replied.

"Yeah, Jessie called. He was concerned."

"Yeah, I don't blame him, and that's not the half of it," Harold said as he pulled out a chair and sat down at the dinner table.

"Are you hungry?" Nancy asked as she put dinner on the table.

"Not particularly, but this looks good, and I would much prefer to eat than mope."

"Well, that's good to hear. If you didn't want to eat, I would really be concerned. I can't think of anything that has ever stopped you from enjoying a good meal. I'm pretty sure I had to drag you away from dinner for the births of both of our children," Nancy said with a smile.

Harold gave Nancy a half-hearted smile and said, "What's that saying, 'live to eat or eat to live'?"

It wasn't much, but at least he was talking.

They both filled their plates and sat down at the table to eat. Between bites, as casually as possible, Nancy said, "Do you want to tell me about what happened?"

Harold stopped eating and looked up at Nancy. The emotion on his face was hard to read. He wasn't angry, and he wasn't sad. It was more a look of disappointment. "You know, I really don't want to talk about any of it, but I suppose I should."

"Why don't you want to talk about it?"

Harold fell silent for what seemed like an eternity. He didn't want to talk about it because even he thought that his behaviour was unacceptable. Nancy would just get frustrated with the weak excuses, point out that he was a grown-up, and tell him to put on his big boy pants and deal with whatever it was that was bothering him, one of her favourite pieces of advice. But this was not a thought that he could share with Nancy, at least not yet.

"I really don't know what to say. I have an almost idyllic life, a wonderful family, a great company, and all the privileges people rightly accuse people like me of having, and yet I'm snapping at every little thing that disrupts my little life plan. It is stupid and embarrassing, and I can't seem to control it. And what's worse, I'm letting the people I love the most see the worst part of me."

Nancy quickly responded, "With the possible exception of that poor guy on the road today."

"Yeah, that poor guy. I can't imagine what he thought when I came out of the car, all guns blazing." Harold managed a half smile, thinking about how stupid he must have looked. "Thankfully, Jessie was there."

"When I talked to Jessie, he said that his view of the situation was very different from yours."

"Not surprisingly, Jessie's view of almost everything is different than mine. What did he say?" Harold responded with no sign of anger.

Nancy proceeded carefully. "Well, discounting Jessie's habit of exaggerating, he said that the man was talking on his phone as he walked in front of you and that you sped off a little early, which was probably what caused the finger. He also said you recognized the guy from church. I said that seemed impossible, given you haven't been to a church for decades."

There was a look of realization on Harold's face as he sat up a little straighter and said, "Fuck, he probably had those little earbuds in his ears, and I was too self-absorbed to even notice. Probably wasn't even the guy I thought he was, and it wasn't from church. The guy I thought he was is a church guy."

"So, it wasn't really anything that this guy did?"

"Apparently not. I seem to be on the edge all the time. And the magnitude of the feelings is overwhelming. They bubble up like a volcano about to erupt, and before I even have a chance to calm myself down, I have said something or done something that I can't take back. I had a meeting with Ramesh and Alison today about our strategic plan, and the only way I could control my emotions was to not have the discussion at all."

"Were they asking for something ridiculous?"

"No, they were being totally reasonable. I was being a dick."

"And you can't think of anything unusual happening in your life."

"Let's see. My daughter wants to quit her great job, my son wants to adopt a child from India or Nigeria, my executive team wants to add a ton of debt so they can fill their pockets, my brother wants us to contribute a lot more money to the foundation, my lawyer cannot seem to take simple instructions, some random guy on the street is flipping me the bird, and I'm having nightmares that are scaring the shit out of my wife."

Harold paused, looked at Nancy, and got a hint of a smile on his face as he reached over, took her hand, and said, "Now that you mention it, definitely different, but nothing unusual."

Nancy laughed, knowing exactly what Harold meant.

"All these things that are bothering me so much may be different issues, but I have spent my entire adult life dealing with issues like these, and at times a lot worse. So why, suddenly, am I having so much trouble dealing with them?"

Nancy smiled at Harold and said, "I was hoping you could tell me." She paused and then added, "Do you think Mark's death has anything to do with it?"

For the first time in the conversation, Nancy saw Harold become defensive. He slowly took his hand away from hers, sat up a little straighter, and responded, in Nancy's opinion, way too quickly and emphatically.

"No, why would the death of someone I haven't seen in thirty years cause all this? It makes no sense."

Nancy proceeded cautiously, recognizing she had hit a chord, which may or may not be the key to all of this. She did not want to lose Harold now. "And the fact that it was suicide doesn't make a difference?"

Nancy watched as Harold visibly calmed himself, dropping his shoulders ever so slightly. "There is no question that I feel worse about Mark's death than I would if some other old friend had died, and the fact that it was a suicide doesn't help. It makes me feel a little guilty that I didn't help him more, but it wasn't me that disappeared. He could have come to me for help if he wanted. I never said no."

"Sorry, do you or don't you think Mark's suicide has anything to do with how you are feeling?"

"Oh, I'm sure it's part of it, but I can't believe that it's a big part of it. Who knows, maybe I'm just getting old and cranky."

Harold got up from his chair, patted his wife on the shoulder, and started clearing the dinner dishes. "I'm sure that anyone hearing that someone they grew up with and was as close as I was to Mark would be a little shaken by hearing that they had died from suicide."

"Did it bother you a lot when Mark moved away?"

"Oh, God. Nancy, that was fifty years ago. I don't remember," Harold flat-out lied. "I was fourteen. Who knows what would have bothered me back then?"

"Maybe if you could remember a little more about your relationship with Mark, it would help with whatever it is you're going through right now," Nancy suggested.

Maybe if I could forget about my relationship with Mark, it would help, Harold thought but said, "Nancy, there really wasn't that much to it. We were kids, we did kid things, and then he moved. Wasting time talking about Mark won't make me feel better. I just need to stop taking everyone else's issues so seriously."

"You think that's the source of your outbursts?" Nancy said with surprise. To her, that seemed much too simple and very unlikely.

"Yeah, I really do. All this stuff with Megan and Jessie, and even the work stuff. I have to just chill a little more, not take it all so seriously."

"But why all of a sudden? Like you said, you've been dealing with these types of things for years. Why are they bothering you now?"

"Because I'm letting them. Plain and simple. What is it you always say? 'Put on your big boy pants.' "

"Maybe you're right. It's certainly worth a try," Nancy acknowledged skeptically. She could not determine if Harold was really convinced that it was all a matter of attitude—which Nancy believed was often the case—or if there was something more that Harold was not sharing, maybe even not acknowledging to himself. "And by the way, about that comment about being old and cranky. You may be turning sixty-four, but you look and act like you're in your early fifties."

Harold gave his wife a kiss and helped with the cleanup. They talked about the foundation, their neighbours, and their plans for the weekend. There was no further conversation about Harold's recent behaviour.

Lying in bed, staring at the ceiling, unable to sleep, Harold tried his best to reflect thoughtfully on the conversation he had just had with his wife. He knew he had avoided talking about anything that was truly bothering him, but he didn't see how dwelling on those things would help, and he knew what Nancy's reaction would be. She would tell him exactly what he had told her, "Put on your big boy pants. There are people out there with real problems." She was right. What did it say about him, acting like an idiot when there were people all over the world with actual problems? Harold doubled down on his after-dinner statement to Nancy. *You have an amazing life. Quit being such a baby about all of your tiny little problems*, he told himself and eventually drifted off to sleep.

CHAPTER TWENTY-TWO

Shane was not feeling well on Thursday morning, so Harold and Shane met virtually, as was now the custom in most organizations. Signing the last will and testament virtually was not a problem, thanks to a bill passed in 2020 due to COVID-19.

"Are you still going to take the day off tomorrow and join me for some quality time in the mountains?" Harold asked as Shane's face appeared on his computer screen.

Shane was working from home that day. However, the background was not Shane's house. It was a stock picture of someone else's office. Harold could not care less about the background, except that having a fake background did some strange things to the picture of Shane himself. Throughout the conversation, parts of Shane's head and body would disappear and then reappear, an ear here, part of the top of his head there, one shoulder, then the other. Harold found it annoying and had told Shane about it, but Shane never made a change.

"I'm sure it's just a twenty-four-hour thing," Shane said.

"Great, I'm really looking forward to a day in the mountains. The fresh air and the exercise will do me a lot of good," Harold said and then switched subjects without giving Shane an opportunity to pursue that comment. "So, I've read through all of your changes, and I think that all of them work how I had hoped they would. Are there any issues from your point of view that would cause me to not sign the will as it is? It looks good to me."

Shane shuffled through the pages for a moment, not really looking at anything. "Harold, I know you're tired of hearing this, but as your lawyer, I'm again encouraging you to reconsider the nature and many of the details of this will. You're making decisions in this document that will seriously affect your family's lives on issues that won't occur for decades. You cannot possibly have the information you'd need to make these decisions. I strongly recommend you reconsider making some changes and leave those decisions to the people involved."

This was far from the first time Shane had made a recommendation on a document that Harold did not agree with. Normally, Harold would have a calm, analytical response, explaining why the structure of the document, or a particular clause, was important to him. It was no big deal. Shane's job was to provide recommendations, and Harold's job was to make the decisions. This time was different, but neither Shane nor Harold understood why.

Harold's commitment from the night before disappeared. Sweat formed under Harold's shirt and on his forehead. He felt like his temperature was rising, and he wanted to yell at Shane. He wanted to use profanities. He wanted to tell him to just do his fucking job.

"Look Shane, I know you are just trying to do your job, and I appreciate it," Harold started, not really appreciating it. "But I have been through this document over and over, and I'm confident that this is the right thing to do for my family. And I think I know them a little better than you do." Harold knew that the last comment was unnecessarily harsh.

"And you've spoken with Nancy? She's comfortable with this document?" Shane asked, knowing that these questions would annoy Harold.

"Yes, she trusts my judgment." Harold was boiling with anger and frustration; he could feel an odd numbness in his left arm, and it was all that he could do to remain civil. The urge to tell Shane to fuck off and then exit the call in a huff was overwhelming, but, for some reason that Harold did not take the time to even consider, his need to have the document signed that day overrode all other emotions.

"Harold, there are hundreds of articles about the problems with trying to rule from the grave. There are so many things that could change between now and when these situations actually arise. How could this possibly be the right time to make these decisions? We could easily change some of these directives into recommendations. It would allow your family to consider your thoughts without being constrained by them."

"Shane, can you give me a moment?" Harold was about to lose control of his emotions. He was sweating, his face was red, his left arm was tingling, he felt like no one was listening to him, and he was experiencing a growing pain in his chest. He turned off his audio and video feeds and shouted at the screen, "Fuck, just do what you are fucking told! I'm not asking for your fucking permission!" That seemed to help.

He poured himself a glass of water from the pitcher on his desk and actively tried to calm himself down, remembering his commitment. After a few deep, controlled breaths, everything slowed down. He regained control of his emotions, and he turned the audio and video back on. "Sorry for the interruption. Some technical issues. Shane, I really do appreciate your advice, and I know you're only trying to do what you think is right. But this is neither your will nor your family. They're mine, and I know what I'm doing. So, hopefully, for the last time, can we simply sign the document and move on?"

Shane was far from convinced that signing this will was the right thing for Harold or his family. He was even less convinced that Harold and Nancy had thought it through. However, he also knew Harold well enough to know that continued badgering would only make him more resolute. There would be a time and a place to have another discussion. For now, he would follow his client and friend's wishes and move forward with having Harold sign the document in a fashion that secured its legality.

"Of course, Harold. What I need you to do is adjust your camera so that I can see you and the document as you sign it. Before you do that, could you hold the signing page up to the camera? There is a code on the bottom right-hand side that will help me confirm you are signing the most recent version of the document." Once Harold had completed these steps, Shane continued. "Okay, now sign the document, and initial every page, front and back, then scan it, and send it to me. Once I have it, I'll witness it and send you a completed document."

Harold knew Shane would check every initial and put his own initial beside Harold's. He appreciated Shane's thoroughness. It had more than once saved Harold a lot of headaches, so he was happy to take the extra steps. As Harold signed, they talked about tomorrow's trip to the mountains, and their plans for the weekend. Once Harold had completed the initials and signatures, they signed off. Oddly, Harold did not feel the sense of relief that he had expected to feel. Instead, the concern that he had forgotten something haunted him. That feeling that you have when you are leaving on a long trip and you are certain that you have forgotten to bring something or do something. Harold could not imagine what it could be, but the feeling persisted.

CHAPTER TWENTY-THREE

Nancy loved practising law. Upon completing her law degree, she went to work for McMurray, MacArthur, and Palmer, a medium-sized legal firm that had a large family law practice. This turned out to be an incredible stroke of luck for Nancy and the firm.

Nancy got pregnant with Jessie at the start of her eighth year at the firm. After a few long conversations with Harold and one of her closest friends, Nancy told McMurray, MacArthur, and Palmer that she would not be coming back to work after her maternity leave. She told them that in the future, she would only work part-time and would do mostly pro bono work for people who really needed representation and could not afford it. Their reaction shocked her and Harold. They offered her a job completely on her terms. Pro bono work was very important to the firm, and the partners felt this was a great way to do more of it.

After talking it over with Harold, she agreed to the job offer on the condition that they would pay her a salary commensurate with the amount that she was working, not the amount that she was billing. They agreed, and it had been a great working relationship ever since.

The arrangement with McMurray, MacArthur, and Palmer gave Nancy the best of both worlds. She could work from home when she needed to, which allowed her to be there when Jessie or Megan needed her, and she could take the cases she felt were in the greatest need.

One thing that did not surprise Nancy was that people without money were not always the ones with the greatest need for legal assistance. It was disturbing to watch parents throw incredible amounts of money into legal fees, fighting for custody of children, not because they were precious and fragile human beings that needed to be protected, but because they were possessions that had to be withheld from the offending party. Nancy felt that she could bring reason to these situations. The legal fees were not as high, but the outcomes were almost always better for the children.

Nancy loved the discipline of the law, and she liked using it to help people, even those who seemed incapable of helping themselves. It fascinated her how easily many of her clients took actions that truly screwed up their lives, and the amount of money they had did not seem to make them better or worse decision-makers. She was dealing with a client right now who, through a series of truly stupid decisions, should probably lose custody of her own children. But given the court's general desire to keep children and their birth mother together, and this woman's financial ability to pay for the fight, she would probably keep the children despite her proven ability to achieve a whole new level of stupidity as a parent.

This particular mom had decided to get back at her ex-husband, who had left her for a younger woman, by going out dancing with some young guy at the local bar. She proceeded to pour herself all over the guy to ensure that the story got back to her ex in full colour. Unfortunately, she had left her seven and nine-year-old daughters at home alone in order to create this little performance.

The thought that maybe the kids were better off without their mother crossed Nancy's mind, but that was not her job. Her job was to act in the best interest of her client. Whether these two little girls had a screwed-up mother was not her concern.

Reflecting on this, Nancy thought, *"Shit, sometimes I really am a heartless bitch. But sometimes there was no right side of the law."*

CHAPTER TWENTY-FOUR

It was Thursday evening and Harold was sitting in his den, trying to write a speech for the upcoming fiftieth anniversary of Bannister Management. He had been putting this off for weeks, not knowing exactly what to say, but he wanted to get at least a first draft completed before the weekend. He had decided to focus most of his speech on Fred Bannister, what he had done for the company, and what he had done for Harold personally. Fred had played a huge part in Harold and Nancy being together, and Harold had never been confident that he had shown adequate appreciation to Fred for the contribution he had made. Even though Fred had passed several years ago, this speech about the company that Fred had started seemed like an opportune time to thank Fred again.

Every time Harold thought of his relationship with Nancy and the lessons that Fred had taught him, he could not help but reflect on the conversation he had just had with Nancy. Why was he having so much trouble being open with her about the will? Everything that he was doing was for her and the children and the children's children. Nancy would see that if he just took the time to explain. But every time it came up, he hesitated.

He decided he would wait until after his birthday, which was less than a week away. He would explain everything, maybe even bring Shane into the discussion. Maybe not. Shane did not seem to understand what Harold was accomplishing. Shane kept focusing on the negative, that the will would constrict some of the family's future decisions. He could not seem to see the value Harold was creating by removing all those tiresome decisions that created frustration, anxiety, and conflict in a family. No, he would explain it to Nancy on his own, right after his birthday. Just him and Nancy, a nice dinner, a bottle of wine. He would tell her about what he was trying to accomplish with the will, explain his father's death, and describe how it was driving him to get better prepared in case anything happened. What he was doing was totally logical. Nancy would completely understand.

Then why haven't you already told her? he said silently to himself.

Looking at the blank Word document on his computer screen, his mind wandered off to the day that he and Nancy had met. They had been at a party that Harold had thrown for Jerry's birthday. Harold had been twenty-seven and Nancy twenty-three. Neither had had a significant other, and neither of them had been looking for one. Harold smiled as he remembered how his heart had almost come to a complete stop when, across a crowded room, he had spotted this cute little blonde with a pixie cut and the most beautiful blue eyes he had ever seen.

In the first two years they had known each other, Harold had found more ways to screw up the relationship than most people could imagine. Nancy, though interested, had been very careful about getting too invested in Harold or the relationship. But she had seen something in Harold she really liked. He was smart, he was ambitious, and he was kind. But he was clearly uncomfortable with close relationships.

When they were together, it had appeared he wanted a more intimate relationship. But every time Harold had got close, something would spook him and he would back off. Sometimes backing off had simply meant going silent for a couple of days. Sometimes it had been something truly bizarre, like the roses incident. Jerry loved to give Harold a bad time about the roses incident. In a bizarre sequence of events, Harold had sent Nancy a dozen roses one day and broke up with her the next. Over thirty years later, Harold, normally a reasonably rational adult, still could not explain what had been going through his mind and often referred to it as the nuclear brain fart.

Fred Bannister, upon hearing the roses story, had given Harold a simple piece of advice: "Get your shit together and figure out how you are going to have a relationship with Nancy, or you are going to lose her."

Harold had made the thoughtful and well-considered decision that living without Nancy was simply not acceptable if he had an option. So, he had got his shit together. He had been far from perfect, especially at the beginning. But instead of running away, he would talk unemotionally to Nancy and tell her what had been going through his mind, and they would talk about a practical resolution. They would have practical conversations about practical issues, and Harold had decided that all his worrying and fretting was not a path to happiness, especially with Nancy. So, he had put on his big boy pants and started acting like a fully formed adult.

A year later, one cold day in late December, standing on a frozen pond that the wind had swept clean, with the full moon reflecting off the black ice, he had got down on one knee, pulled a diamond ring from his pocket, and said, "I'm not sure exactly what to say because the words at my disposal simply are not sufficient or adequate enough to let you know how I feel about you. I cannot see myself living the rest of my life without you. You make me laugh, you make me smile, and you make me feel things that I have never felt in my life. You make me feel loved. But, more than all of that, you make me want to be a better man. You make me want to live a better life. Nancy Blair Jamison, will you marry me?"

Nancy had looked down at the man she had known she loved and always would love and said, "No." She had said there was no way in hell that after all of his ups and downs, she was going to say yes until she was damn sure that he was all in. "Remember roses one day, break-up the next? We are not doing that again," Nancy had said gently and firmly, but with a smile. It had taken Harold another year to convince Nancy that she could depend on him and that he was not an emotional basket case.

He had made some big strides after his conversation with Fred, but Nancy had needed to be certain that he was not going to revert.

In the year between the two proposals and every day since, Harold had made a point of looking on the bright side of life. Every morning, he would look at himself in the mirror and think about how good he had it. His commitment to being more positive about himself and his life had created a positive effect on his relationship with Nancy and everyone else. It also had had a very positive effect on his moodiness, which became increasingly less regular and less severe. Everyone, including Harold, had seen the change in him and correctly attributed it to Nancy. She was definitely the rock in this relationship.

"Hey, can I interrupt you for a moment?" Nancy said as she walked into the den.

"Of course. What's up?" Harold responded.

"I thought I might cancel my plans for the weekend. Maybe you and I could spend some time together and talk a little more about how you are feeling. The girls will understand." Nancy was not crazy about cancelling on the girls, especially because she could not tell them the real reason, but she was comfortable knowing that she would figure something out.

"That is very kind of you, sweetheart, but totally unnecessary. I'm feeling a lot better already. You should go to the cabin this weekend, and we can talk when you get back."

"Are you sure?"

"Yes, I'm sure."

"Okay, if you're sure."

"I'm sure. Have a great time at the cabin."

Leaving the den, Nancy was pleased that she had offered to cancel the trip. It was the right thing to do. But she was even more pleased that Harold had said no. This was one of the many things that Nancy liked about Harold. He didn't blubber and whine about his problems. He dealt with them. He wasn't like her clients. She didn't have to handhold Harold through to a solution. He would figure it out on his own.

CHAPTER TWENTY-FIVE

Nancy and Harold were up early the next morning. She was heading to the cabin with her friends, while he was heading to the mountains with Shane for a combination of snowshoeing and cross-country skiing, something Harold had never done before. Carrying his snowshoes on his back while he cross-country skied would be easy, and he had extendable poles, so there was no need for two sets. He wasn't so confident about what he was going to do with his skis while he snowshoed, but Shane would have the answer.

Shane was even more opinionated than Harold, which periodically annoyed Harold when Shane was giving him personal advice, but he usually appreciated it when getting legal advice. Shane was much more of an outdoorsman than Harold, or he was much more interested in googling information about the outdoors. Harold was never sure which it was because Shane, like Harold, was great at sounding like an expert on every subject, regardless of his true level of expertise.

"Have a great time," Harold shouted as Nancy walked out the back door.

"You too," she responded and added, "Love you."

"Love you too."

Harold looked at his watch. Time to get moving. He had told Shane that he would pick him up early so they would have lots of time in the mountains. The weather was perfect: not too cold, but cold enough to expect soft fluffy snow in the trees, where they would spend most of their time.

Harold dialled Shane's number and waited as the phone rang two, three, then four times. On the fourth ring, a gruff-sounding voice answered, "Hello."

"Hey, is this Shane?" Harold inquired.

"Yeah, sorry, I feel like shit. I'm not sure if it's a cold or the flu or the black plague, but whatever it is, it feels a lot worse today," the gravelly voice replied.

"And?"

"I feel like shit. I'm sure I mentioned that," Shane quipped. "Seriously, sorry, I can't make it today; I was really looking forward to some fresh mountain air, but my whole body aches, and I'm pretty sure you don't want to spend a couple of hours in a car with me right now."

You're absolutely right, Harold thought and quickly responded, "No problem, your health has to come first. Maybe next week. We might even get lucky and get a nice dump of snow between now and then."

"Yeah, it'd sure make the skiers happy. Let's talk next week when we're both back in the office, and hopefully, I'm feeling better. We can work out a plan then. Stay safe."

"Great, take care of yourself," Harold signed off.

Harold knew Shane was absolutely right in deciding not to go. He also knew it would really piss him off if Shane went and gave him whatever was making him so sick. Yet he could feel the anger and frustration bubbling up inside of him. *Fuck*, he thought. *Why are people so unreliable? How do you even catch a bug these days, between social distancing, Zoom calls, and washing your hands every five minutes? How does anyone manage to get sick?* He knew, intellectually, that his thoughts were irrational and totally unfair, but that did not stop the growing anger.

Harold thought for a moment about phoning his brother Jerry, or even one of the kids, to see if they had any interest in heading to the mountains. Looking again at his watch, Harold decided it was too late to be asking anyone to take the day off work and spend the day in the mountains. This seemed to increase his irrational anger. Why hadn't Shane told him yesterday that he was not going to go? Harold would have made other plans.

The right thing to do would have been to change into his work clothes and head to the office, but that would invite another conversation with Ramesh and Alison, which he definitely was not in the mood for. He was angry and determined not to let someone else ruin the plans he had made. He had taken the day off work, he had his gear all packed in the car, the weather was almost perfect, and he had let everyone at work know he would not be in today. Nancy was off to the cabin for the weekend with some girlfriends, and he did not want to spend the day sitting around the house.

In a moment of self-pity, something that Harold normally avoided but had recently become a reoccurring theme, he said, "*Fuck it,*" and decided to go on his own.

Harold threw on his ski jacket and ski gloves and headed out the door, too angry to even consider that this might be the last time he would ever be in the house where he and Nancy had spent the last twenty-eight years raising their children.

Harold was sixty-three years old. He made thoughtful and often overly conservative decisions daily in business and in life. He knew the perils that existed in the mountains, or he should have. No one would ever understand how it never crossed his mind that what he was doing was foolhardy and irresponsible. Harold, supposedly, no longer made unexplainable decisions, like sending roses one day and breaking up the next.

CHAPTER TWENTY-SIX

The drive to the mountains had calmed Harold significantly and allowed him to take his mind off his problems and focus on the amazing scenery that surrounded him. Harold could not help being awestruck by the enormity and ruggedness of the Canadian Rocky Mountains. He had a very basic understanding of the formation of the Rockies and thought it would have been incredible to have been there to watch the massive pieces of earth and stone be thrust into the air by tectonic forces, to form giant edifices of rock and earth thousands of feet in the air. That it took millions of years to occur and happened a hundred million years ago meant nothing to Harold. In his mind, he could see the tectonic plates smashing into each other, buckling the earth, then slowly driving the centre of this great collision upward for hundreds and then thousands of feet. Jaded rocks pierced the clouds, as if trying to escape the forces that confined them to the ground.

Harold, impressed with the symphony of sound and action that his mind created, had completely forgotten the YouTube video called *70 Million Years in 2 Minutes* that Jessie had shown him ten years ago. The video was a magnificent portrayal of the formation of the Himalayas, but having completely forgotten the video, Harold was free to convert the sound and images to the formation of the Rockies.

Without fail, when Harold spent time in the mountains, the thin line between the total isolation of the tree-covered mountains and the highways and towns that existed within them always impressed him. In ten minutes, you could walk from the highway and find yourself totally alone in the middle of immense fir trees that could hide both the sight and sounds of civilization. And if you were not on a trail and not paying attention, you could easily find it difficult to make your way back.

As he approached his destination, Harold, now completely calm and feeling much more like himself, was reconsidering his decision to venture into the mountains on his own. He knew there were risks, but he felt like he desperately needed some alone time to think through what had been happening to him. Cavorting with nature could not possibly hurt. It had taken him close to two hours to drive here. It would be a shame to turn around and drive home. "Shit can happen, but I'll be careful. No unnecessary chances," he said to himself.

Harold parked in a small parking lot near the Continental Divide and pulled out his equipment, poles, backpack, snowshoes, skis, special boots that worked for both cross-country and snowshoeing, sunglasses, and toque. Harold loved that most Americans did not know what a toque was. For a reason he could not explain, it made him feel uniquely Canadian. With each piece of equipment he pulled out of the car, and with each step of the process of getting suited up, Harold kept debating the go-or-don't-go decision in his head.

Standing at the trailhead, all ready to go, Harold looked down the path and thought once more about the wisdom of proceeding. It was a bright sunny day; he wasn't going far, and he really did not want to turn around and drive home without taking the opportunity to get a little exercise and enjoy the mountain air. Conversely, Harold thought, *the mountains are a place where things can go wrong very quickly, even if you're being careful.* As he was standing there, paying no attention to the people around him, trying to decide, a voice came from behind him.

"Get moving or get out of the way. The sun's not going to last forever."

Harold did not know who belonged to the voice, but he immediately wanted to turn around and confront the stranger, which, even in his sudden state of anger, he knew was a bad idea. Instead, he planted his poles and pulled himself forward, quickly increasing his pace in an anger-driven effort to put some distance between him and the stranger. He hoped the movement would allow him to outrun the feelings bubbling up inside of him.

The first part of the journey, which Harold was far too angry to remember, let alone enjoy, was on cross-country skis, which made packing the snowshoes very easy. Harold had simply strapped them onto his backpack. It is quite surprising how much distance he could cover on a pair of cross-country skis in a short time, especially when he was angry. In the hour and a half that Harold skied, he put a little less than seven miles between himself and the car. He was not paying close attention to where he was going, but because he was on a ski trail, it didn't matter. It was a clear day with no snow in the immediate forecast, so he was comfortable that he could simply follow the well-defined tracks back to his car.

He had decided to proceed out of anger, but now that he was in the midst of the experience, he decided he would enjoy it. He figured he would take four hours—two hours out and two hours back—and stick to the trails marked out by the park's staff. No need for concern, but out of habit he made a mental note that he was travelling mostly due west.

This was the first time Harold had ever been in the mountains by himself. As he switched from his skis to his snowshoes, he momentarily questioned the plan to leave the cross-country trail, which was clearly visible, easy to navigate, and well-used. He was aware of his lack of significant knowledge of how to survive in the wilderness or the full array of potential dangers in the mountains. While trying to find an effective method of strapping the skis to his pack, he even considered putting the skis back on and heading home. But Harold had experienced this anxiety before on long bike rides, runs, or hikes. Whenever he cut the plan short, he would always finish regretting that he had not gone the full distance. He felt it would be no different today.

If he stopped and turned around now, he would find himself sitting in his car an hour earlier than he had planned, annoyed at himself for taking the easy way out. Besides, he was only snowshoeing for an hour, not enough time to even get off the path ahead of him. Turning around now would be easy, too easy. He checked that his snowshoes were tightly secured to his boots, grabbed his poles, and started on the next phase of his adventure at a nice, comfortable pace.

Harold had tried everything he could think of, but it was simply impossible to strap the skis on the pack in a way that would not interfere with his movement on the less-travelled hikers' path through the trees. The snowshoe trail was nothing like the openness of the well-marked cross-country ski trail he had just been on. While the path was very visible, it was narrow and had not been used since the last snowfall, which meant he would break the trail in deep, undisturbed snow. The trees were not overly thick, but there were a lot of overhead branches and fallen trees that he would be ducking under and climbing over. Harold knew that the skis, which were taller than he was, would be continually banging into the trees or getting caught on them. He finally used a bungee cord to strap the skis to a tree where they would be easy to find.

Harold was not worried about the skis. No one would take them. Snowshoe tracks in fresh snow were even easier to follow than cross-country tracks, so he knew he would easily come back to the exact spot on his way back to the car.

Harold made a point of sticking to the well-marked hiking path through the trees. The snow on the path included about a foot and a half of powder, much more than he had expected. This was dramatically different than skiing. It was relatively slow and often methodical as he crushed the snow and created a secure footing with each step. Harold thought that in only thirty minutes of this slow, deliberate pace, he probably would not get far from the cross-country ski trail he had just been on, which was more than fine with him.

CHAPTER TWENTY-SEVEN

Harold took his time and stopped periodically to enjoy the incredible and unusual winter scenery. The undisturbed snow ahead of him glistened in the bright sunlight that wove its way through the trees. The bright January sun made the snow sparkle like a million tiny diamonds had been sprinkled all over the trees by the woodland fairies. Periodically, Harold would see an insect crawling across the top of the snow and was amazed that something so small could survive in these conditions.

Harold laughed to himself at how much being a father and grandfather had changed his thought process. Woodland fairies and the survival of insects would not have been the first things to come to his mind some thirty years ago when he had first met Nancy. This was what came from years of watching Disney movies and reading children's books with your children and grandchildren. They became well-adjusted and picked up reading and writing at an early age, and you became fanciful and creative and started picturing woodland fairies in your mind.

Without thinking about it, every so often, Harold would look back to make sure that his tracks were easy to see. They were like giant footprints on an otherwise completely empty canvas. They would be impossible to miss. This was not like following your own footprints on a crowded beach where there were many other conflicting prints, and sometimes the sand was so hard your foot simply did not make a mark. This was a two-foot-long and ten-inch-wide shoe print into deep snow every step of the way. It would take inches of fresh snow and probably some strong winds to make these prints disappear, and neither of those was expected to hit this area today or tomorrow, let alone in the next hour.

As Harold walked out of a grove of trees, he looked to his left and recognized that he was standing on a path at the top of a long hill that led to a flat valley. The snow on the hill was deep and untouched. Although Harold knew it would mean slogging back up the hill, he could not stop himself. The urge was too great, and the experience would be too invigorating. So, he turned to look down the hill and ran as fast as his sixty-three-year-old body would allow him, hands, poles, feet, and snowshoes flailing in every direction. He was barely able to keep his balance while hollering at the top of his lungs.

When he came to a stop at the bottom of the hill, Harold looked back at his tracks and acknowledged that the hill was steeper than he had expected and that this was probably not the smartest decision he had ever made. But it was worth it. He began the long climb back up to the hill to get back on the trail.

It had been about thirty-five minutes since Harold had started his snowshoe trek; he was feeling good, and the weather was beautiful, so he decided to go for another ten or fifteen minutes. There were a lot of fallen trees in the area, which was not a concern to Harold. He simply had to be sure his snowshoes had a good grip before putting all his weight on them. He did not want his feet slipping out from under him and impaling himself on a piece of branch sticking out of the ground or the trunk of a tree.

No sooner did the thought cross his mind than Harold felt his right foot slip. It was an instantaneous occurrence that only allowed for a completely automatic reaction. There was no time to look at what he might land on if he fell and no opportunity to look for a soft or safe landing area. The foot that held all his weight was shooting off uncontrollably, and if he did not react quickly and appropriately, he could find himself in a lot of trouble and a lot of pain.

Without thinking, Harold's other three appendages shot off in supporting directions to stabilize himself. Each pole-laden hand searching for the security of something stable; his other foot flew forward, looking for solid ground. All three immediately sank fast into the soft powdery snow. Harold's muscles tensed, ready to absorb the impact when it came, but the muscles were useless to Harold if his poles and feet failed to find solid ground.

Without warning, there was an impact. His knee, wrist, and elbows buckled to absorb the instant jolt, his hands and feet frantically adjusting their positions to regain control without losing contact with the solid ground they had found, and every muscle in his body fired in an effort to regain his balance.

In an instant, it was over. The entire experience had not lasted for more than two or three seconds, but Harold had broken out in a sweat trying to recover. It happened too quickly to be frightening as it was happening, but the moment it was over, and he had a chance to think about how dangerous an injury could be when he was alone in the mountains, Harold felt panic set in. It lasted only a moment, but it was incredibly impactful.

He refocused himself; these mountains are unquestionably beautiful, but if he did not treat them with the respect that they deserved, they could be very dangerous. This wonderland of white was breathtaking in so many ways, but at that moment, he was much more focused on the unknown dangers it masked under that beauty.

Harold decided maybe it was time to head back. Being out here by himself was probably not the time to take any unnecessary risks. Stepping carefully over a small fallen tree, Harold placed his right snowshoe on a pile of broken twigs, branches, and fallen leaves. He pushed down on it to check its strength. When he was confident, he shifted his weight onto his right foot and lifted his left foot over the fallen twig. His feet were beside each other when he heard the cracking, but before Harold could react, he knew there was no longer anything holding his left foot up, and his right foot was uncontrollably slipping into the hole that had been created by the left foot.

The fall was instantaneous and, from Harold's initial point of view, uneventful. He did not feel his head bang against the tree trunk as he flew by it. He did not feel the jagged ends of the branches cut through his jacket and pants and into his skin. Harold did not even feel the two-point landing that badly sprained his left wrist and broke his left ankle. All he felt was the sensation of falling and then the sudden stop and the complete darkness that immediately surrounded him.

All the worries of the world were gone as Harold lay unconscious, broken, and bleeding at the bottom of a hole, twenty feet deep, alone in the middle of an endless wilderness.

CHAPTER TWENTY-EIGHT

As Harold slowly regained consciousness, his first instinct was to check for injuries. His head hurt, and he felt dizzy, sleepy, and slightly nauseous. He was certain he had a concussion, but in his present state, he could not assess how bad it might be or what that might mean. His jacket and pants were ripped and there was more than a little road rash on his skin. He was bleeding, but not badly. The odd thought that he would not bleed to death crossed his mind. Having his eyes open, even in the limited light, hurt. He knew falling asleep was a bad idea, but he couldn't stay awake. Everything hurt, especially his head. He could find neither the strength nor the motivation to move. Lying there with his eyes closed, unable to stop himself, he faded off into a deep sleep.

Hours later when Harold woke up, it was nothing like waking from a good night's sleep. His eyes opened slowly. He was uncertain where he was, and he was completely disoriented. Harold looked at his phone. He had been asleep for well over three hours, and the dizziness and throbbing pain in his head were still there. Thankfully, he no longer felt nauseous; at least, he didn't as long as he stayed still. The moment he tried to sit up, the dizziness increased and the nausea returned. So, he rolled over on his back so he could look around and assess the situation he was in.

It was dark around him, except for the light coming from the hole he had fallen through, which was at least twenty feet above him. Being unable to move, he instinctively inspected the ceiling he had just fallen through. From this angle, with no snow to cover the trees, it was clear that dozens of small- to medium-sized trees had fallen or been purposely piled in this spot to cover what for all intents and purposes appeared to be a large, oddly shaped, natural hole in the ground. The ceiling of the hole looked a little like that of a thatched roof, except there was no uniformity to the tree trunks and branches, and thanks to Harold, there was now a large hole near one edge of the ceiling. Somehow, he had managed to experience the incredible misfortune of stepping on what was likely the only spot that could not hold his weight and that was large enough for both him and his snowshoes to fall through.

The trees had given way so quickly that there had been no time to adjust his footing to stabilize himself. His memory, although still very foggy, allowed him to piece the fall together. He recalled falling down and slightly forward as the ground had disappeared from under him. His body had shifted to the right and bounced off the snow, and his head had bounced off the trunk of one of the trees. As he had tried to keep himself upright and find some footing, his right foot had slammed through the hole created by his left foot, and his entire body had followed close behind. As he had been falling, he had instinctively grabbed for anything that would stop the fall, but whatever he had grabbed had simply fallen with him. Having landed first on his left foot and then almost simultaneously on his left hand, he now remembered hearing a crack, but he could not remember feeling any pain as he had crumbled to the ground.

Harold, adjusting slowly to his surroundings, realized he could not see the edges of the hole. With surprising calm, he considered that he may not be alone in this hole in the ground. It was possible he was the unwelcome visitor of some very unhappy animal, which had just been disturbed from a long winter's nap. It also occurred to Harold that his entry into the hole might not be the only entry. Slowly and carefully, Harold adjusted his pole in his good right hand so it felt more like a weapon than a support system. He reached for his cell phone, turned it on, and used the light to survey the entire area of the hole, which was not particularly easy in his prone position. Each time that he lifted his head to get a better look, the dizziness got worse and the nausea would return. To his relief, it appeared he was alone, at least for now. To his dismay, the only entrance and exit appeared to be directly above him and considerably out of his reach.

It was not clear if the hole had been constructed by someone or had simply been an accident of nature. The hole was easily twenty feet deep and about twenty feet long and eight feet wide, with sides that were almost perpendicular to the ground. The wall farthest from him and the one to his right were both sheer rock faces that looked oddly similar to a sheet of granite. There were changes in colour but virtually no cracks, creases, or ledges that could be used to climb the wall. The other two walls appeared to be densely compacted dirt and gravel.

There were a few roots sticking out of the dirt that were big enough to grab hold of, but none that were large enough to support an adult's weight. Without moving, Harold was able to scratch at the floor of the hole. It wasn't frozen, and at least the first few inches were dirt. He was sure that if he started digging, it would not be long before he hit solid rock.

The way the trees were stacked to create a roof was sloppy and unstructured. However, it could easily have been intentional. Even the weak spot that he had fallen through could have served as the entry. The light from his phone did not reveal any colour. Everything, even the trees above him, appeared to be some shade of black or grey. If it had been built by someone, why, and what purpose would it have served?

Whatever its origins, whatever its purpose, Harold was certain he needed to get out of the hole as quickly as possible. The more time he took to get out of there, the more things could go wrong.

Lying on his back, he was unable to make any significant movement without increasing the symptoms of the concussion. He slowly started to feel the throbbing pain coming from his broken ankle. The pain intensified with every moment that passed. Within an hour, it was beyond excruciating.

As he lay flat on his back on the ground, unable to even lift his head, he contemplated the circumstances in which he now found himself. Harold did not scare easily, but his fear suddenly overwhelmed him. Sweat-through-your-ski-suit fear. This was not a little tumble that he was going to joke with Nancy about. This was not a "you're lucky you got out" situation, and this was definitely not his functional paranoia. Harold was in real trouble. He was very likely going to die in this hole.

"What the fuck is wrong with you, Bower?" he screamed, immediately regretting it. But the horror of what he had just done to his family—to the wife he loved more than life itself and to the children and grandchildren that were everything to him—implanted itself in his all-too-foggy mind. He knew in that moment that they would come to hate him for this one act of stupidity. All the good, all the love, all the support was going to be flushed away because of this one stupid act.

As Harold lay there, wallowing in his own despair, unexplainably, the concept of confirmation bias suddenly popped into his mind. He realized once his family hated him for this one stupid, selfish act, they would re-examine his entire life; all the faults and mistakes would suddenly become the focus, and Harold had made lots of mistakes. Until now, they were either forgiven or ignored, but after this, they would become who he was. In Harold's mind, as he spiralled down, he had made nothing but mistakes. Because of his insane stupidity, he was going to leave a legacy worse than his father's. It was a moment of total recrimination for all those selfish moments of weakness, of not putting his family first. At that moment, Harold saw nothing but this and every other wretched mistake he had ever made. In his present state of mind, he believed these mistakes would now define his entire life.

"Who the fuck goes into the mountains alone? What fucking idiot would be this stupid?" Harold continued to spew the hate he felt for himself as he slipped further and further into a cycle of self-loathing. His head was spinning more with each word.

He was sweating. There was a growing pain in the centre of his chest. He felt a strange pain growing in his jaw and neck, and he was certain he was going to throw up. Harold had read enough about the symptoms of a heart attack; he knew exactly what was happening.

"Fuck," Harold said out loud as he fumbled for the bottle of Aspirin in his coat pocket. "Not now, for Christ's sake, not here." The pain was increasing exponentially. His mind was racing. It was nearly impossible to focus. He pulled the Aspirin bottle out of his jacket pocket and popped it open. The pills fell out all over him and onto the dirt. He grabbed two, popped them into his mouth, and started chewing. The pain, numbness, and perspiration got worse.

Roll onto your side, Harold's mind screamed at him through the searing pain. *You're going to die if you don't*, was the last thought he remembered. As he threw himself over onto his left hip, he heaved. Vomit came spewing out of his mouth, and everything went black.

CHAPTER TWENTY-NINE

Two hours later, Harold slowly regained consciousness. The pain in his chest was almost completely gone. He was no longer perspiring. The dizziness and nausea were also gone, but the pain in his ankle was worse. Looking at the vomit on the dirt directly in front of him, Harold found the Aspirin bottle and began picking the pills out of the dirt and putting them back into the bottle. He was certain the Aspirin had saved him, and he was not about to waste a single pill.

The simple effort of picking up the pills had brought back the symptoms and exhausted him. Despite the pungent odour of the vomit, Harold could not find the strength to do anything about it. For more than an hour, he lay on his back in the growing darkness, staring at the hole, certain his life was over. He contemplated the slow and painful death he was about to experience and the pain his actions were going to create for the people he loved most. The thought that maybe he shouldn't have taken the Aspirin crossed his mind. Maybe it would have been better for everyone if he had just died.

Harold slowly fought his way back to reality, forcing himself to think rationally and thoughtfully.

"You're not done yet, Bower," he said out loud. "Quit feeling sorry for yourself, get off your ass, and fix this. This is not what you are going to be remembered for."

This was not the first time Harold had been in a difficult position, and he was damn sure going to do everything he could to ensure it was not the last.

"Okay, son, time to climb out of this tomb," Harold commented to no one. He did note that he was talking very purposely to himself and not in a quiet voice but much more like a coach giving the team a pre-game pep talk. Maybe that's what it was. Maybe it was his way of dealing with his sudden and palpable anxiety, knowing he was utterly and completely alone. Maybe it was his version of a pep talk. He wasn't sure and didn't care. Whatever it was, it was his first step to getting himself in the frame of mind he needed to survive.

The first thing he needed to do was deal with the vomit, but the moment he tried to sit up, the dizziness and nausea returned. He lay back, hoping the symptoms would subside. They did, but they didn't completely go away. He quickly realized that for now, trying to do anything would be fruitless and would likely create even worse problems. But he had to do something with the vomit. The smell of it was making everything worse, and he was concerned it would cause him to vomit again, which he really did not want to do.

He pulled himself up into a sitting position, drew his legs up toward his chest, and removed his snowshoes. Then he used one snowshoe like a shovel to mix the vomit into the dirt and throw the vomit-filled dirt as far away from himself as possible.

The process was excruciating, and the feeling that he just wanted to lie down and go to sleep increased with every bit of effort. When he had done as much as he could to reduce the smell, he allowed himself to lie back and rest.

He had read about the dangers of sleeping with a concussion and the need to have someone wake you every few hours, but that was not an option. His head was pounding, he was exhausted, and he lacked the strength to do anything but stare at the hole above him. The fight to stay awake seemed fruitless. The light from the hole was quickly fading, and Harold slowly surrendered to the urge to sleep.

CHAPTER THIRTY

It was Friday evening at 8:00 p.m., and Nancy was surprised when Harold's phone repeatedly went straight to voicemail, signalling that he was on the phone, was out of a service area, or had turned his phone off. None of which seemed likely, especially over the time Nancy had been trying to call, which was now getting close to two hours. It was unlike Harold to not answer his phone, especially when they were away from each other. Because Harold had travelled so much for business when they were raising their children, he had developed the habit of calling to offer some support when he was away. No matter what was going on, he had phoned home every single night. When the travel had diminished dramatically in later years, Harold had maintained the tradition. So not hearing from him felt strange.

Nancy decided to wait until 8:30 p.m. and try again, and if she still couldn't get a hold of him, she would assume that he was sitting at home watching a movie with his telephone either turned off or out of battery. Not something Harold would normally do, but it also would not be the first time.

"Did you get an answer?" June, Nancy's best friend, asked as Nancy walked back into the living room of the cabin.

Nancy and Harold had purchased the cabin twenty-four years ago, for cash, because Harold had always said that if you had to mortgage a cabin, you should not be buying one. He had a lot of economic and lifestyle theories that Nancy chose not to debate or, in some cases, even listen to. Her interest was in what they were going to do or not do, and she seldom cared what Harold's rationale was for either.

"No, it's still going straight to voicemail. He's probably watching a movie and doesn't realize his phone is off," responded Nancy. "Harold has an amazing ability to shut out the world when he's watching TV, especially if he's tired or stressed," she said as she picked up her glass of red wine and took a sip. "When they were building the company, and he would come home after a long day, he could turn on the TV and literally disappear inside of it. The kids could be fighting right on top of him, and he wouldn't even notice it."

"And he'd sit there all night just staring at the TV?" questioned June.

"Oh no," laughed Nancy. "He was a very active father. He coached both of the kids in one sport or another, and always went to their games and often their practices, even if he wasn't coaching. And if you really needed his attention when he was watching TV, you could get it if you were willing to shout his name three or four times."

Nancy was pensive for a moment, then said, "Harold's a great dad and a great husband, but when he gets transfixed on the TV, it's amazing to watch what can happen around him without him taking any notice." She laughed and took another sip of wine.

Nancy and her friends were having so much fun chatting, drinking wine, and playing games that she completely forgot about trying to call Harold again until she was getting ready for bed, and by that time, it was 1:30 a.m., and she certainly was not going to call him at that hour.

Harold would be up early, he always was, and he would be making phone calls, even if it was Saturday. She could call him when she got up, after he had figured out his phone had been off all evening.

CHAPTER THIRTY-ONE

The intense pain in his ankle, which had made for a fitful sleep, woke him early the next morning. And given his concussion, that was probably a good thing. His head felt a little better this morning, and he had no nausea to speak of. He wasn't sure if the smell of vomit was completely gone, or if he had just got used to it.

Looking up at the opening above him, he decided he needed to get to work finding a way to get himself out of this hole. He sat up slowly. His symptoms did not increase, which encouraged him to continue. He slowly got himself into a kneeling position and then tried to stand. The moment he put even the tiniest amount of weight on his left leg, he let out a "Holy sweet Mother of God," which he did not mean as a prayer.

He immediately fell back to the floor of the hole, landing on his left arm, which solicited a protracted scream that stretched the well-known F-bomb into a twenty-four-letter word and rekindled the fog in his head.

When the pain and the fog finally subsided, Harold checked his wrist and ankle. He was pretty sure the ankle was broken but was not sure how badly. There was no blood, so he could assume the bone had not broken through the skin. He loosened his boot just enough to feel the bone around the ankle. To his untrained touch, it felt like the bones had been crushed, and it was already beginning to swell. Harold decided he needed to keep his boot on or he would never get it back on. He re-tightened it immediately.

Taking off his glove, he could see that his left wrist was already swelling and discolouring. He could move it, but it was painful.

Probably only a severe sprain, but it would be of limited use to him for at least a few days, which was going to make the effective use of a ski pole extremely difficult.

Looking around the poorly lit hole, Harold again started to dwell on the enormity of his situation. At the bottom of a deep hole, unable to move, and with no one to help. The fear of what he was certain he was about to experience set in. Never in his entire life had he felt so helpless, so scared. The intensity of the fear overwhelmed him. It became the only thing in his life at that moment. He felt no physical pain; he felt only a consuming sense of despair. Darkness surrounded his every thought. There was no hope, no solution, only a slow and painful death. He felt the desire to simply get it over with, to no longer feel the anguish that was consuming him. He wanted to give up, to make the pain stop. Not the physical pain, the infinitely worse psychological pain.

The old saying "a coward dies a thousand deaths" crossed his mind, and he realized that if he allowed himself to give up, the journey to death would be even more painful. He knew that no matter how bad the situation was, he could never hasten his own death. He looked for a ray of hope; he searched for a solution. Not because he was certain he would find one, but because searching for a solution was in his nature.

He forced his mind to focus on his surroundings. The walls of the hole were almost perpendicular to the bottom; he could not possibly crawl out of here and even if he could, based on what he could see of the trees covering the holes, the only way out was the way he had come in. The rest of the trees would be much too heavy to lift, especially in his present condition.

The opening in the roof was at least twenty feet above the bottom of the hole. To get out of the hole on his own, he would need to get close enough to the trees to grab onto one of the tree limbs and then pull off some kind of gymnastic miracle move to elevate himself through the hole. Probably impossible if Harold were at his best and twenty years younger, and if there were no snow to deal with. In this situation, he needed a miracle, like having someone who just happened to be driving through the trees with a cherry picker find him.

He had no idea at that moment how to get closer to the trees covering the hole. Even if he could get closer, he could not use his left arm effectively, so he could not pull himself out, and he could not walk on his left ankle, so even if he got out, his chances of making it back to the car were slim and none, and slim had just left town.

At least for now, the best thing he could do was try to find someone to help him.

The first thing that Harold thought to do was check to see if anyone was near, so he started shouting. At first, he started hollering "Help" every five seconds, but that caused the dizziness to return. So, he stopped for a while. When the dizziness subsided, he tried speaking in a loud voice, "Is anyone out there?" then "I have fallen in a hole and can't get out!" knowing it was unlikely anyone outside of the hole could hear him, even if they were there. Lying there, knowing that, for the moment, there was nothing he could do about his situation, he allowed his mind to wander and began to wonder if the company that made those safety buttons for old people made anything that hikers could use in the mountains. Then he chastised himself for wasting his time on pointless trivia.

Even though it was almost impossible for anyone to hear him, Harold determined he would commit to making whatever noise he could for as long as it was light. He had to do something.

Shouting hurt his head, and banging his poles together did not make enough noise and exhausted him quickly. Exhaustion brought on nausea and the desire to go to sleep.

As he lay there, losing his resolve to not think about dying, he began contemplating the frightening possibility of freezing to death or dying from thirst in this hole, never seeing his wife or children again, when two powerful feelings came over him. The first was that if he died down here and left Nancy alone, she would never forgive him. The second was that he really had to pee.

Peeing out in nature was nothing new for Harold. He had done it often, as had most of the male friends he had hiked, skied, or snowshoed with. But this was different. Harold was more than likely going to be down here for a while, waiting for someone to find him or recovering enough to get himself out, and he did not want to be lying in his own urine, waiting to be rescued. He had several empty baggies in his backpack that he had brought along to take garbage home, and he thought he could probably pee in them, seal them up tight, then throw them out of the hole, but it was neither a short throw nor a big hole. What if he caught the bag on a branch? He could end up covered with his own urine, and if he was in here for any significant length of time, he might need those baggies for something more substantial. After all, with all the fibre in his diet, Harold was a regular type of guy.

Harold decided his best bet was to pee in the hole, even if it was a little small. Crawling around on his knees and one arm, he found the lowest point in the hole, which was the corner farthest away from the hole he had created by falling through it.

Using one of his ski poles and his good arm, he dug a hole about sixteen inches deep; he was fortunate the ground was not frozen. He got on his knees, peed into the hole, and then threw enough dirt back into the hole to completely absorb the pee. He hoped it would not stink too much, but felt that whether it did or didn't was not one of his bigger problems.

All the moving around had brought back the dizziness and a little of the nausea, and had intensified the ever-present pain in his ankle. He was shocked at how exhausting this relatively small amount of effort had been. Lying on his back, trying to recover, Harold could not fight off the urge to fall back to sleep.

CHAPTER THIRTY-TWO

Nancy dragged herself out of bed at eight o'clock the next morning to make some breakfast for everyone. Even though she was not a coffee drinker, she had filled the coffeemaker and set it on automatic before she had gone to bed to ensure her friends would have coffee if they happened to get up before her.

This was definitely not your bacon, eggs, and hash brown crowd, so making breakfast involved putting out yogourt, fruit, granola, Cheerios, and milk, and making a few pieces of toast. This was the type of hosting that she enjoyed, easy peasy.

When everyone had finished breakfast and Nancy had put everything away, she thought she should give Harold another call before they went out on their carefully planned daylong hike. While everyone else put together and packed up a lunch for the hike, she went into the living room to call Harold.

The phone went straight to voicemail again, which did not surprise Nancy. Harold was probably talking to someone from work. Saturday seemed to mean nothing to Harold. Every day was a workday.

Nancy went and helped with the lunch. Everyone got dressed up warm for a cold winter hike and headed for the car. Just before leaving the cabin and going out to the car to join her friends, Nancy gave Harold one more try. Voicemail again. *God, can that man talk*, was the entirely justifiable thought that went through Nancy's mind as she headed for the car.

The conversation was lively and far-reaching. It started with everyone sharing their winter vacation plans, and then went to the joy of grandchildren. Someone brought up the bumper sticker, "If I had known that grandchildren were this much fun, I would have started with them," and they all had a good laugh.

The hike that they had chosen was covered with a thick layer of snow that had been compressed by the hundreds of people that had walked on this path before them. They would not need snowshoes or skis for the hike. A warm pair of winter boots would suffice.

The conversation continued through most of the hike, but in the rare moments of silence, Nancy's mind would wander back to Harold and the oddity of his phone repeatedly going directly to voicemail. *Maybe,* she thought, *Harold had gone through another experience like the one with the pedestrian, and his phone was the victim this time.* She couldn't see Harold throwing his phone against a wall in anger; however, she could not picture him telling someone that he was going to rip off his finger and shove . . .

"Nancy. Nancy, did you hear me?"

As Nancy reconnected with reality, she realized she had been walking along in a dream world, paying no attention to where she was walking or the conversation going on around her. The group had stopped walking in the middle of the path, and her three friends were all staring at her.

"What?" Nancy asked.

"Where did you go? Beth was asking you about work, and you were a million miles away."

"I'm sorry," Nancy said with a forced smile. "I was off in dreamland. Must be the beautiful scenery and the clear mountain air. What was the question?"

Beth laughed, "Oh Lord, I can't even remember. Nothing important, just making conversation."

"Well, okay. How about this for a response? Work is going well. But as I have told you often, as much as I feel good about what we accomplish, the situations that these families find themselves in would break my heart, if I had one," Nancy said with a chuckle.

She made a conscious effort to remain present for the rest of the hike. Whatever the issues were with Harold's phone, she decided they could be dealt with later. Now, it was time to enjoy the beautiful weather and splendid company.

CHAPTER THIRTY-THREE

When Harold woke, his head was feeling a little better, but the ankle continued to hurt like hell. It was a throbbing pain that seemed to pulse with the beating of his heart. He had considered taking a couple of Aspirin for the pain, but he was certain that he had read that it was dangerous to take Aspirin or Advil if you had a concussion. Something to do with bleeding.

Harold turned on his cell phone to check the time. It was already just about three o'clock. The chances of anyone finding him tonight were becoming less and less likely by the moment. People would be exiting the forest, not coming into it at this time of the day.

Not willing to simply sit and hope, Harold tried to be productive, but doing anything, including taking a piss, brought back the symptoms and immediately exhausted him. Even if he could overcome the pain in his broken ankle, which at the moment he couldn't, he was incapable of doing the simplest task for more than a few minutes at a time.

Given the time of day, he knew it was unlikely he would attract anyone's attention, even if he could make some noise. So, he started planning to spend another night in the hole. This one, he would ensure, would be much more comfortable.

The preparation for spending the night in the hole seemed to lift Harold's spirits. Finally, something that he had some control over. If he had to spend another night in this hole, at least he was prepared; the hole gave him shelter from the wind and insulation from the cold, and his clothing was specifically designed to handle seriously cold weather. So, as long as the temperatures stayed above −20 degrees Celsius, he was unlikely to die of exposure, even if he did not have additional sources of heat. He had an extra down-filled jacket with a hood in his pack; he had a thermal blanket and more than a dozen foot and hand warmers to stick in his jacket if he really felt that his body was losing heat.

Setting himself up for a decent night's sleep and quickly checking his backpack helped Harold convince himself that his life was not in any immediate danger. He had food; he had not even eaten his lunch from yesterday yet. Plus, there was also an additional selection of edibles that Shane had convinced him to always keep in his pack. He was reasonably warm; he had enough water for a few days if he rationed it; and he was comfortable that someone would start looking for him, or at least for the owner of the abandoned car, by sometime tomorrow. And with the size of the snowshoe prints he had left behind in the otherwise untouched snow, he should be easy to follow. This was definitely not an ideal situation, but he was starting to feel that there was no need to overdramatize his current circumstances.

Suddenly it struck Harold. Was he cool, calm, and collected, or was he simply in shock? He had always had a high pain threshold, so as much as the ankle hurt, it was not intolerable. If he could just get himself to the point where he could put in more than a few minutes' effort, he was certain that he could get himself out of this mess.

Harold turned his phone on again, 5:10 p.m. He realized he had not even looked to see if he had service. He had just assumed that he did not. He was right, no service. For the moment, he did not have the urge to fall asleep, which was encouraging. He knew that this was going to be a long night; he was safe, but he had absolutely nothing to amuse himself with. Nothing to read, he couldn't go out for a walk, and he had no TV or radio. He had music and a few games on his phone, but how long would that last? He decided not to waste the battery. There might be a more important use for the phone. He turned it off.

Lying on the thermal blanket to keep the dampness of the ground from seeping into his clothes, Harold stared at the hole, watching the diminishing light, realizing it would soon be dark. He knew that here in the mountains, he would experience the meaning of "total darkness." Unless there was a clear sky and a big moon, it would become so dark in his hole that he would be unable to see his hand in front of his face. There would be no discernible difference between having his eyes open or shut. On the other hand, if it was a cloudless sky, the hole that Harold had fallen through might give him a small view of the stars. Seeing the stars in the mountains, where there was no ambient light, was amazing, something a city dweller could never understand.

Lying there with nothing to occupy his mind, the throbbing pain in his ankle became his focal point. It hurt like hell, and nothing he did relieved the pain, even a little. It was going to be a long night.

Suddenly, Harold heard a noise. It wasn't exactly footsteps, but it sounded like feet shuffling on the dead trees above him. Snow, brushed from the tree limbs that covered the hole, floated down onto his face. With an instantly awakened sense of hope, he struggled to stand on his one good leg. He was just about to holler for help when into the hole popped the snarling, growling face of a full-grown wolf.

The wolf circled the hole, sniffing and pawing at the trees and branches, apparently trying to understand what he had found and what he should do. Could he smell Harold? Could he smell the blood? Harold could do nothing but watch as the wolf determined his next step. As the wolf pushed down with its left front paw on a branch at the edge of the hole, it gave. The wolf's left front leg slipped into the hole, pulling the wolf's body toward the opening. Harold and the wolf cried out simultaneously as both realized the danger of what was about to happen. As Harold watched, unable to do anything to affect the outcome, the wolf instinctively scrambled in an effort to find a foothold that would stop it from falling into the hole with Harold.

CHAPTER THIRTY-FOUR

The radio on the desk of the RCMP station crackled, warning everyone that a call was coming in. Constable Jennings, the evening officer, was charged with the responsibility of taking and logging each call and, where necessary, providing the officer with advice for action. He put down his coffee cup so he could type a record of the call into his computer.

"Constable Jennings, this is Constable McGuire. The grey BMW X5 licence number MBX 472 that I called about last night is still in the parking area near the Continental Divide."

"Does it appear to have been moved at all?"

"Negative, Constable. It appears to have been undisturbed since last night. There is still no sign of activity in or around the car."

"Is there any possibility the car could have been abandoned?" Constable Jennings asked.

"Possible, but unlikely. The car's in good condition. There are no flat tires, and nothing suspicious in or around the car," replied Constable McGuire.

After a brief pause, Constable Jennings remarked, "I just checked again, and the car still hasn't been reported stolen."

"Okay," replied Constable McGuire. "How would you like to proceed?"

"Do you think this could be a drug swap and the car is the delivery tool?" asked Constable Jennings.

"Nowadays, anything's possible, but why would it be there this long?"

"Good point. I'll check with missing persons and get the information on the vehicle registration. I'm sure that we'll get some phone numbers and an address. That's about all that we can do for the moment."

"Okay, I'll drive past this location once more tonight. If anything changes, I'll let you know. I sure hope that this doesn't turn into another search and rescue situation," commented Constable McGuire.

"Yeah, you and me both."

CHAPTER THIRTY-FIVE

The wolf regained its footing but barely backed away from the opening. Whatever the wolf could smell in the hole was clearly appealing enough to the wolf that it would continue to put itself in danger. Again and again, it ventured to the edge of the hole, sometimes backing off before anything happened, sometimes slipping again and having to scramble to stop from falling.

Harold felt helpless as he sat and watched the wolf and its relentless efforts to get to him. He hoped the wolf was not stupid enough to fall into the hole, and he was concerned that the wolf, through all of its efforts, would find an alternate path into the hole. What a paradox. Ten minutes ago, Harold would have loved to find an easy way in and out of the hole, but now he was frantically hoping no such path existed.

Harold told himself that, as long as there was no other entry, he was in no real danger. The wolf would snoop around the edges of the hole, but there was no way that it was going to jump into a twenty-foot-deep hole, especially when it really did not know what it would find there.

The problem was not this single wolf or any immediate danger; the problem was Harold's ability to get out of the hole if this wolf and potentially its pack were hanging around the opening. He also did not want it scaring off potential rescuers, and there was still the unlikely possibility that the wolf could fall into the hole, just as Harold had, although he acknowledged animals were smarter than humans in this sort of situation.

Harold decided he needed to be more forceful in scaring the wolf off. Having sat down earlier to rest, he stood again, on his one good leg, took his ski pole in his right hand, and threw it like a spear at the wolf and accompanied that with some very aggressive shouting.

It is crazy what we decide to shout when we are in trouble. Did Harold really believe that shouting obscenities at the wolf would be more effective at scaring the wolf off than simply making aggressive noises? Maybe he thought the wolf would be offended and leave. Whatever his reasons were, Harold started shouting the foulest comments at the absolute top of his voice while he repeatedly threw his ski pole at the wolf.

"You mother-fucking piece-of-shit wolf. Get the fuck out of here. I will rip your fucking throat out, you worthless piece of shit. God damn you, get the fuck out of here, you four-legged piece of rat shit." Harold went on and on. The shouting and the pole-throwing were exhausting, and his headache was getting worse by the second, but none of it had much effect on the wolf.

The dance seemed to go on forever. The wolf would stick its head into the hole. Harold would shout obscenities and throw the pole, never making contact, and the wolf would then back away for a few minutes, only to come back again. Finally, after countless attempts, Harold made contact. A very well-placed shot of the sharp point of the ski pole hit right under the chin of the wolf and sent it howling and running off like a scared rabbit. Harold hoped the pole had penetrated the wolf's skin, but there was no visible trace of blood on the tip. The way the wolf had taken off, Harold felt confident that it was not coming back any time soon for any reason.

All the effort had exhausted Harold, brought back the symptoms of the concussion, and significantly increased the pain in his ankle. He lay back down in an effort to calm the overwhelming urge to vomit. Despite the pain and discomfort, the need to sleep overwhelmed him again.

CHAPTER THIRTY-SIX

When Harold woke, it was dark. There was no way that there were still people on the trail and no one, at this point, would know he was missing. His car in the parking lot, in his opinion, would probably not yet cause someone significant concern even if they saw it, and there was a pretty good chance that they wouldn't have seen it yet. He was not even certain that anyone checked the parking lots.

Harold settled back onto his blanket. The pain was really intensifying, and he knew the more he thought about it, the more it would hurt. He really wanted to take a few of the Aspirin. But he doubted it would help that much, and he was certain the risk was too high. So, he abandoned the idea.

As he lay there, trying to get his mind off the pain, he started thinking about his guitar. At this time of night, he would often go into his den, pull out his guitar, and play a few tunes. He loved to sing and play his guitar even if he wasn't very good. It gave him enjoyment, and he never did it in front of anyone except Nancy and their children, and none of them cared if he was good or bad. Harold figured that all of them simply shut the noise out, just like he used to shut their noise out when they were young. It is amusing what the human ear cannot hear when it does not want to.

He thought about how funny it would be if someone walked by the hole and heard the singing. If it happened, he hoped they would not decide against rescuing him because of how bad his voice was. He could picture it in his mind, a middle-aged couple snowshoeing through the deep snow and tight trees. The husband would look over at his wife. "Sweetheart, do you hear that noise?"

"Yes, dear, I do," she'd reply. "What could it possibly be?"

"I'm not sure. It sounds like it could be two moose mating or an animal dying a horrifying death," he'd muse.

"Do you think we should go and see what it is?" she'd ask.

"No, we'd better stay away. Regardless of which it is, we won't be able to help and it could be dangerous," he'd suggest.

"You're probably right, but it's hard to walk away from something that's in such obvious distress, even if it's from mating," she'd respond, giving her husband a look of reproach for never having made her feel the need to make these types of noises.

Harold laughed to himself. It was now pitch-black, which meant a cloud-covered sky. He looked around but could see absolutely nothing; he wondered if that was what it felt like to be blind and immediately dismissed the idea, realizing there was, of course, a massive difference. As he played with the experience of not being able to see anything, he suddenly had the feeling that he was no longer alone. There was something or someone in this hole with him.

In that moment of palpable fear, he did not know what to do. He felt like a child who was afraid to look under his bed for fear the monsters living there would gobble him up. Was the wolf there waiting to pounce? Was it another animal that had found its way into the hole? Perhaps this was some animal's regular home and Harold was intruding. He had checked for an alternate opening earlier and found nothing, yet the feeling of another presence was so strong he was certain there was something there.

If he reached out, he could get his hand ripped off. If he did nothing, he could get his throat ripped out. Harold thought for a moment that if he made some aggressive noise, it would at least buy him some time, but nothing would come out of his mouth, no matter how hard he tried. *Do something, you dumb piece of shit!* Harold's mind screamed at him.

CHAPTER THIRTY-SEVEN

Nancy was a little miffed when her call again went straight to voice-mail. Just because there were no children to care for was no reason for Harold to suddenly become incommunicado. Considering Harold's recent erratic behaviour, Nancy again considered the possibility that, in a fit of anger, he had destroyed his phone. Even if that was the case, there were other phones, and he could probably get a new one quickly and easily. There was simply no excuse for Harold's lack of consideration, and Nancy was determined to let him know how unacceptable it was if she could ever get through to him.

Then Nancy remembered their house phone. They still had one, but other than scams and robocalls, no one ever called that phone anymore, and neither she nor Harold ever used it to call anyone else. She decided to give it a try. Not surprisingly, no one answered. Harold would probably have ignored it even if he had heard it, and because it was in the kitchen and Harold was probably in his den, there was a very good chance that he wouldn't hear it.

The girls were waiting in the living room, planning to play some *Trivial Pursuit* and some new game called *What Do You Meme?* that was apparently a lot of fun. Nancy decided to hell with Harold. If he couldn't bother even keeping his phone on, she was not going to ruin her evening worrying about it.

The original *Trivial Pursuit* had been filled with questions about history and what had been then current-events, but the new edition they were playing was mostly about movies and TV shows, two subjects Nancy knew practically nothing about. The game was fun. The other ladies, especially Nancy's partner, were gracious about her total lack of knowledge when it came to television, and quickly suggested that they should turn it into a drinking game.

"Okay, every time Nancy says that she's never heard of a show, we have to drink."

"Oh, my God," responded Nancy. "I don't think that we have enough wine. How about taking a drink every time I get an answer right?"

"Nancy, I think that you've misunderstood the purpose of a drinking game. We aren't trying to stop drinking," was the instant reply.

The *Trivial Pursuit* game went on for a little over an hour and was filled with good-natured ribbing for incorrect answers and often, in Nancy's case, no answer at all. At the end of the game, the winner was chided for spending far too much of their time watching television.

Nancy enjoyed the jokes and conversation, but her periodic lack of engagement in the game allowed her mind to continually slip back to her inability to contact her husband. His lack of consideration was negatively affecting her ability to enjoy her weekend, and she resented it. It crossed her mind that this phone issue may not be simply an oversight; it could very well be a passive-aggressive act caused by some unknown issue that Harold had arbitrarily decided to be offended by. Amid the merriment that surrounded her, Nancy decided that enough was enough. If Harold wanted to make himself miserable, that was one thing, but making everyone around him miserable had to stop. Whether Harold liked it or not, when she got home, they were going to have a serious conversation and clear this shit up once and for all.

The ladies' decision to shift to the *What Do You Meme?* game forced Nancy to stop thinking about Harold. The game was more Nancy's style and required her to pay attention, especially if she wanted to deliver a worthwhile response, which was the key to everyone enjoying the game. Thanks to the laughter, the wine, and her good friends, Nancy eventually stopped thinking about her troubled husband and his phone issues and enjoyed the evening with her friends.

That Harold might actually be in trouble never crossed her mind; had it crossed her mind, she would have immediately dismissed it.

CHAPTER THIRTY-EIGHT

Harold finally grabbed his cell phone with his bad arm and his ski pole with his good one. Ready to fight, kind of. He fumbled to turn the phone back on, and finally, the screen lit up, instantly filling the darkness with light. Quickly he flashed it from side to side, almost frantically trying to find the intruder. After a few moments, Harold realized there was nothing there. No matter how he felt, he trusted his eyes, and they were clearly telling him he was alone. The cell light faded off. Harold knew there was nothing in the hole, but he still felt the strange presence. This was something totally different than he had ever felt before. Those previous presences had felt strange but somehow connected to him. This felt like an intruder, a foreign body about to invade his space. He turned the cell light back on to convince himself that it was nothing more than his paranoia. As the light faded, he lay back and tried to go to sleep.

"Did you want to talk?"

Springing up from his blanket, Harold frantically searched for the button on the cell phone that would provide him some light and hopefully some answers. "Who's there?" he blurted.

"The light is unnecessary. You will not be able to see me," said the voice that seemed to have no source.

"What do you mean I won't be able to see you?" a perplexed and frightened Harold mumbled while he flashed his cell light in every corner of the hole.

"I am a spirit. I have no physical form so you cannot see me with or without the light, which, I realize for humans, makes believing in my presence more difficult," the voice commented in a calm and reassuring manner.

Harold continued to probe the full expanse of the hole with the light of the cell phone anyway, not believing for a minute that he was conversing with a spirit, but there was no one there, only the small and completely empty giant hole in the ground.

"Who are you?" Harold demanded.

"I do not have a name, but for the purposes of this conversation, you can call me Herman."

"Okay, Herman, if you have no physical form, how do you talk?" Harold asked, not knowing if he was talking to someone, something, or himself. Was this a dream, a reaction to the shock, or was the concussion perhaps much worse than he had thought? Maybe he was dead.

"You are very perceptive, and no, you are not dead. I am not actually talking. I am simply sharing my thoughts with you. Your mind translates it to sound to make it easier for you to comprehend."

"You aren't talking? That makes no sense. And why do you sound like you are reading the news?"

"Well, I was trying for something that sounded trustworthy, like Walter Cronkite. I thought it would be a nice touch. And just because the fact that I am not talking does not make sense to you, it does not make it any less true. A concept I gather that most humans, especially older white males, have a hard time comprehending."

Harold had no idea what was going on. He was talking to someone who wasn't there. It answered questions that he had only thought of asking. It was beyond bizarre and more than a little frightening. Maybe his mind was simply creating an illusion to stop him from thinking of the pain and fear. Maybe he was experiencing an auditory hallucination because he desperately needed someone to talk to. He had read about them, and apparently they were more common than you would think and often happened to perfectly healthy people under significant stress. Of course, Harold had no problem admitting that he was under significant amounts of stress, and the voice was not reducing that stress. Maybe he was losing contact with reality.

"We seldom communicate with intelligent physical forms, but it seemed extremely important to you, and you do not seem otherwise occupied, so it appeared to be an opportune time. Do you want to talk?" the voice repeated.

"Do I want to talk about what?" Harold queried. "What is it you think is so important to me?"

"It appears that you are obsessed with what will happen after your death. Your thoughts and actions seem to be centred on trying to control what will happen, but you are doing everything in a vacuum because you have no knowledge of life after death, and to be perfectly honest, it does not appear that you have any comprehension of the purpose of living. I am here to help you with that."

"You're going to teach me the meaning of life? Are you sure you have the right person? I'm not a big believer in the whole afterlife, spirit-world thing," Harold responded.

"Let me see. What is your full name, address, and date of birth?" The voice then paused. "Yes, I have the right person. We are not telemarketers; we do not pick numbers randomly, and we never get wrong numbers or wrong people. And again, just because you do not believe in spirits does not mean that we do not exist. You have spent months making decisions about your life and the lives of a lot of other people, all based on your idea of what life is all about and the perception that you are going to die soon. Do you not think it would be helpful to understand what actually happens when you die, and the reason behind your existence?"

"This is all very confusing. My interest in what happens after death has been focused on what happens to my family and loved ones. I don't remember talking or even thinking about life after death."

"Harold, for an incredibly intelligent physical life form, you are pretty slow on the uptake. You are making decisions about how to live the rest of your life and trying to make decisions about how your family and friends live theirs, yet you have no idea why they are alive at all. You would do more research into the purpose of a building's existence before you bought it than you have put into the purpose of your life or anyone else's life."

"And you are going to tell me the purpose of life," Harold said with a chuckle. "I've heard that promise before."

"Yes, I am going to tell you what I believe is the purpose of life, of yours and the lives of every other intelligent life form. I will also share with you the reality of the course of life, and then, once fully informed, you can make your own decision about your life's purpose," Herman said, without a trace of impatience.

"So, you came because I'm making decisions about the rest of my life without having key information, and I'm guessing you think the decisions that I'm making are wrong," Harold responded, becoming more convinced that Herman was a figment of his imagination or a symptom of the concussion.

"Well, yes and no. I responded because your spirit and your physical form are in conflict, and your physical form has been unwilling to listen or even consider alternative ideas. Talking to your human form is just the easiest method of communicating with both of you at this point in your spirit's development."

"So, do you show up every time someone and their spirit are in conflict about how to live their life? Why have I never heard of this before? This seems like something religions would jump all over."

"We never 'show up,' as you call it. That would suggest that, like humans, spirits have a physical space that confines us. We do not. The physical form and the spirit form are in regular conflict. Why your spirit's specific request is being responded to is very difficult to determine and something that I also have never experienced before. This direct spirit-to-physical-life-form communication is very unusual but not unprecedented. And as far as you not having heard about this happening to anyone else, would you have believed them?"

"Good point. You said 'spirits.' Are there more of you?"

"Yes, you will be visited by three spirits. Pay them heed, for your very soul depends on it." Harold was certain that he heard Herman laugh. "I have always wanted to say that to a human. Yes, there are billions of us, but it is unlikely that you will hear from others."

"What do you mean spirits don't have a physical space like humans? And if you do not have a physical form, what separates you from the billions of other spirits?" Harold queried the unseen intruder.

"You humans think of everything as an object that has dimensions and exists in a place and a time; even vapour and air have dimensions and exist in a place and time. A spirit has none of those things. It has no physical form or component, and it is nowhere and everywhere at the same time. We neither come to you nor leave you, in the manner that humans conceive of it. What separates us from each other is consciousness, our individual sense of existence."

This was more than a little confusing for Harold. "So, what you are telling me is that when you die, you become a spirit that is everywhere and nowhere at the same time, and the only thing that separates you from a million other spirits is your personal sense of existence. Is that correct?"

With absolutely no sign of frustration, the spirit responded, "So far, I have not been talking about human death at all. I was simply explaining the nature of a spirit in a manner that will allow you to understand how it compares to the physical forms that have surrounded you throughout your present life. I said billions, but the actual number is unknowable, and yes, it is your personal sense of existence that separates you."

"So, are you saying that when we die, our spirit does not go to heaven or hell? Because if you start talking hellfire and brimstone, I'm out. I have not believed in that crap for a long time. It's nothing more than a concept designed to control the masses," Harold said while wondering exactly how he would go about exiting a conversation that he was not even sure that he was actually having.

"So far, I have not even said that humans have a spirit. The fact is you egotistical humans, as usual, have it backward. Humans do not have spirits; spirits have human forms for part of their journey. And no, when a human or physical creature's body ceases to function, the spirit does not go to heaven or hell," was Herman's definitive reply.

"So, where does it go?" Harold was thinking this was getting interesting. If this was a hallucination, his mind was going to have to come up with something out of the depths of his subconscious to respond to this one.

"It is hard to understand, but it does not go anywhere. It is a spirit. It is not controlled by space and time. It has no physical dimensions." Then, in what almost sounded like a humorous voice, Herman said, "Harold, you are going to have to get a quicker grasp on the basic principles if we are to get anywhere in this conversation. A spirit is not a thing that you can touch, feel, or physically limit. It doesn't go anywhere."

"Okay, I get it. A spirit has no physical form. So, are you and my spirit the same things?"

"We are the same, but our abilities and our awareness of our individual circumstances are very different."

"So, when I die, my spirit gets all of these special capabilities that you have."

"No."

"Okay, you've lost me again."

"Partially because you continue to think of it as your spirit, but perhaps some broader explanation is needed."

CHAPTER THIRTY-NINE

Harold sat back on his blanket in the pitch dark and tried to make himself as comfortable as he could, sitting in a hole he could not escape, with a sprained wrist and a broken ankle, talking to someone who wasn't there. He was absolutely certain none of this was actually happening. He was what you would call a meat and potatoes kind of guy—not that he ate a lot of either, Nancy made sure of that—but he was not much into philosophy or spirituality or mysticism. It was all very strange and very out of character for Harold, but he had no place to go and no TV to watch, and this seemed like a great way to pass the time, even if it was a dream or a concussion-induced hallucination.

Herman, the spirit, began to explain, "We live in an infinite universe, no beginning and no end that any spirit or physical life form is aware of. That universe has two types of intelligent inhabitants: the physical and the spiritual. The members of the spiritual world begin their existence by experiencing life through a physical life form. This allows them to take in information slowly while their abilities mature. Because there is so much to experience and because each life form is so limited in its duration and the variety of experiences available to it, a single spirit will be a part of hundreds of thousands of physical life forms."

"Why is it that only a limited duration with limited experiences is available?"

"Because the physical laws of the universe limit all life forms, regardless of where they are. Although life forms try, and to some degree succeed, to extend their lives or overcome distances with speed, infinity is something they can only conceive. It is not something they can experience."

"So, humans are simply vessels for spirits to have experiences through. Is that what you are saying?" Harold queried.

"I am saying exactly that, but the way you say it makes it sound like humans are a set of clothes that you throw away when you are tired of them. That is not the relationship at all. In fact, it is nothing like that."

"Okay," countered Harold, quite enjoying this hallucination. "What is it like?"

"Think of a massive obstacle course, in fact, an infinitely large and infinitely complex obstacle course. That is the universe and the life forms that live within it."

"You mean a track of things that you run through, climb over, and crawl under? That type of obstacle course?"

"Well, yes, but way more complicated. This obstacle course is an unending series of challenges, disappointments, and victories. Think about all the challenges that people face on earth, and then think of all the challenges that people on earth could face but seldom ever consider, like a giant comet hurdling through space and smashing into your planet, or the molten centre of the planet erupting and splitting the planet in two, and then multiply all of those possibilities by infinity. That is how much there is to experience."

"And you are saying that one human life is not likely to experience a significant portion of what is available to be experienced."

"That is a big part of what I am saying. While each human form is important, they simply do not last long enough to truly enjoy the abundance of available opportunities. On the other hand, a spirit has no such time limit, at least not one we are aware of, so they go from one life form to another, experiencing the wonders of life and the universe. But it is also important that the life form and the spirit believe that the life they are experiencing is their one and only life. As I am sure you can imagine, knowing that this life was only one tiny portion of your existence, would dramatically alter the quality and nature of the experience."

"But are you not concerned that by giving me this information, you will alter my life experience?" Harold paused for a moment. "Sorry, and my spirit's life experience?"

"No, because your nature will be to question whether this conversation actually happened. You will and are, right now, wondering if this is real, or strictly a figment of your imagination brought on by your recent obsession with death and your current circumstance. When we finish talking, you will have a new concept of life, but you will be no more certain of whether it is a fact or a theory."

"Hmm, that is probably a fair assessment. I already don't believe that this is happening. So, for the sake of the experience, tell me, if the spirit is all-knowing and infinite by nature, why do they need life forms to experience things?"

"There are a lot of different reasons. First of all, spirits are not all-knowing, and second there are certain things that you can only experience with a physical form, like birth, sickness, injury, hunger, death, a good bottle of wine, and of course physical orgasms. A spiritual orgasm is very enjoyable as well, but experiencing a physical orgasm first is the best way to appreciate, fully, a spiritual one."

"Seriously, a spirit has come to me to tell me about the wonders of the universe and life after death, and you're telling me it's all about orgasms?"

"I did not say that it was all about orgasms. I was just saying they are one of the many things best experienced first with a physical life form. And by the way, as good as the human orgasms are, there are other life forms with much better orgasms. And yes, I would suggest that the longer you are around, the more that you will appreciate the value of a full-blown spirit-altering orgasm."

The spirit paused, apparently taking a moment to reflect on past orgasmic experiences. Then he continued, "Anyway, as the spirit matures and gains knowledge through the experiences that they gather during hundreds of thousands of lives, they need the physical form less and less. They begin experiencing other spirits and the universe without the need of the physical, so rather than touch or taste, they simply know. And that is when the true expansion of knowledge and awareness really begins."

"You mentioned hundreds of thousands of lives lived by one spirit. Wouldn't that get a little repetitious?" asked Harold.

"Actually, I probably underestimate. It is probably millions of lives. And is repetition a problem? Consider that there are eight billion people in earth's civilization today, living very different lives, and multiply that by all the civilizations on all the other planets. I am comfortable that most intelligent life forms can stay engaged."

"You keep mentioning other life forms and other planets. Are you saying that there is intelligent life somewhere other than on earth?" Harold blurted out.

"Wait, are you saying that there is intelligent life on earth?" Herman quipped. "I have been waiting forty thousand years to use that line. Spirits do have a sense of humour."

Harold smiled, thinking that even his hallucinations were doing a poor job of trying to be funny.

Herman, after getting over his pleasure in his own humour, continued, "The dimensions of the universe are unknowable. Do you really believe that humans are the only life form? There are many life forms, some like humans, some not. Some of your science fiction writers have done an amazing job of guessing at many of the life forms that really exist out there."

"You mean that some of them are right? Creatures like that actually exist out there somewhere?"

"Well, you are not going to run into Yoda or Chewbacca, but there are some life forms that are pretty darn close to these, and many others. As I have said, think infinite. That covers a lot of possibilities."

Harold's musings about his favourite sci-fi characters and the possibility that they might actually exist were interrupted when Herman began talking. "But let's go back to the acquisition of knowledge. The pursuit of knowledge through experience is the greatest joy of our existence, regardless of what life form we exist as. It would be so sad, incredibly illogical, and incomprehensibly cruel if we were born into this incredible and infinite universe and we only had a human's minuscule life to enjoy it, to explore it, to experience its many wonders."

"What do you mean by our 'minuscule life'?"

The spirit audibly laughed. "Good question, and maybe a poor choice of words. But it is getting late, and your physical form needs its sleep to recover, so why do we not pick this conversation up at another time?"

"You mean I'm not sleeping? Isn't this a dream?" Harold asked, thinking that none of this was really happening and that the voice was going to tell him it was not a dream, even if it was.

"It is not a dream," the spirit responded, just as Harold knew it would.

CHAPTER FORTY

Harold could feel the hot breath on his face. It smelled of whisky, which mixed with the body odour of this man that he hated, and it made him want to vomit. Father Brown pushed him against the wall, holding him there with his fat greasy hands.

"Where is he, you little piece of shit?" the priest whispered into his ear.

"I don't know where he is, and if I did, I wouldn't tell you," Harold responded.

The priest licked Harold's cheek.

"Oh, you'll tell me. You know you'll tell me. You know you'd rather tell me where to find him than have to replace him."

Harold squirmed, humiliated, knowing that this disgusting piece of humanity was probably right. He did not have the courage to replace Mark, or the strength to do anything to stop what was happening to Mark. He wanted to beat the priest to death with his own hands.

The priest pushed his body against Harold's and slowly ran his hand down the front of Harold's chest, over his stomach, and down to his waist, where he stopped to undo Harold's belt.

"Maybe you should replace him. I'm sure your father wouldn't mind. Your father thinks I'm a prince of a man and would never believe a bad word about me."

Harold squirmed to get away, to remove himself from the priest's grasp, but the priest was twice his size and had him pressed against a wall so hard he could barely move.

"Leave me alone!" Harold screamed.

But the priest only smiled and went on to undo Harold's pants.

Harold felt an object next to his right hand. He grabbed it. The thickness and weight of it were immediately recognizable to Harold. It was a ball-peen hammer. He swung at the priest, surprising him but not hurting him.

The priest stepped back to assess the situation, smiled, and gave a little laugh. "The child has a weapon. Good, this will make it more interesting." The priest lunged toward Harold, who jumped back and swung the hammer. It landed hard on the priest's shoulder. The priest slumped from the pain of the blow, and Harold swung again, hitting the priest on the head. The priest fell to his knees.

Harold leaped forward, aimed the hammer at the centre of the priest's head, and swung with all of his strength, connecting squarely at the top of the forehead. The contact made a sickening sound as the hammer crushed his skull. Consumed with anger, hate, and guilt, Harold kept on smashing the hammer into the head of the priest again and again, screaming at the priest to leave him alone, over and over. The priest slumped to the floor, unconscious. Blood poured from the gashes on the priest's head and covered everything, but Harold continued to swing, landing blow after blow.

The movement and the screaming woke Harold. He was sweating and swinging his arms in the air. In a moment of disorientation, Harold did not know where he was. It took him only seconds to realize that he was still in his hole. Staring into the darkness, Harold knew what had triggered the nightmares, even if he refused to admit it to anyone else. Was everything that he was going through all related? Were the fits of anger, the terrible decisions, the nightmares, and the apparent visit from the spirit world all related to the actions of a fourteen-year-old? Was losing his grip on reality his final punishment for what he had failed to do so long ago?

Once Nancy had committed to enjoying the day with her friends and forgetting about Harold and his recent behaviour, the four of them had a great day and evening of hiking, telling stories, eating, drinking, laughing at each other, and playing games. Nancy had managed to completely forget about phoning her husband, which she felt a little bad about.

It was now well after midnight, and Nancy decided it was far too late to be calling him now. She decided that it could wait until morning.

As the recent events of his life tumbled through his mind, Harold slowly faded off, knowing even sleep was not a reprieve from the guilt Mark's suicide had rekindled.

CHAPTER FORTY-ONE

Harold woke up early and cold. He realized he should have taken some additional precautions to stay warm. Simply bundling up in his thermal blanket and warm winter clothing had definitely not been enough. He had at least a dozen hand warmers in his pack and thought this might be the right time to start using them. Somewhere in one of those survival articles, he had read that if you placed the hand warmers under your armpits and near your groin, it would help ward off hypothermia.

When he looked in his pack, he was pleased to see he had far more hand warmers than he had expected. Nancy must have dumped some in there from another backpack.

Sticking hot hand warmers onto sensitive skin was considerably different from putting them into your winter gloves, but they appeared to work just as the article had said that they would. Harold was not toasty warm, but he was, almost instantly, much more comfortable.

He took only a few minutes to contemplate what he could remember about last night's nightmare. The subject matter was clear to him, as was his guilt associated with that subject matter. It was even clear that Mark's suicide was the trigger, but what did all of this have to do with everything else he was experiencing? He could not make the connection, but what he did know was that he could not allow any of it to stop him from getting out of this hole and back to his family. He could worry about the rest of it when his family no longer had to worry about him.

Harold spent most of the day alternating between trying to stay calm by convincing himself that he would not die in this hole, eating and drinking very little to buy time, digging and refilling holes to pee in, and trying to find an obvious way out of the hole that could be accomplished by someone who had a wrist that he could barely use and a broken ankle he could not stand on. Knowing that he could not yet walk, his efforts at trying to escape his hole included making noise and yelling for help, hoping someone would hear him.

As much as Harold wanted to get out of the hole, he was trying to be realistic. If he got out and could not walk back to his car, or at least back to the cross-country trail where someone would be likely to find him, he would probably put himself at greater risk than he was by sitting in the hole for a couple extra days. Risk assessment had been one of the key sections covered in a training session on strategic planning he had taken only a few weeks ago. It crossed Harold's mind that it was too bad he had neglected to ask them how he would assess the risk of staying in or leaving a hole in the middle of the Rocky Mountains when you had a broken ankle and were running out of water. He chuckled as he thought about how helpful that information would be right now.

He kept picturing his giant footprints in the untouched snow that would be impossible to miss. Surely the combination of his car parked for days in the parking lot, the skis strapped to the trees, and the footprints would lead them right to him in short order. However, Harold knew that if they did not find him soon, his risk profile would change significantly, and his only hope for survival would be to find a way out of the hole on his own. The concept of not being found frightened him. But for now, he was safe, so he settled in and prepared for another night in his new home.

CHAPTER FORTY-TWO

Harold had just settled in for a long winter's nap, a thought that caused his mind to wander back to the many Christmas Eves when he and Nancy had read *The Night Before Christmas* to Jessie and Megan. The thought of the four of them huddled together on the king-sized bed put a smile on his face and a lump in his throat.

Tonight he had taken the time to put new hand warmers in his armpits and near his groin before he bundled himself up in his thermal blanket and warm winter clothing. He knew that the hand warmers would not last all night, but he wanted to be warm as long as possible. He would deal with the morning in the morning.

When he heard the voice again, he was more than a little surprised. He was pretty certain that he was not yet asleep, so it probably was not a dream. If it was caused by him hitting his head, why had he not heard from the voice all day?

"Hey, Harold, Herman here again. How was your day?"

"I thought you were everywhere and nowhere at the same time; do I really have to tell you how my day was?"

"No, not really. I was just trying to be polite. And I thought that there might be something that you really wanted to share with me."

"Can't you read my mind? You seemed to be doing that yesterday."

"Only when my attention is focused on you. Could you imagine if we were reading everyone's minds all the time? The amount of information would be, well, infinite, and the noise, even for a spirit, would be overwhelming."

"And spirits are not capable of infinite?" Harold asked.

"Not even close," Herman responded. "Now where were we when we stopped talking? Oh yeah, what did I mean by your 'minuscule lives'? I don't mean that they are unimportant; I mean, they are so very short. It took hundreds of millions of years for the earth to form and for humans to develop. The lifespan of your human form is far too tiny for the spirit to develop, grow, and have all the life experiences necessary for a spirit to understand and explore the magnitude of the infinite universe and the incredible things they will encounter in a life that appears to have no end."

"I don't understand. I thought spirits were, how did you put it, nowhere and everywhere at the same time? If you are everywhere, why don't you know everything?"

"Because even as a spirit, we still have the limitation of absorbing only so much input at any given time. So, while we may be everywhere, our attention still has limited capacity. For me to read your mind, I have to be paying attention to your thoughts, and I cannot read them faster than you have them. What a spirit can do is absorb a huge amount of information very quickly. While a human may stare at a sunset for half an hour and still miss many of its components, a spirit absorbs and enjoys every aspect of the sunset immediately. However, we cannot experience multiple sunsets at the same time. Our attention moves from one to the other incredibly quickly, but we must actively change our focus. We are not omnipotent. We are simply different."

"Okay, now I'm curious. Did you spend your day focused on me?"

Herman laughed. "To be honest, you moved so slowly today I could have watched a hundred sunsets and visited a thousand civilizations and still not missed anything that you were doing."

"Wow, it sounds like you had a full day. How long does it take for a spirit to become all-knowing and to find eternal bliss?"

"I do not know, and no spirit that I have encountered and shared knowledge with has claimed to be all-knowing. Although we have great lengthy spans of happiness, we still face times of sorrow."

The voice seemed to become quiet. "It is difficult to watch the pain experienced by young spirits because of the actions taken by them and their physical forms in a million lifetimes, but life experience, whether joyful or painful, is our only known path to growth."

Harold interrupted. "Why would a spirit feel bad about something that the life form, as you call it, does or did?"

"Because your spirit is an important part of the driving force behind all of your voluntary actions. Together the spirit and the physical form decide if you study or go out drinking. They decide if you treat people well or treat them badly. Like dealing with human teenagers, it would be so much easier if we could simply tell the young spirit what to do and what not to do, but like a teenager, the spirit's learning process requires the application of free will. It is an essential part of the process."

"You cannot communicate with these young spirits?"

"About as well as you humans communicate with teenagers. I am on a roll." Herman chuckled. "We can communicate easily with other mature spirits, but we have very limited ability to communicate with the very young ones, the ones that are still experiencing everything through a physical form."

Smiling at Herman's efforts at humour, Harold continued, "Is my spirit a young spirit?"

"Ignoring again that you are missing the point that it is not your spirit, I actually have no way of knowing, but the fact that I am here gives me the impression that it is not that young."

"So, is that why you can communicate with me—and I assume the spirit that uses my human form—because my spirit is not so young?"

"That is an excellent question, and I do not have an answer. I think it is partly because I am not being asked what you should do. It is likely a tear in the fabric of time and space that, somehow, one of us has slipped through."

"Wow, are there really tears in the fabric of time and space? That is so cool. What about wormholes?"

"Ha-ha." Herman chuckled again, obviously enjoying the conversation. "I was just kidding about that, but I guess anything is possible. I have never experienced a tear or wormholes. To the best of my knowledge, the only way for physical life forms to travel through space is the old fashion way, following the laws of physics. But black holes—there are lots of black holes, and they are super cool inside if you are a spirit. Not so fun if you happen to have a physical form."

"Because a physical form gets distorted in a black hole?" asked Harold.

"Ripped to pieces, right down to its molecular form," quipped Herman.

"Given all the varieties of shapes and sizes that we see in sci-fi films, is all physical life pretty much the same? If we could find a way to travel extreme distances in short periods of time, could we coexist like they do in Star Wars? All kinds of creatures hanging out at the same intergalactic bar? That would be incredible," Harold said, changing the subject.

"You again want to put easily understood parameters around what is beyond your life form's ability to understand, but it is not possible. There are some life forms that I am aware of that are very different in appearance to humans but live on a similar planet to earth and depend on the same environment that humans depend on. However, the number and types of life forms are as infinite as the universe, so while some may be compatible, others would be completely incompatible. And the reasons for that incompatibility are as infinite as the universe. Going back to your question about things getting repetitive, no, not even in a million lifetimes. Spirits experience and grow through life forms that are beyond our comprehension."

"Wait, you said 'our' not 'your.' Are you saying that there are life forms that even you do not comprehend?"

From the total darkness came what sounded like a chuckle. "Yes, I am saying exactly that and much more. I am still a relatively novice spirit. In my brief existence, I have had the opportunity to commune with only a small percentage of the spirits that exist without physical forms and the infinite universe that we live in. My limited ability to absorb more than one experience at a time and the infinite number of potential experiences means that there are an unknown number of life forms of which I am not yet aware. And of the many of which I am aware, there is so much about them I do not yet understand."

"How old are you?"

"We do not exist in human years or consider numbers for our age, but as a spirit without a physical form, I watched your earth develop from a mass of molten rock to what it is today. I can recall many of my physical forms prior to that, but my powers of recall have not developed sufficiently to recall all of them."

"What you are saying is that you are billions of years old, and you are only a novice spirit, that there are spirits much older than you."

"What I am saying is that I do not know how old I am. I cannot recall my entire life, and I have communed with spirits that recall viewing events as a spirit that occurred when I still experienced life through a physical form. Every spirit that I have shared knowledge with knows of a spirit that can recall viewing events as a spirit while they still experienced life through a physical form. What I am saying is that if there is an oldest spirit out there that can recall the beginning of time, I have not met them or any spirit that has. For a life form that invented the word 'infinite,' you do not seem to have a very good grasp of its meaning." When Herman made the last comment, Harold could clearly hear the kindness in the jab.

It baffled Harold. What this spirit was telling him differed greatly from any religious concept he had ever heard of. If this was a hallucination, where were these ideas coming from? The more questions that he asked, the more confused he was by the answers. Was there no God? Was there no heaven and hell? If the Bible was not the word of God, whose word was it? And that was just the big stuff. What about the detailed stuff, like was Harold living his life in the manner that he was supposed to? Was he teaching his children the right things? What were we supposed to be accomplishing during our lives and why? Now that he had someone to talk with that knew so much more than he did, he wanted answers.

The spirit interrupted Harold's thoughts as if he was listening to them. "Excuse me, to be clear, I am here to give you some information about what happens after a human dies, what is out there beyond the human form, and what the process of the life experience is like. I am not here to tell you how to live this life or any life. That is something that you will need to figure out on your own."

There was silence and Harold thought that the spirit must have left, or whatever it was that spirits did.

"No, I have not left. And you are right, that is not what spirits do, as I have explained. I was just thinking that you need your sleep, and you need to elevate that ankle if you want to keep the swelling down," commented the spirit.

"Two excellent ideas, but before I fade off to sleep, can you tell me if anyone knows I am missing yet?" Harold asked.

"The police have noticed your car and are trying to determine why it is parked where it is. Nancy and several other people have been trying to call you, and your son Jessie stopped by your house to talk with you, but so far, they all just think they keep missing you. And because you are notoriously horrible about returning text messages, no one has bothered sending you one. So, no, at this point, no one knows you did not make it home," responded the spirit.

"I can't believe how stupid I was, going into the mountains in the dead of winter all by myself. I'm such a fucking idiot." Harold was spinning into a cycle of self-loathing and repudiation that would continue until he faded off into a sound sleep. The spirit said nothing. It wasn't like Harold was wrong, but he didn't need anyone or anything to help support his position.

CHAPTER FORTY-THREE

Harold woke up very early on Sunday morning. He had gone from beating himself up to trying to analyze the repeated nightmares about Father Brown to desperately having to pee. It was a truly shitty night's sleep, even for someone stuck in a hole.

It was normal for Harold to wake up early, almost every morning, having to pee, but he was almost always in a nice comfortable bed, dressed only in a T-shirt and boxers, and mere steps away from a functional toilet. When you were sleeping on a thermal blanket completely clothed and had to pee into a hole that you had to dig before you could pee in it, waking up early to pee was far more inconvenient. All of this and a badly sprained wrist and a broken ankle were all a giant pain in the ass.

After repeating the entire adventure of the night before and damn near peeing himself, which at this point would be more problematic than embarrassing, Harold finally got himself into a position to relieve himself. It was great until he realized, in midstream, that he also desperately needed to take a shit.

Harold then spent well over an hour building himself a toilet that would allow him to slide his ass over it without standing or squatting.

The next forty minutes would have been a great comedy skit for Monty Python. However, it wasn't that funny, at least in the moment, for Harold. First, he dug a hole in the shape of a toilet, which even he did not understand. A round hole would have worked just as well. But at that moment, the shape of the toilet seemed critically important. Then he wriggled around, trying to get his pants down low enough that he wouldn't accidentally urinate on them. Once they were down around his calves and he was sitting bare-assed on the dirt, he began to wiggle, squirm, and slide himself into position over the hole.

The hole (or whole) setup was far from ideal as his sprained wrist and his broken ankle, along with having his pants down around his ankles, made sliding his bare ass across the cold dirt extremely painful and incredibly uncomfortable.

Once he got himself in position, he couldn't seem to go. What had seemed so urgent over an hour before when he had started the process suddenly seemed impossible. Realizing that he had no place to go and thinking about how hard it had been to get there, Harold decided to just stay where he was. If his balls and penis froze and fell off, well, too fucking bad. He was done worrying about it.

Eventually, Harold relaxed and did his business, then it was time to clean up after himself. There was a little toilet paper, in his backpack, for shitting-in-the-woods , so he wiped himself off. He did not want to leave the tissue or the shit where it was and he did not want to bury it because if he was still here tomorrow, he would need the toilet again. Given that he was digging mostly with his hands, he really did not want to be digging in a hole where he had just buried a pile of his own shit.

Harold bumped, wriggled, and slithered around on the dirt and finally got his pants back on and done up, then he started the cleanup.

Fortunately for Harold, Nancy had never removed the roll of doggie bags she had kept in each backpack. Harold had never been a dog person, or someone who appreciated any sort of pet, but due to his present circumstances, he was very happy they had once owned a golden retriever. He packaged up his shit in the compostable doggie bag and managed on the third try to throw it out of the hole.

Harold spent the rest of the day elevating his ankle, throwing dirt and small sticks out of the hole, hoping someone might notice, making noise in a breathtaking variety of fashions, and urinating only when he absolutely had to.

The headaches, nausea, and fatigue were significantly less prevalent today, but they still came back every time he exerted himself. He desperately wanted to escape the hole, but as he was so far unable to push himself enough to seriously mount an escape, he settled for planning his escape from the hole. Looking around, he noticed the pile of branches that he had dragged into the hole with him when he had fallen. If the gift that he had received from Jessie four Christmases ago was still in his backpack, he was pretty sure that he knew how to get out. He carefully searched, looking in every pocket, checking the bottom of the backpack thoroughly. Just as he was about to give up, his fingers felt something hard. He reached into the depths of the backpack and extracted the prize.

Nancy got up and repeated the early morning process of the day before, thankful that her friends were so easy to take care of. She considered phoning Harold, but she was more than a little angry with him and wanted to tell him so to his face. They were all planning to get on the road by 11:00 a.m., meaning she would be home by 2:00 p.m., so she decided to wait until she saw him in person to deal with all his recent issues once and for all.

The morning was a pleasant, unhurried process of four very dear friends talking about their upcoming week, enjoying a quiet and peaceful breakfast, taking their time packing the car, and only notionally acknowledging that at this moment, none of them had a care in the world. In the glow of the morning sun and the wonderful companionship, Nancy's frustration with Harold quickly became only a blip in the road.

Three hours after leaving the peacefulness of the cabin, Nancy arrived home, and after doing a quick tour of the house, was surprised to see no sign of Harold and, more perplexing, no sign that he had been in the house since Friday. Harold was not a messy person, but he wasn't a neatness fanatic either. If he had been in the house, there would have been signs of him making himself something to eat, having a glass of wine, or eating a late-night snack. But there was nothing. The house was exactly the same as Nancy had left it, and in over thirty years of marriage, that had never happened, not even once. Something wasn't right, but at this point, Nancy had no idea what it could be.

"Hey, Don, have you talked with Harold in the last couple of days? He seems to have turned off his phone, and I can't get a hold of him." Nancy had called the neighbour, who was one of Harold's closest friends, hoping that he would have some information that would calm her hopefully irrational fears.

"No, last I heard, he was heading to the mountains. I haven't heard from him since Thursday. I'm sure he'll show up before dinner. You know how Harold hates to miss dinner," Don joked.

"Yes, of course, I'm sure that you are right," Nancy responded, not at all sure that Don was right, but there was no point debating it with him and certainly no point alarming him at this point.

Because the trip to the mountains was three days ago, it did not immediately occur to Nancy that she might want to contact Shane Richards. If it had occurred to her, she would have immediately dismissed it, certain that Shane would say that he had not seen Harold since Friday.

Nancy was reluctant to contact Jessie or Megan. She did not want to worry them unnecessarily, and so far, all she had was an uneasy feeling and a clean house. Not much to go on. She was certain that if he had been in an accident, even if he could not call her, it would take about two minutes for the police to figure out who Harold's emergency contact was, and she would get a call.

At this point, Nancy was not certain at all how to proceed. Thinking about all the failed calls, she then, and only then, began to wonder if it was possible that Harold had been missing since Friday. The mere thought of that turned her stomach and sent a shiver through her body. Then she wondered if he was missing at all. How foolish would she feel if she reported him missing only to have him walk into the house fifteen minutes later with a perfectly reasonable explanation? The idea that he had gone into the mountains on his own was inconceivable.

She finally decided that if she was going to act like a panicked wife, she would do it with someone who could do something about it. She looked up the phone number of the local police station. She didn't know what she would say, but it seemed like the obvious place to start.

Just as she was about to make the call, the house phone rang. Nancy didn't recognize the number but decided, given the circumstances, to answer it anyway.

"Hello," Nancy said.

"Hello, this is Constable Jennings from the Canmore RCMP office calling. Is this Nancy Bower?" the voice asked.

"Yes, this is Nancy."

"Is your husband Harold Bower?"

"Yes, Harold's my husband. What's this all about?" Panic was beginning to set in. She was already imagining a list of things that this officer might say, and none of them were good.

"Ms. Bower, we've been trying to get a hold of your husband, but the phone number we have for him goes directly to voicemail, and he hasn't called us back. Does your husband drive a grey 2018 BMW X5 with the licence plate MBX 472?"

"Yes, that's my husband's car. Why?" *If he had been in an accident, why would they be calling him?* rushed through Nancy's mind.

"Are you aware of any reason why your husband's car would have been parked for the last two nights in a parking lot near the Continental Divide?"

Nancy was desperately trying to not get ahead of herself. There must be all kinds of reasons that the car was there, but she could only think of one.

Nancy did her best to calm herself, knowing that her overreacting was not going to help anyone. "Constable Jennings, I've also been trying to get a hold of my husband since Friday evening, and as you said, his phone has gone to voicemail every time. He and a friend of his went into the mountains on Friday, and I'm concerned that something bad has happened and they're still in there."

The constable responded calmly. "Ms. Bower, it's too late to start a search party tonight, and it's too early to panic, so why don't we start by you phoning everyone who might know anything about your husband's whereabouts, including his friend or his friend's family. He may very well turn up safe and sound with a perfectly reasonable explanation about his car."

"What should I do if I can't find him?"

"Call me back, and we'll figure it out from there."

Nancy immediately called Shane. When she heard Shane's voice answer the phone, her emotions swung in a multitude of directions. *If Shane is okay, Harold is okay. If Shane is at home, why is Harold not at home? If Harold has absentmindedly worried the hell out of me, I'm going to kill him.*

Nancy tried to regain her composure as she responded to Shane's calm hello with an equally calm response. "Hello, Shane. How are you?"

"I'm getting better, but still dealing with an annoying cough and a runny nose. But I'll be back in full gear in a couple of days," Shane responded, not understanding what the call was about, assuming that Nancy was calling to talk to his wife. "Did you want to talk with Clair?"

Nancy completely ignored Shane's comment about Clair. "Sorry, did you say that you were sick?"

"Yeah, damn flu, that's why I couldn't go snowshoeing and cross-country skiing with Harold on Friday. Didn't he tell you?" Shane responded in a fashion that suggested he assumed Nancy already had this information.

"You didn't go to the mountains with Harold on Friday?" Nancy asked, hoping that she had misunderstood.

"No, I was really sick. I'm really surprised that Harold didn't tell you."

"Shane, I haven't spoken with Harold since Friday morning. His phone has been going to voicemail, and I just got home from the cabin. Would you know if Harold went to the mountains with someone else?" Nancy said, almost pleading.

"To be honest, Nancy, I wasn't even aware that Harold went to the mountains. Are you sure about that?"

"The Canmore RCMP called and told me that his car has been parked up at the Continental Divide for two nights. I can't imagine why his car would be there if he isn't."

"Have you tried Jerry or the kids? Maybe one of them knows where he is and why his car's there."

"No. So far, I've only spoken with you and our neighbour, Don, but I'll call Jerry and the kids right away. Is there anyone else that I should call?"

"Nancy, you call Jerry and the kids. I'll call Steve Simmons, and anyone else I can think of who might have gone to the mountains with Harold, or who might have seen him in the last couple of days. I'll call you back as soon as I have some information for you. In the meantime, Nancy, don't panic. I'm sure there's a perfectly good explanation, and Harold'll show up safe and sound before the end of the night."

"Thanks, Shane." Nancy was focused on phoning Jerry and hung up the phone without saying goodbye. Neither she nor Shane noticed.

She called Jerry first, not wanting to alarm the kids if she did not have to. Jerry answered after the first ring, incredibly chipper for a Sunday evening.

"Hello, Jerry Bower here."

"Hey, Jerry. Nancy here. Sorry to bother you on a Sunday evening. I'm sure that you're trying to have some downtime. I was wondering if you happen to have spoken with Harold recently?"

Jerry's voice instantly went from chipper to concerned. "Nancy, that's a very odd question, especially from you. What's going on?"

A tremble entered Nancy's voice, and for the first time since she had discovered the clean house, she was having a real problem holding it together. It was all she could do to stop herself from bursting into tears. "Harold hasn't answered his phone since Friday, and the RCMP in Canmore called and said that his car has been sitting in a parking lot at the Continental Divide for two nights. Jerry, I'm afraid that Harold's in the mountains, and he's in trouble."

"Nancy, I'm sure there's a simple explanation, and Harold is somewhere safe and sound."

Nancy could tell by the tone in Jerry's voice that he was no more comfortable with that explanation than she was. They both knew that if Harold *could* call, he *would* call. There was no way on earth that Harold would let her and the family worry about his whereabouts if he had any ability to let them know what was happening. Nancy knew, and she knew Jerry knew, that Harold was in serious trouble.

"Jerry, do you really believe that?" Nancy asked.

"Nancy, it doesn't matter what I believe. Right now, we need to assume that Harold is safe, and we just need to do whatever we can to locate him. I'll be right over. You can't be alone right now." Jerry responded in a manner that Nancy knew that his coming over was non-negotiable, which she was completely fine with at that moment.

As soon as Nancy got off the phone with Jerry, she phoned Megan and then Jessie. Their reactions to the call were both almost identical to Jerry's. Surprised immediately that their mom was asking if they had heard from their dad, and certain that if he could call, he would have called. Both insisted on coming over. Nancy agreed.

Minutes after Nancy got off the phone with Jessie, Shane called back. No luck. No one had heard from Harold, no one had any idea where he might be, and no one had any suggestions about who Harold might have gone to the mountains with, or at least no suggestions other than the people who were all accounted for.

Nancy immediately phoned the constable back and let him know the results of her calls.

"Ms. Bower, perhaps you should come out here first thing tomorrow morning. I'll call search and rescue tonight."

As Nancy hung up the phone, she heard Jerry walking in the front door, followed by Megan only a few minutes later and Jessie a few minutes after that. None of them lived far away, and it was easy to tell, by looking at them, that they had done nothing to prepare for the visit other than throw on a coat, gloves, and a pair of boots. They all had that Sunday evening, haven't done anything but brush their teeth look. Even the clothes they were wearing looked like they'd slept in them.

Nancy could not care less how they looked. She was glad they were there. She gave each a giant hug as they entered the house, and she continued to fight the urge to cry. Now was not the time. Now was the time for sober discussion about what to do next.

Nancy explained about the call with the RCMP officer from Canmore and her plan to go to Canmore first thing in the morning. She promised them she would call each of them regularly throughout the day to keep them informed.

Jerry was the first to respond. "Nancy, I think that I should go to Canmore with you tomorrow. You'll need some support, and maybe there's something that I can do to help. If you're all right, I'm going to go home and put some gear together, and I'll pick you up first thing in the morning."

Nancy simply said, "Okay."

Jessie and Megan also insisted on coming with Nancy and Jerry to the mountains and doing whatever they could to help. They took turns going home, getting some things in case they had to stay in Canmore overnight, and letting their partners know what was happening. Neither wanted to leave their mom alone for even a moment.

CHAPTER FORTY-FOUR

Harold looked into the darkness. He was not sure why he had been hearing voices, and he did not expect to continue to hear them, but he asked anyway. "I'm more than a little confused by what you have told me. Could you answer one simple question? Is there a God?"

Herman did not respond right away. The pause was so long that Harold assumed he was alone and probably always had been.

"I do not know," was the almost inaudible reply.

"What did you say?" Harold said, making it sound more like a condemnation than a question.

"I do not know," repeated Herman with a little more conviction.

"You don't know? What do you mean you don't know? You're a spirit that's been around since before the dawn of time. You can be anywhere and everywhere, and you don't know if there is a God? What are you talking about?" Harold was angry and perplexed. If this was an illusion, it was a fucking annoying one. "How is that possible?"

"I was not around before the dawn of time; I do not even know when the dawn of time was, or even if there was a dawn of time. Remember infinity. You do not understand how much there is to learn. As I mentioned earlier, your human word 'infinite' means something, and despite your earthly views of life after death, all knowledge is not immediately accessible, even in the spirit world."

"Aren't you the least bit curious about whether there is a God? If your entire existence is now centred on seeking knowledge, isn't that kind of an intriguing piece of knowledge to pursue? Isn't that kind of the ultimate piece of knowledge?" asked Harold as he considered what it would take to get a better-quality hallucination.

"You are absolutely right. Knowing whether or not there is a God is the most important piece of knowledge that could ever be gained, the Holy Grail of knowledge." Herman said the next word with a strong emphasis to make a point. "*So*, do you not think it would stand to reason that it probably would not be particularly easy to acquire, especially for a novice spirit, let alone a spirit that still experiences all life through a physical form and is not yet even aware that it exists as a spirit? My guess is that this piece of knowledge may very well sit on the other side of infinity."

"So, you don't know if there is a God? Do you *believe* that there is a God? Does the evidence point to there being a God?" asked Harold, putting a heavy emphasis on the word "believe."

"I can tell you what knowledge I have gained and what knowledge I have not gained, and I can tell you what I believe based on that knowledge. But I cannot tell you factually that there is a God, and I cannot point you to a spirit that can state factually that there is a God."

"Okay, what do you know?"

"I know that the life of a spirit is a very long journey of learning through an infinite number of experiences and that, although you do not appear to remember from one life to the next in the first part of your journey, all the experiences of those lives stay with you. Eventually, as your spirit matures, and you no longer experience everything through a physical life form. You begin a slow process of remembering more and more of the experiences from those lives. I know that throughout what appears to be the eternal existence of a spirit, you encounter many other spirits, and all of them will be an ongoing part of your journey."

"So, my wife and I could spend eternity together?" thought Harold out loud, suddenly taking the conversation in a totally new direction.

"First, when your present life form dies, neither your spirit nor your new life form will remember your wife or anything else from this life. It could be thousands or hundreds of thousands of years before you recall the experiences of this life. So, you will not spend eternity with your wife and children in the way that humans think of spending eternity. As your spirit and the spirits of those you have loved grow and change, you will encounter each other again and again, and you will eventually recall that you have spent many lives together, in a variety of life forms, and that you have spent many lives separate.

"There will be so many spirits that you, and everyone you have loved, will have spent time with. There will be so many 'loves of your life' because there are so many lives. To a spirit, time and space have no meaning, and your ability to 'spend time' with any other spirit is nothing at all like 'spending time' as you know it. So, yes, you will be able to spend eternity with your present wife and children. But spending time being with their spirits simply does not mean what it means to you in your present life form."

"I wish you would quit referring to me as my present life form. And frankly, going from life to life and being torn away from the people that you love sounds less than appealing to me."

"Sorry, but that is probably because you continue to think of your existence and your wife's existence in terms of the life that you presently inhabit. Your physical life form and your spirit see themselves as one inseparable entity, which is dominated by the physical form, but that is just not the case. I know from a human point of view this could sound less than appealing, but as the spirit grows and comes to understand the journey that it is on, all of this will make much more sense. But it is a long journey, and it is not a simple one to explain."

Herman continued, "We do not know where it all began, why the universe exists, why we are capable of ever-expanding knowledge, why there is no apparent death of a spirit, or why there seems to be a never-ending stream of new spirits. We spirits do not understand the full meaning and nature of infinity any more than any other life form understands it. Actually, that is not accurate. There are some civilizations that still have a very myopic view of the universe. So, we have a better understanding of infinity than most other life forms."

Harold contemplated for a moment and then thoughtfully commented, "But once you recognize yourself as a spirit, you don't die, your friends and family don't die, you don't hurt each other, you don't want for any material things?"

"Yes, that is a simplistic but accurate statement, but keep in mind that it is an evolution, not a revolution," responded the spirit.

"Okay, well, even if it is a slow process, that sounds a lot like heaven to me. All the spirits living in peace together, sharing knowledge, caring for each other. So, what happens to the spirits of all the mean and nasty people in this world and all the other worlds?"

"What do you mean, what happens to them? They are spirits. They travel the same path as all other spirits. In fact, you may find that in many of your lives, you were one of those 'mean and nasty people,' as you call them."

"Are you saying that people get to mistreat each other, get to steal, kill, molest, lie, and cheat, and there is no final reckoning, no power that delivers the appropriate punishment for those horribly hurtful actions? What about Hitler? What about Stalin? Are they not punished for what they did?" Harold's voice was up an octave, and he was visibly agitated.

Calmly, the voice responded, "We know of no judgment day where the ultimate judge hands out the ultimate reward or punishment. There is only learning, understanding, and coping. It is all part of the process of growing and maturing."

Harold was now shaking. "So, the priest who manipulated a young boy into a hurtful and harmful sexual encounter gets treated the exact same way as the poor child who had to endure the horrific experience? There is no retribution, not even a shitty next life as a rat or cockroach?"

"That is an oddly specific example. But no, each spirit simply goes on to their next experience."

"This is fucking crazy! Are you telling me those bad people just get to move on in the spirit world? That there is no fucking reward for being a good person during your lifetime? That fucking idiots that hurt, torture, and kill people on earth are not punished? I mean, the concept of eternal damnation seems over the top, but, fuck, nothing at all? Is that what you are telling me?"

"Harold, I am not sure that I should tell you anything. You are getting awfully upset, and I am not sure that I am helping you with your quest for answers. You need to understand the answers are simply not as easy and basic as you and the rest of humanity want to believe."

Herman paused to allow Harold to respond. When he said nothing, Herman continued. "If you cannot deal with what is really out there, including its limitations, I may be causing you more harm than good. You profess to not buy into the hell, fire, and brimstone of earthly religions, but the concept of punishment for what you perceive as horrid actions seems critical to your sense of right and wrong. Maybe we should quit while you are still likely to consider this nothing but a dream or a hallucination."

Harold desperately tried to get his emotions under control. He had completely lost sight of the fact that this might all be happening in his mind, but he desperately wanted some answers, even if they were only coming from his subconscious mind. "I'm sorry. You're right, I'm overreacting. Please explain how spirits are rewarded or punished for their behaviour."

There was a long silence that seemed to make the darkness even darker. Finally, the spirit responded in a calm, low voice, "Harold, is this about Mark?"

Herman's mention of Mark visibly startled Harold. "No, this isn't about Mark." He paused. "Nothing's about Mark. I don't know what you think you know about Mark, but this conversation has nothing to do with what happened to him."

Herman, still speaking softly, replied, "Harold, would you like to tell me about Mark? You think about him a lot, but you have never talked to anyone about what happened."

Harold was again shocked by Herman's words. "What do you mean I think about him a lot? I can't remember the last time I thought about Mark."

"Harold, you know that is not true. You think about Mark and Father Brown almost daily. You have even started having nightmares about them."

"It was decades ago. I don't want to talk about it. There's nothing I can do about it now. Just drop it."

The subject clearly bothered Harold, and it showed both in his tone of voice and his body language as he crossed his arms across his chest and turned his head away from the direction he believed Herman's voice to be coming from.

"Harold, you were a child who made a mistake. You are now an adult. Do not keep making the same mistake," Herman said softly and kindly.

Not knowing how much Herman actually knew, Harold responded aggressively. "What're you talking about? I didn't do anything to anyone."

"How has telling yourself that been working out for you? Do you feel at peace with yourself?"

There was an extended pause as Harold rubbed his face with his hands, took a deep breath, and finally said, "I should've told Mark to tell everyone as soon as he told me about Father Brown. Instead, I did nothing, and I convinced Mark to do nothing. How could I ever feel at peace with that? Are you going to tell me it was okay, that I was only a child? Me saying nothing allowed that piece of shit to do the same thing to other young boys. How is that ever going to be okay?"

"You are right. It will never be okay. You should have told Mark to say something. You should have helped Mark tell someone. However, I will tell you that you were fourteen years old, and that this was not a burden you or Mark should have had to carry. I will tell you that had you said something, you would not have been telling Father Brown's superiors something that they did not already know. I am going to tell you that you made a horrid mistake, but not owning up to that mistake and moving on is an even worse mistake."

"I don't know how to," Harold said, sounding defeated, wanting desperately to let go, but fearing that letting go would be giving himself absolution that he didn't deserve.

"It is not about absolution, Harold. It is about accepting the imperfections of who we are, of who a fourteen-year-old boy was, vowing to do better and moving on. You cannot undo the past."

"How do I make it up to Mark and all the other boys?"

"You cannot. Mark and the others are travelling on their own journey. They do not benefit from you holding on to this. They gain nothing from your continued desire to punish yourself. You can only learn from your mistakes and try to do better. There is no way to undo them."

There was a long silence.

Finally, Herman spoke. "We have talked of many things tonight, many of which are very hard to comprehend. You have a lot to think about."

Harold looked around at his hole, his broken ankle, and his sparse supplies, and in a moment of despair, said, "Does it matter anymore what I think? Look at me. Do you really think that I'm going to find the strength to climb out of this hole and make my way back home? Let's be realistic, Herman. Isn't it all over but the crying?"

Herman replied with a soft smile that Harold could hear in his voice, "Harold, it is never over. Remember infinity. But let us not give up on this life just yet. I am going to leave you for now. You need your rest, and you will want to conserve your strength if you are to save your physical form from destruction."

"When will we talk again?" Harold asked.

"When the moment is right," responded the spirit, knowing that there was more to the Mark story that Harold needed to tell, but only when he was ready.

Immediately, Harold could sense that he was alone again. He called out, but there was no reply. Lying there in the darkness, thinking about that moment fifty years ago when Mark had told him what had happened. Thinking about how weak and selfish he had been. Mark had forgiven him many times over the years. Even when Mark had refused to testify at Father Brown's trial, years later, refusing to relive the pain he had suffered, he had still forgiven Harold and insisted that none of it had been his fault. But Mark had never known the entire story. If he had, Harold was certain that he would have never forgiven him. How could anyone?

CHAPTER FORTY-FIVE

Harold woke early on Monday morning, feeling much colder than he had expected. The temperature must have dropped after he had fallen asleep. He wasn't shivering, which was a good sign. He was probably not hypothermic yet. He started stretching to increase his heart rate and increase his circulation. First thing this morning, he would have to get some new hand warmers out.

"Get up, get moving," Harold chided himself, and as he rolled over on his blanket, his eyes became riveted to the most terrifying sight he had ever encountered. Completely frozen in place physically, Harold's mind sped off at warp speed. He would never see his beautiful wife or his children again. He would never play with his grandchildren, watch them grow, and share in their accomplishments. He had wasted so much time throughout his life. There was so much more he could have done, so many things he could have accomplished, and so many people he could have helped. Only moments before, he had convinced himself it was only a matter of time before someone would find him, but now, when they finally found him, they would find nothing but his remains. He was doomed, and there was nothing he could do but sit and wait and watch it happen.

Directly in front of Harold, piled at least two feet high, was a soul-crushing mound of fresh snow.

Harold knew the moment he saw the size of the mound that his chances of being found had gone from almost certain to almost impossible. Yesterday, his tracks would have led the searchers right to him. All they would have to do would be to find his car, which would not take long. Now, when they found his car—which they would within hours of Nancy reporting him missing—they would have no idea in which direction to even begin. This snowfall would cover everything, but more importantly, it would cover his tracks. This much snow would make it impossible for anyone to track Harold's path. There was no possible way that they would find this hole. His tracks would have been obliterated, and his chances of survival had been obliterated with them.

Harold was sweating. His head, chest, and arms were all starting to hurt again. He needed to calm down, get control of himself, and recalculate his situation. What he had thought would be a short and reasonably comfortable stay was now likely to be a long and increasingly difficult one. He had to consider what he had left in his pack and ration it out carefully. In desperation, Harold realized that every mistake he made from now on would dramatically reduce his chances of ever seeing his family again.

He breathed deeply and slowly. He had to calm down. Panic and self-pity were no longer options. He took deep breaths through his nose, all the way down to his diaphragm, held it for five seconds, then exhaled slowly through his nose. *Let all the air out. Hold it. Now, calmly and slowly repeat*, he told himself, trying to get control so he could think clearly.

What was now clear was that Harold's only way out of this situation would either be pure dumb luck or his own determination. Someone arbitrarily wandering by Harold's hole at the moment that he was making a lot of noise seemed about as likely as winning the lottery or getting hit by lightning.

As much as he wanted to believe in the possibility of someone accidentally finding him, Harold decided he had to accept that there was only one way that he was going home, and that was on his own two feet. He chose to ignore the other, more obvious way, which was in a body bag.

His mindset needed to change, and it needed to change immediately.

CHAPTER FORTY-SIX

"Search and rescue are already at the site, setting up a command centre," remarked Constable Reid, who had taken over the case from Constable Jennings, who worked the evening shift. "The blizzard last night has unfortunately wiped out any tracks that might have given us a clue which direction your husband might have gone."

Nancy, Jerry, and the kids had driven up to the RCMP detachment first thing that morning, but the blizzard, which had dropped well over a foot of snow, had made driving horrendous. They had just about ended up in the ditch a couple of times, which in no way helped to calm everyone's already frayed nerves. The drive, which normally took ninety minutes, had taken just about three hours.

"How long do you think it'll take to find him?" Nancy asked, knowing full well the constable would have no way to answer that question, but she was afraid to ask the actual question that she knew was on everyone's mind.

"There's simply no way to know. Your husband could have left this parking lot on at least four different cross-country ski trails, and if he was snowshoeing, there's no way to tell where he could have gone. So, at this point, we don't know in which direction we should focus our search," replied the constable.

"We have our snowshoes and our gear. Can we go up to the site and help?" asked Jerry, who had been given the difficult job of driving this morning.

"I know that you just want to help, and I can't even imagine what you must be going through, but with all of this extra snow, it'll go much faster if we leave the search to the people who have been trained for this type of situation. If you like, you are welcome to go up to the search site and talk with the search commander."

The search commander, Jack Holloway, was very experienced in this type of situation. He had got into this work because he loved the mountains. He stayed in it because he came to understand the incredible fear that the lost people and their families were experiencing, and he wanted to do everything that he could to help.

Constable Reid had contacted him, and he knew the missing hiker's family was on their way to the search site. He was trying to decide what he should and should not say to them. The chances of an inexperienced hiker lost in the mountains for three days still being alive, even in these temperatures, were pretty small. Someone would either have to have an incredible amount of natural survival instincts or a whole lot of luck. However, whether the hiker was likely to be alive would not affect their search and rescue process. They had specific procedures for this type of thing, and they would follow them, regardless of what any of them thought about the likelihood of finding the hiker alive.

Every family asked, almost immediately, "Do you think they're okay?" No one wanted to use the words "dead" or "alive." Jack had always taken the position that he'd hold off saying anything one way or the other if it was likely they'd have a definitive answer within a day or two. There was no point squashing their hopes or giving them a false sense of security when they would likely know for sure in a couple of days.

Jack knew all too well from experience that the real problem was that they might not know in a couple of days. It might be spring before they found the body. How could he prepare them for that? It was too horrid to even contemplate, so for now he would just wait. This was the part of the job that Jack disliked, but he knew it was the most important part of why he was there. As he saw Nancy and the others get out of their car and start walking toward him, he thought about the fact that, in his world of search and rescue, seventy-two hours after someone had gone missing, they changed the terminology from a "rescue" to a "recovery" mission. Something that he decided not to share with the family.

"Do you think he's okay?" was the first thing out of Jessie's mouth as soon as the introductions were complete.

"Folks, it's way too early to make any predictions. There are still far too many variables," Jack responded to avoid giving them his true opinion, "but you could help us a lot by telling us as much about Harold as possible. Dana here is going to take the four of you over to our van and ask you a bunch of questions. Please give her as much information as you possibly can. Some of it might not seem important to you, but the more information we have about Harold, the better our chances are of a good outcome."

Jack knew that the information the families provided seldom actually helped in these situations, but it kept the family occupied and made them feel like they were contributing. He looked out at the forest that engulfed him and thought, *If this guy is still alive, it will be a fucking miracle. Why do people insist on being so goddamned stupid?*

CHAPTER FORTY-SEVEN

Harold had never been in a situation anything like what he was presently experiencing. But he had been in enough tough situations to know that to have any chance at all, he had to be calm and thoughtful. Every decision he made, every drink of water, every bite of food had to be carefully considered. He knew he could not survive long enough in this hole, and in these conditions, to wait for his ankle to heal sufficiently so that he could walk on it, or at least walk properly. The effects of the concussion were diminishing every day, but they were not gone and could easily last for days, maybe weeks. But he had minimal supplies and still had to be strong enough to find his way out of the hole and then out of the forest, which, he acknowledged, might have become impossible with this snowfall. Right now, he could not allow himself to think about that. He had to focus on the best way and time to get home. He was on his own.

Water was his first concern. He had two good-sized water bottles. One was empty, the other was now only a little more than half full. The fresh snowfall provided an opportunity. His first goal was to get as much snow into the hole as he could, so he spent his first hour throwing things at the tree covering above him. The first few throws were incredibly successful, and the pile of snow grew significantly; however, less and less additional snow came down with each throw.

He then packed the snow into the empty bottle and poured the water from the half-full bottle over it to melt the snow. Using his shirt to sift out anything other than the water, he eventually filled both water bottles. Then he pulled out his largest plastic bags and did the same with them until all the snow he could collect, without also gathering a bunch of dirt, had been converted into water. This was a slow process, and it needed the aid of his body heat to make it work. He assumed he had to keep the water as warm as possible so it did not lower his body temperature too much when he drank it. He pulled out his ski pole and dug another hole, where he buried all the water except the two bottles that would be his water for the next couple of days. Thanks to the plentiful supply of hand warmers, he could melt the water without making himself too cold.

The food in his pack had originally included his lunch for the Friday hike, plus a half dozen packages of granola bars that each contained two bars and eight good-sized packages of dried fruits. It was not much, but Harold knew that food would not likely be his problem. This much food could keep him alive for a couple of weeks, and his actual fear was the cold. Right now, they were experiencing a reasonably warm stretch. Daytime temperatures were just below freezing, and nighttime seldom went below −15 or −20 degrees Celsius. Harold was pretty sure someone could survive for quite a while at that temperature, especially in this hole, out of the wind, with the ground and the trees as insulation. His fear was a cold front that could easily drop temperatures to −35 degrees Celsius or worse. In the Canadian Rockies, it was not a question of if. It was a question of when.

Harold now knew he could not wait for someone to find him. He had to get himself out of this hole and back to safety. But how? His ankle and arm were still in a fair amount of pain. Everything he had accomplished up to this point, he had done either crawling on three of his four limbs or butt-scooting around in the dirt. He had not tried to put any weight on his leg and wouldn't until he had to. He could use his left hand but not with any strength, and lifting anything with it was totally out of the question, but they would heal, and every day that went by, Harold knew he would have more use of both his wrist and ankle. There was still a chance. He just needed to stay calm and not do anything stupid.

In all of this fuss to stay alive, Harold had all but forgotten about his visitor from the last few nights. Had he really been talking to a spirit? Of course not, he determined. It was a dream or a hallucination brought on by the pain, the shock, or the isolation.

Whatever it was, Harold did not have time to dwell on it. His focus right now had to be on making a plan to get out of there. He studied the walls of the hole carefully and decided to approach the situation with two different strategies at the same time, not abandoning either until he had to.

It was Monday afternoon, and there was little chance someone would be in the area, but Harold shouted anyway. When he was tired of shouting, he started through his repertoire of songs.

The second strategy was to find a way to crawl out of this hole and walk back to the highway. The first problem was how to get out of the hole. It was far too deep to jump, and the walls were too steep to climb, even if there were footholds, and there weren't. But thanks to Jessie's Christmas gift that he had found last night, Harold already had an idea. The gift was a large Swiss Army knife with a very sharp blade. In his mind, the plan not only seemed plausible but also seemed easy to implement. At least in Harold's mind.

Gathering up the branches that he had dragged into the hole with him, he began creating his own footholds. Looking up at the top of the hole, he figured he only needed seven or eight. How he was going to drive them into the side of the hole, how he was going to stand on his broken ankle while he did it, and how he was going to get from the wall of the hole over to the opening were all things he would figure out later. For now, his focus was on creating the eighteen-inch pointed sticks that would lift him out of this hole.

He desperately wanted to get out of the hole and get back to his family, but he was smart enough to know a desperate act could easily be a disastrous act. Right now, this hole in the ground was his refuge, and as painful as waiting would be for him and probably Nancy and the children, he knew it was better to focus first on methodically building his escape, one step at a time. Then he would worry about how he was going to find his way back to his car. There was no reason to rush. His tracks would not become any more hidden than they were right now, and the stronger his ankle was, the better. And there was still an outside chance that someone could find him.

Throughout the day, he whittled the branches, stopping only to rest his hand for short periods of time. He made as much noise as he could but had to stop often to give his head a rest. When his head didn't hurt, he hollered, hooted, and even sang. He particularly liked the fast-paced songs like "Twist and Shout" and "Johnny Be Good." They seemed to warm him up and lift his spirits.

Harold would find his thoughts wandering off to all those great family weddings and how much he and Nancy loved to dance. He hadn't really cared much about when, where, how, or even if any of his children got married. The world was changing, and Harold was comfortable changing with it. But he was always hoping they would find some excuse to dance. Lying in a hole, singing to attract the attention of someone who might not even be there, Harold was struck with the realization that it was pretty sad that he had spent years hoping someone would get married so he would have an excuse to dance with his own wife.

The sun was beginning to set, Harold had not heard a sound from outside of his hole, and he was pretty certain no one outside had heard him. Nancy must know by now that he was missing. She had probably phoned his cell repeatedly, never leaving a message because she felt messages were unnecessary. At some point, she would have phoned friends and family to see if they knew where Harold was.

When she spoke with Shane, Nancy would have probably figured out that Harold had stupidly gone into the mountains on his own. Harold felt horrible about what Nancy and the kids were likely going through. The RCMP would have found his car, and had it not been for the snowfall, they most likely would have been able to find him. He figured the RCMP would probably already be assuming that he was dead; he hoped they had not told Nancy.

The first night would be a sleepless night for Nancy and his kids. It would be the night they would all wonder why their father, who never made rash decisions, would choose to do something so stupid. Nancy would have phoned everyone they knew, trying to find out where he was, but no one would know. His wife and his children were probably going through hell worrying about him, and there was absolutely nothing that he could do about it. The wrenching in his stomach was almost unbearable. Why had he not stopped after skiing? Why had he been so stupid as to go alone? Why had he picked now to become a mountain man?

CHAPTER FORTY-EIGHT

"Good morning, everyone. My name is Dana and I'm so sorry to meet you under these circumstances." The young lady, dressed like a veteran of the mountains, showed them into the van and got each of them a place to sit down.

Ostensibly, Dana was there to gather information about Harold that would help them find him, which was not entirely untrue. If any information did come up that could be useful, and some often did, she would highlight that and get it to Jack as quickly as possible. The colour of the clothes he was wearing, the type of material in his clothes, if any of them had hiked or snowshoed with him before, especially if it had been in this area. People often moved toward things they knew, even subconsciously.

After all the introductions had been made, Dana began asking questions, starting first with those that might provide some immediate assistance.

"Have any of you been in this area with Harold before? We find people are drawn to the familiar."

They all looked at each other, hoping that someone would say yes, but no one did. They had all been in the mountains with Harold many times, but not anywhere near this location.

"When you've been in the mountains with him, does he prefer to stick to trails, or does he prefer to adventure?"

Jerry answered first. "My brother, he's a by-the-book kind of guy, never lets the trail out of his sight." Everyone agreed. Dana made a note.

"What kind of a pace does he like to set? Is he a front-of-the-pack, middle-of-the-pack, or back-of-the-pack type of guy?"

Nancy smiled and said, "That depends a lot on who he's with. He's very fit, but he's sixty-three. I guess I would say middle of the pack."

"Great, you gave us a description of what he's likely wearing. Is there anything else that you think might help, like an unusual coloured toque or gloves?" Dana asked.

"Nothing like that, but his basic blue ski jacket is reversible, and the other side is a bright florescent orange. But I've never seen Harold wear it with the orange side out. He thinks it's ugly," Nancy shared.

"Let's hope that he's not concerned with fashion right now. The orange would be much easier to spot than basic blue," Dana offered as she wrote down the information, pulled out a yellow highlighter, and drew a line through what she had just written.

Then Dana shifted from questions that would help them find him to questions that would help them assess how long to continue to look. This was necessary but always difficult, especially if a family member happened to ask how this information was going to help them find the missing person. The fact was that search and rescue, even with their great volunteers, had limited resources. At some point, someone was going to make the call on whether to continue expending those limited resources on this singular situation. The information Dana was about to gather would inform that decision.

"So, could you do your best to tell me what supplies Harold has with him? I know that you probably don't know for sure, but your best estimate would really help."

The four of them listed the items they were aware of: the extra jacket, the thermal blanket, granola bars, dried fruit, and a well-equipped first-aid kit. Nancy remembered she had dumped a couple of dozen hand warmers into that backpack because she was giving a couple of old backpacks away.

"How has his state of mind been recently?" Dana asked.

All four knew why Dana was asking, and all four wanted to defend Harold. Megan even started by saying, "Dad's always in a great state of mind, always upbeat, a glass-half-full type of guy."

Nancy put her hand on Megan's hand and smiled at her. "Megan's absolutely right, but lately Harold's been dealing with some issues. Nothing he couldn't handle, and certainly nothing to do with where we are now, but he hasn't been the same old Harold." No one disagreed.

"Would you call it a depression?"

"No, not at all," Jessie piped up. "No, certainly not depressed. More like easily angered. He'll be happy as can be one moment, then snapping someone's head off the next, and then back to being the nicest guy in the world the next. Just short little spurts of anger. No depression."

"Do you know if he's been seeing anyone regarding emotional or psychological issues?"

All of them responded "definitely not," before they all realized how judgmental they probably sounded, even though that was not their intent.

"Okay, let's talk about his physical condition. On a scale of 1 to 10, for a man of sixty-three, where would you put Harold?"

There was some debate between the eight perceived by Megan, who knew very little about how fit most sixty-three-year-old men were, and the ten perceived by Jessie as he thought about the speed and dexterity Harold displayed getting out of his car to chase down the pedestrian. Dana assured them a precise response was not necessary. "How about medications?"

"Other than over-the-counter painkillers that he uses very periodically, no medication at all," Nancy replied.

It was clear that Jerry was surprised by this response by the look on his face, but he chose not to say anything.

"Any family history of heart disease?"

"Yeah, our father died of a heart attack," Jerry responded.

Dana looked up from the paper that she was writing on. No one else took much notice. "Can you tell me a little more about the circumstances?"

"He dropped dead of what they called a widowmaker in the middle of dinner," Jerry shared, having long ago lost any emotional connection to the story.

"How old was he at the time?" Dana asked.

The look on Dana's face and the knowledge of what his answer was going to be suddenly caused a shiver of fear to shoot through Jerry like a small bolt of electricity. He was suddenly very aware of every word coming from his mouth. "Well, you have to understand, our father was the very opposite of Harold. He was badly overweight, smoked like a chimney, drank a lot, and, well, you know, his lifestyle was killing him. Not at all like Harold. Harold takes amazing care of himself. He's as healthy as a horse."

By this point, all four of the others were staring at Jerry, wondering what on earth this was all about.

Dana was the first to talk. "I'm sorry. How old did you say your dad was when he died?"

"Sixty-four."

"Really?" Nancy responded immediately, not really sure what to make of the number. "The pictures I've seen of him make him look much older. I'd always assumed that he was in his early seventies when he died."

"Yeah, Dad lived pretty hard and died young."

Dana looked back down at her paper and asked, "Are any of you aware of Harold experiencing any physical conditions that might suggest some undiagnosed health conditions?"

Suddenly, everyone was cautious, looking from one person to the other, not knowing what to say and what not to say.

"Dana, could you give us a few minutes? This is a lot all at once," Nancy asked in the controlled voice of a lawyer who knew how to handle uncomfortable situations.

"Of course," Dana responded, not at all surprised. These were not naïve people. They knew what was happening.

When Dana had left the van, Jerry was the first to speak. "Are you sure that Harold isn't on any medication?"

"Not that I'm aware of. Why?" was Nancy's reply, not sure why Jerry was asking and no longer certain she really knew the answer.

"I've been on a statin for five years to control my high cholesterol levels. I just assumed Harold was going through the same thing. It's typically an inherited condition."

"Christ, Mom. This could explain some of what Dad's been going through. Shit, I thought that he was going to have a heart attack that day when Phillip and I came over to talk to him," added Jessie.

A hundred questions pulsed through Nancy's mind. *Is he sick? Why didn't he tell me? Is he lying in the snow, dead? Will they stop the search if they know?* And many more. She looked up at her family and said, "Okay, let's get Dana back in here and tell her what we know. No speculation, no guessing, only what you know for sure." She looked at each of them in order across the room. "Do you all understand?"

They all nodded.

CHAPTER FORTY-NINE

The moment darkness completely engulfed the hole, the voice came back again.

"Harold, how are you feeling? I see that you have found a new hobby. Does the wood have a particular purpose?" Herman asked, referring to the pile of thick pointed sticks beside Harold.

"Stairway to heaven," Harold quickly replied.

"Would you like to continue our conversation?" Herman asked, knowing Harold was not leaving anytime soon.

Harold was feeling good and said so, but because he was feeling good, he was more than a little surprised to hear the voice again. He went with it anyway. "Yes, I would very much like to continue our conversation. I'm ready for the whole truth and nothing but the truth, even if Nicholson doesn't think I can handle it."

"Yeah, that was a good movie."

"You watch movies?"

"We watch lots of things in lots of different places. Infinity is a lot of time to kill."

Harold laughed, something that he did not think was possible under the circumstances.

"So, where did it all begin?" Harold started.

"We do not really know where or how it all began or if there was a beginning. There are many theories, but no facts. Logically, you would think that there would be, but I am not sure exactly how logic and infinity coexist. Maybe, as difficult as it is to understand, the universe was always there. Maybe life forms and the physical universe have always existed; they just keep changing. To some extent, you can trace the coming and going of life forms and things like planets and stars, but spirits are not like humans. There is no birth event that other spirits are aware of, and there is no need for care and nurturing as there is for a baby human or the other physical and intelligent life forms that exist throughout the universe.

"By the time we spirits are aware of a new spirit, it has been through hundreds, maybe thousands of physical life forms, and although everything this new spirit has experienced stays with them, at this stage in its development, it lacks the capability to recall anything but the life they are experiencing at that moment. Because the spirit is so young, they see themselves as more physical than spiritual, and they use terms like 'soul,' 'life source,' and the 'spark of life' to describe something that they feel but do not understand. That lack of understanding is key to the spirit fully experiencing each physical life. If the spirit knew this was just one of many lives, the experience would be completely different. It is important that they feel this is all there is, my one chance."

"But you're telling me. Won't it affect my experience?"

The spirit chuckled. "As we discussed earlier, in this life, I am comfortable that you will never trust that this really happened. You do not even trust it now, while it is happening. In your next life and all of your future lives, you will not remember this happening."

"Sorry, I'm a little lost. Could you explain how this memory thing works with you spirits? Don't you keep losing your brains every time you move to a new physical being? How can you possibly keep the memories?" Harold interrupted.

"This one will be easy for you to understand now, though as little as one hundred years ago, it would have made no sense at all. It works very much like a computer. Your brain is the working computer for your physical self. Everything you see, hear, feel, touch, smell, or experience goes into your memory banks, and as long as you are physically healthy, you can remember everything."

"I don't feel like I remember everything," Harold quipped.

The voice went on, "But you do. As long as your brain stays intact, what you have difficulty with is recall. Everything is there, but all physical beings, even the very smartest, have a relatively limited ability to recall what is in their memory."

"So, all the information from my entire existence is stored somewhere in my brain?"

"No, only memories from your present life are stored in your brain. But all the information that your brain collects is automatically uploaded to your spirit, much like your computers upload to the cloud, except your spirit has infinitely more memory than the cloud."

"Seriously, my brain is uploading. That's so cool. So why can't I access it, and is that why some people can remember previous lives?"

"You can't access it because so far you cannot even knowingly access your own spirit. You still experience almost everything through your human brain. Your human form and spiritual form experience life together, but your spirit does not yet realize it exists without the human form. While many life forms believe that they have a spirit or a soul, they have never experienced it as something separate from their human form. Your spirit thinks that it is the human form and that its existence depends on this life form."

"But a lot of humans believe that our soul goes on to heaven or hell after the body dies."

"That is true, but they believe that the soul goes on to heaven or hell based on the actions of the human. The soul is not independent of the human body."

"What about people that believe in reincarnation? According to you, they have it right."

"They have it partially correct, but they still do not feel their spirit as a separate entity. They have a theory that they like to put their faith in, but they have nothing to prove the accuracy of that theory."

Harold, puzzled, asked, "So, I'm just a temporary vessel for my spirit?"

"Your body is a temporary vessel for you. You and your spirit are the same thing. You simply have not matured spiritually enough to recognize it. Remember that, at this point in your existence, and for a long time to come, you believe that your physical form is the dominant entity," the voice said calmly, never seeming to run out of patience with Harold's questions.

"Are you telling me that spiritually I'm dumb?" Harold asked with a smile.

The spirit chuckled and responded, "No, you are not dumb, but like a human baby, you are very young and have not had the time to develop the abilities of your spirit."

"You mean like sixty years young?"

"No, as we discussed earlier, spirits do not deal with time. And for all we know, every spirit has always been, but some started their journey of experience sooner than others. However, to put it in more human terms, when I say 'young,' the point that I'm trying to make is that your spirit may have started its journey only one hundred thousand years ago. You need to keep reminding yourself that infinity is a long, long time, and if you believe that evolution takes a long time on earth, it is a blink of an eye compared to spiritual evolution."

"So, what is the process of the evolution of the spirit, in fifty words or fewer?"

"I'm not sure that I can explain it all in the time that we have together, especially using words. Spiritual communication is so much more efficient than using the very limiting process of finding appropriately descriptive words. Basically, your spirit somehow comes into existence or has existed forever, and for reasons that we've not yet been able to uncover, starts the journey of discovery. That is when it attaches itself to physical beings to experience life and existence, take actions, and deal with those actions' outcomes. At this stage, the spirit and the life form are very simple. They do not knowingly communicate with each other in the physical world or the spiritual world; they simply exist and experience."

"Are you saying that the baby spirit experiences life through simple creatures like an amoeba?"

"Well, that may be a stretch. But the fact is, we just don't know because of the inability of a spirit that has not been through the journey of discovery to communicate with us. We can't be sure, but none of us recall being an amoeba. Although, I have to say that I have lived through some life forms that might have made being a single-cell animal look more exciting. Sorry, spirit humour.

"What we know is that by the time we can communicate with the spirit, it has travelled a long way on the path of discovery. It has started to see itself more as a spirit than a physical form and has changed its focus from physical pursuits to spiritual pursuits. But it still has little to no recall of previous lives."

"What stage is my spirit at?" Harold asked.

"It is impossible to know, but your spirit appears to be more advanced in its journey. It is not fully aware of its existence beyond you. It cannot communicate with other spirits, and that is not the focus of your spirit's existence. Your spirit is still focused on sharing this existence with you, its physical form. Your experiences are your spirit's only experiences at this point in its evolution. Like you, your spirit is not aware of what happened before this life nor what will happen after it. However, your spirit somehow communicated with me."

"So, my spirit and I are separate beings or life forms?"

"Yes and no. The you that is your spirit is the life force within the you that is your physical body. It is the part of your existence that will go on after your physical body dies. It is you as much as your body is you, but at this point, neither your spirit nor your physical body fully understands the true nature of their mutual existence. Your spirit has no recall of previous lives, so like you, it does not know what happens when your physical body dies. Your spirit has much to learn, and to accomplish that, it may repeat similar lives over and over."

"Is that frustrating for the spirit?"

"Not at all, because neither the physical form nor the spirit knows what they are missing and will not for a long time. Even when the spirit starts to recall all of their lives, even the most similar ones are still very different."

"So, why do some people on earth seem to know a lot about their previous lives?"

"Sometimes the stories are more imagination than memory, but every so often there is a glitch, like a computer glitch, and partial memories come flooding through to the spirit and then from the spirit to the human brain. It is actually quite amazing; our spirit world does not know why it happens, or what it means. So far, it has not been a sign that the spirit is ready to move on to the next level. And it does not continue from one physical life experience to the next. It is simply one of many unexplained phenomena that exist in the infinite universe."

Harold was impressed by the simple explanation for something that he had always wondered about. Some people who talked about their previous lives seemed like charlatans, making up stories so convincingly that even they believed them. But others seemed like very sincere people who were as shocked by these memories as everyone else was.

If this type of glitch happened, there must be other high-level interactions that happened between our spirits and their human hosts. But now that Harold kind of had a basic understanding of life after death, there were so many other questions that he wanted answers to.

"So, what would a colossal achievement in the spirit world look like?"

"Overcoming the oppression of guilt, being able to share a moment of genuine joy with a multitude of spirits all in the same moment or—"

Harold interrupted. "Hold the phone. What do you mean overcoming the oppression of guilt? What guilt? What oppression? Do spirits feel pain?"

The voice in the dark laughed and laughed hard. "Of course, spirits feel pain. Nothing like humans and not physically, but yes, they feel pain. Spirits spend a great deal of time learning to deal with those feelings of pain and helping other spirits deal with that pain."

"And what specifically causes a spirit to feel pain?"

"As a spirit becomes more and more aware of its existence, it recalls more and more about its previous lives. Some memories are of love and acts of kindness and joy, of friends and loved ones, and of the joy they shared. But some are of hatred and greed and jealousy and acts that are mean, hurtful, and sometimes incomprehensibly horrid. When a spirit first remembers its previous actions, it is like a dream, but as they mature, they realize they committed those acts, and the pain can be devastating. Depending on how heinous the act was, how many there were in how many lifetimes, it may take a long time for a spirit to get past it, and I mean a long time, even in the spirit world."

The spectre of Mark immediately entered Harold's thoughts. "I thought you said a spirit does not suffer for the sins it commits in the physical form."

"I said that it is not punished, that there is no judgment for their acts. I did not say that a spirit does not suffer. The suffering that they experience is self-imposed," Herman said, knowing exactly what Harold was thinking. "As the spirit recalls their many physical lives, they also begin to understand the ludicrous nature of the justifications they used to rationalize their behaviour. They have developed an incredible level of empathy because a molester in one life may have been molested in another life. An army general who sent soldiers to their death in one life may have been a poor soldier forced to fight for a cause he could not understand in another. The suffering comes from truly and completely understanding and feeling the suffering that you caused.

"A spirit who understands how unimportant and fleeting possessions and power are can no longer rationalize their actions. 'I also suffered' and 'I had to do it' are no longer reasonable excuses. 'I had no options,' when you have the experiences of a million lifetimes to call on, is shown to be a lie.

"In the enormity of infinity, the physical issues of earth seem tiny and unimportant, but causing pain and suffering for others actually becomes more important and harder to justify. Spirits who have lived millions of lifetimes realize they had choices. They know what every participant would have experienced, and they know that they could have done better, so much better."

"But no one judges them? No one imposes a penalty or punishment for their behaviour? They do not have any concern about repercussions if someone finds out? They don't ever get to feel that they have paid their debt?" asked Harold.

"No, there is no concern about what anyone thinks of them or their actions. At this point in a spirit's existence, it has experienced a million lives and clearly understands the difference between right and wrong. When the spirit examines its existence, it clearly feels joy for having created joy and it feels pain for having created pain. But there is no outside force demanding retribution or offering absolution."

"Is there only black and white? Is there no grey left?" Harold wondered out loud.

"Oh yes, there are lots of shades of grey. Sometimes our actions create pain for some in order to create joy for others. Throughout our many lives, we face no-win situations where, no matter what we do, we are going to cause pain for someone. Sometimes our actions cause pain of which we have absolutely no knowledge. There are moments of a little joy and a little pain. The spirit sees the kaleidoscope of situations it faced and the spectrum of emotions it created in a million lives. The blackest will cause its pain and the whitest will create its joy."

"But eventually the spirit gets over the pain caused by the blackest and moves on?" Harold was feeling bad for the spirits.

"They eventually learn to exist with who they are and what they have done, but they never forget. Like humans, spirits try to make up for their immoral acts with a mountain of altruistic acts. The spirits who are the most giving and caring in the spirit world often committed the worst acts in the physical world, but no spirit is without scars of regret."

Harold thought for a moment, trying to apply what Herman was saying to his existing life. "So with each successive life, I will become better because I'm learning from my previous life, even though I cannot remember it. Is that correct?"

"No, you are again trying to create order where there does not appear to be any. The process of a spirit evolving away from the need for a physical form appears to have nothing to do with how good or bad you are during your physical life. The change seems to correlate more to the growing self-awareness of the spirit, but what triggers that is far from clear."

"So, moving closer to the spiritual world is not dependent on how good we are in our physical life?"

"No, there is no direct relationship. It is not a reward system; it is an evolutionary process. Think more like a baby in the womb. The baby does nothing to earn its way into the world. It simply develops to the point it is ready to emerge as an independent life form."

"Yeah, but a baby could be premature."

"Okay, not a perfect example, but you get the point."

"So, I will suffer for eternity for what I did, or didn't do, when the priest abused Mark. Is that what you are saying?"

"Not at all. You will suffer with it, and a million other mistakes you will make, for as long as you do not deal with the full reality of the action and your role in it. If you refuse to accept accountability for your mistake, you will continue to suffer because deep down you know the truth, even if you continue to hide it from yourself and others.

"When you accept your accountability, fully admit your role, and are totally honest with yourself, you can stop feeling the pain and accept the mistake that was made. If you created joy, that never becomes a bad thing, and if you created pain, it never becomes a good thing. They are what they are. Accept them, acknowledge them, and then move on."

"And which do you think it is with me? Don't you think that I have accepted my accountability?" Harold asked, challenging Herman.

"I do not know. Only you know that. You said that you feel bad for the terror experienced by all these boys who you know nothing about. Is that really what haunts you? Is that what you cannot forgive yourself for?" asked Herman, who, because of his ability to read

Harold's mind, knew exactly what Harold was not admitting, had never admitted, and had been haunted by for fifty years.

"Yes, it is. If I had said something or encouraged Mark to say something, maybe that would have been the last straw. Maybe somebody would have taken real action, not simply sent the priest to another parish."

"If you had said something? Why would you have said something? It was Mark's story, was it not? Should Mark not have spoken up? What point would there have been to you speaking up? You were not there. You only knew what Mark told you."

"I was never molested, if that is what you are implying."

"So why should you have spoken up?"

There was a long pause, Herman leaving Harold with his thoughts, allowing him to unravel the past that Herman was fully aware of. But Harold had lied about it to himself so often that he did not know how to migrate to the truth, even to someone who was probably nothing more than a figment of his imagination.

"Because I knew," was Harold's slow and tortured reply.

"You knew what?"

Harold looked up at the ceiling of the hole, trying to stop the tears that were streaming from his eyes. "I knew about Father Brown before he molested Mark." He paused, having trouble finding the words. "I had walked in on him and another boy months earlier. Father Brown was exposed, and the boy was holding on to the priest's . . ." Harold could not say or even think the word.

"They both looked directly at me. No one said anything. I turned and ran away. Herman, I saw that with my own eyes and said nothing, not even to Mark. I might not have been able to stop what happened to all the other boys, but I could've stopped what happened to Mark. He was my best friend, and I did nothing. I was too much of a coward at the time and I've been too much of a coward my entire life to tell anyone the truth.

"Herman, how will I ever measure how much pain that one stupid decision caused? How do you ever forgive yourself for that?"

Herman's response was kind but emphatic. "You cannot."

CHAPTER FIFTY

Jack Holloway had made a point of sending the family back to the RCMP detachment before the search team started coming out of the forest. The sight of the searchers giving up for the day, regardless of how logical it might have been for everyone else, always added stress to an already stressful situation for the family. He had promised that he would meet them there at around 8:00 p.m. and give them a complete debriefing of what had happened that day. Jack was about five minutes late as he walked into the conference room at the RCMP detachment.

"Did you find anything?" was the question Jack heard as soon as he entered the room. It came so fast he was not even sure who it came from, other than it was a male voice.

"So far, nothing that would give us any suggestion that we are close, or even looking in the right direction," Jack responded, thinking, *This never gets any easier.* "Folks, have a seat, and I'll walk you through what we've done up to this point and what we know."

Jack then spent the next hour walking the family through the information that they had. He showed them a map of the area, with the area that they had searched today shaded in green. Jack had purposely made the map scale such that it caused the green-shaded area to look as big as possible. Green, because Jack had determined that it seemed to make the families feel like action was being taken.

He talked about the area of the search and how they had based it on the distance that Harold would have likely covered in the two to two and a half hours he would have likely been moving away from his place of origin. Jack explained the variety of natural shelters that

Harold might have found in the area that could have kept him safe, completely missing the hole that Jack did not know existed. He then outlined what the search process would look like tomorrow, showing them on the map the area that they expected to cover, not overselling it but trying to give the family some comfort.

Throughout his description of the search results and plan for tomorrow, Jack made a point of using Harold's name as often as possible. Jack had learned this lesson the hard way during the first search in which they had given him the responsibility of talking to the family. He had made the mistake of continually referring to the lost person as "the hiker." The hiker's mother had absolutely lit into him, screaming that this was a human being with a life and people who loved him who were scared to death that they would never see him again. This was not a pair of shoes someone had misplaced. The mother was absolutely right, and Jack had never made that mistake again.

Jack continued to struggle with whether or not to tell the family that Harold was unlikely to be found alive. The only thing that stopped him was the mild weather and the information that the family had provided about the supplies that Harold would likely have been carrying. If he had some water and that many hand warmers, had some idea of how to use them, and was smart enough to find shelter, he just might beat the odds. Jack knew enough to know that it was still too early to be making any predictions.

After the briefing, Nancy, Jerry, Megan, and Jessie decided to stay as close as possible to the search site and rented a few hotel rooms in a nearby town rather than drive back home. They all knew they would want to be there first thing tomorrow morning, and the roads were still not great.

"Don't worry, Mom. They'll find him. He's strong and healthy. If anyone can survive out there, it's Dad," Megan urged as they all tried to force down some dinner.

"Yes, I'm sure you're right, sweetheart. All that exercising will finally pay off," Nancy responded with a very weak and unconvincing smile.

"The weather has to help," said Jessie. "It's barely been below freezing for the last few days, and you know Dad is dressed up like the Michelin Man. Didn't you say that he had a thermal blanket and an extra down-filled jacket in his backpack?"

"Yes, I'm sure that he did. You know how much your dad hated being cold." Everyone noticed the use of the past tense, but no one wanted to point it out, and Nancy could not bring herself to correct it.

For the next couple of hours, the family drank some beer and wine and told Dadisms, as they called them—all the things that Harold did that made him uniquely him. Every one of them was trying to accomplish the same thing: stopping themselves and everyone else from thinking about where Harold was right now and the very real possibility that none of them would ever see him alive again. Unfortunately, when they finally all went to bed, after assuring each other that tomorrow was going to be a better day and telling each other not to worry, everything was going to be okay, never seeing him again was all any of them could think about, and worry was all they could do.

CHAPTER FIFTY-ONE

Herman knew that at this moment, a hand on Harold's shoulder would be incredibly helpful, but he had no hand to give, so he tried his best with what he had. "Harold, you made a mistake. You cannot fix it, you cannot change it, and trying to control everything else in your life will not make it go away."

"So, I should just pretend that it never happened?"

"No, you have been pretending that it did not happen, and look how that has worked out. Accept that it happened, accept that it was your fault, acknowledge the limitations of a fourteen-year-old, and try to do better."

"I have been trying to do better."

"Are you sure? Are you trying to do better so that others do not suffer, or are you trying to do better so that you do not have to suffer?"

"I don't know what you mean. What difference does it make? I'm trying to take action while I can, to stop the people that I love from having to suffer," was Harold's not-so-emphatic response.

"Okay, if you say so." Herman knew now why he was talking with Harold and the message that he needed to share with Harold, but he also knew that he could not tell Harold. Harold had to figure it out for himself, in his own time. Deciding that changing the subject might be the best option for the moment, Herman continued. "Let us leave that for now and talk more about the difference between the spirit world and the physical world.

Any opportunity to stop talking about Mark and Father Brown was more than good with Harold. The difference between the physical world and the spiritual world was becoming a more interesting question with each conversation. *In our world, we grow through experiences like falling in love, playing sports, attending school, attending the theatre, getting a job, having babies, raising children, and complaining about the government. With no physical form, what type of experiences could exist in the spirit world?* Harold wondered about all of this, but said nothing.

Herman, responding to Harold's unspoken thoughts, said, "We can experience all the intellectual and emotional things that you do. We do not have to create a picture or produce a play to share the beauty of what it could be. We do not raise children, but we help each other grow, and we definitely get to enjoy the beauty of an infinite universe, sights that your mind could not even imagine, we have experienced.

"What we do not experience is the sense of limitation that life forms experience. A desire to experience more creates our urgency, not a limitation created by time. And falling in love? A spirit falls in love continually. We have the knowledge that love has no limits. Loving something or someone does not limit our ability to love something or someone else. More importantly, we are not possessive about being loved. We do not need to own someone's love. We are happy to share it. There is lots for everyone." Herman said.

"Okay, that concept of lots of love for everyone may take some getting used to. Is it because we have such a relatively brief life span that we are so focused on possessing things?" Harold responded, still thinking of the concept from an entirely human point of view.

"Yes, but it is not just the limitation of time in your life span; it is the limitation of everything in the physical world. In the spirit world, there is no need for envy or greed. The power to control others does not exist. You cannot want for what others have because you are free to have it if you choose. In the physical world, there is constant unfulfilled desire, even among the nicest, kindest, most giving people."

"And that's bad?" Harold asked, assuming that he would be told that it was.

Herman laughed. "No, it is not bad; it just is. I believe that if this universe was actually designed by a creator, the brief lives and the pressure to have things, for yourself or your loved ones, was an intentional feature to encourage life forms to create as many experiences as possible chasing worldly possessions, chasing love, and chasing acceptance or adulation from others."

"So, it is okay to chase worldly possessions? Seems pretty shallow, coming from a spirit," Harold remarked.

"That is because when you are thinking of worldly possessions, you cannot help but include the limitations placed on those worldly possessions by your civilization and the limits of the physical world. There is nothing intrinsically bad about possessions. What you come to understand as you evolve as a spirit is that there is also nothing intrinsically good about them either. Where there may be an issue is where some people do not have the basic requirements necessary to sustain life, while others are concerned about the size of their fifth house and their private jet. These are the type of issues that a spirit may come to regret in the fullness of time."

"So, we should all live in a commune and share everything evenly. Is that what you're saying?" Harold puzzled.

Herman chuckled, "Communes, another thing that humans may come to regret in the fullness of time. No, that is not what I am saying. In the physical world, it is not that simple. Living down to the lowest common denominator tends to pull everyone down, not up. Giving away everything that you own may make you feel better for a moment and help someone else out for some period of time, but it will not solve the problem.

"What I am saying is that the physical world, whether it was designed or simply evolved, is full of experiences that can be good and bad or neither all at the same time. This is the beauty of it. The physical world is full of unanswerable questions because of its physical limitations. In your world, people often talk about the ethical dilemma that would be caused if you were driving a car and you were forced to choose between hitting an old man or a young child. The physical world appears to have been designed to force intelligent life forms to make those types of decisions."

Harold smiled. "But in the spirit world, you experience all the great things and none of the bad. You don't experience sickness, you don't get injured, you don't want for food or money, and you don't worry about the clothes you wear or the car you drive. How is that not heaven?"

The spirit laughed. "You, of course, make an excellent point. Compared to the many terrible things that happen in the physical world, feeling bad about your past actions, while you want for nothing, sounds pretty good. So yes, I guess it is at least closer to heaven. However, I think you missed the most important difference between the physical and spirit worlds."

"Really? And what is that?"

"We no longer have to make a choice between ourselves and others, or between the old man and the young child. Anything that I have, I can give freely to any and every other spirit without diminishing what I have in the slightest. There is no scarcity of anything that we need or could want. Imagine that in human terms."

"Well, that certainly explains a little about why you are not obsessed with whether there is an actual heaven. It is probably not that big of an upgrade from the spirit world," joked Harold.

"Good point, unless, of course, we find out that there is a hell and that we are all headed there. Would that not be a kick in the ass, if we had an ass to kick?" responded Herman with a laugh.

Harold pondered for a moment. "So let's assume for a moment that there is a God, or something like a God. How much do you believe that this God really has to do with what goes on here on earth or in any other civilization in the universe?"

"My belief," Herman responded, "is nothing. Based on what I have experienced and the information shared with me, the physical world was designed, or for some unknown reason evolved, or just always existed to be riddled with problems, opportunities, and challenges. That includes every physical structure and every life form, all of which are amazingly designed but also fatally flawed. There are simply too many defects in the physical world, too many win-lose situations, to believe that any physical form or life force could ever avoid triumphs, defeats, and eventually, destruction. The universe appears to be an infinite obstacle course designed specifically for the enjoyment or challenge of the life forms and spirits that inhabit it."

Herman continued, "Take death, which we in the spirit world see strictly as just another event in a long series of events. Our experience is that all physical life forms die eventually. Modern science and good living might extend life for a short period of time, but inevitably every physical life form in the universe dies."

"Wow, death is an event. Seems like a pretty enormous event to me."

Herman laughed. "Well, yes, it would to you because you see it as an end, the final event, while we see it as only another experience in an infinite number of experiences. The universe understands that without disappointment, we will not recognize accomplishment. Without sorrow, we cannot appreciate joy. Somehow, the universe exists with that balance. The desire for more is an integral and necessary part of existence for physical and spiritual life forms. It drives us to experience the infinite universe, which appears to be why it exists. In the physical world, you learn to experience life."

"Hold it. You said that the universe exists with balance. How do you explain the dramatic imbalance in the spectrum of human lives?"

"You are again thinking of existence in terms of the very limited life form that you are presently experiencing. In the fullness of time, the physical things that you possessed will mean nothing."

"So, it is a waste of our time to focus so much energy and effort on achievements and possessions? In the long term, it is all going to average out anyway?"

"Harold, I think the problem may be that you are looking at it all wrong. You and all the other life forms, including spirits, do not exist for the outcome. We exist for the journey, the infinite journey. Miley Cyrus has it pretty much spot on in her song 'The Climb.'"

Harold paused, pondering this last statement carefully while trying to ignore that a spirit, amid a deep philosophical discussion about the infinite universe and life after death, had just cited Miley

Cyrus as an expert on the subject. It was amusing to Harold, but he thought Jessie would be thrilled with it. "So, what we do matters?"

"Oh, it absolutely matters, but it matters because it is part of the journey, not because it is the end of the journey or because it determines the end of the journey."

"So, my entire existence has no beginning and no end, and everything that I achieve is only meaningful from the point of view of gathering experiences. Is that what you are telling me?"

"Yes, that is what I am telling you. But that part is not different from what life forms already believe. All intelligent life forms believe that your experiences matter; it is just a question of why they matter. If you believe there is nothing after death, then what you did during your life is all that matters because there is nothing else. If you believe you face a final judgment, where you are judged for your actions and then sent either to heaven or hell for eternity, all that matters is what you experienced in life because that will define where you go after death. There are a variety of other beliefs, but regardless of what you believe happens after death, the only thing that matters while you are alive is the experiences you create during your life.

"What I am saying is that, based on what I know happens after death, what you do in this life does matter, and matters forever. There is no end point. Being proud of your actions matters a lot because those actions will follow you for eternity. Like Miley says . . ."

"So doing good things is important," Harold commented.

"Absolutely," Herman responded. "But as far as we know, the only real reward you receive for doing good things is what so far appears to be the eternal knowledge that you did good things, and more importantly, that you did not make others suffer to gratify yourself and fulfill your personal needs."

There was a long pause in the conversation as Harold tried to absorb everything that he had heard. Then he asked, "So, in your opinion, after your hundred million years or so of existence, is there a God?"

Herman laughed again, quite enjoying this conversation. "The God that most of the human religions on earth have conjured up?

No, I do not believe that God exists. And my existence provides some pretty good proof that I am right. But I do believe that there is something more to all of this than even an ancient spirit can see. I struggle almost as much as you do with the concept of no beginning and no end, so I do believe that something created the multitude of environments that we live in, both physical and spiritual, and that whatever that something is created spirits and intelligent life forms to experience the beauty of life.

"I believe that whoever or whatever created this infinite universe has infinite patience and infinite time to allow all of us to learn to love and enjoy each other and the incredible, and constantly changing, nature of this infinite universe. I believe that whoever or whatever created us and the evolution we experience wants us to be happy and has created an environment that will allow us all to get there in the fullness of time. They have the infinite patience to sit back and allow us to experience it. I believe that free will is the most important gift that was given to us, and any interference would compromise that free will. So, I believe that there is absolutely no interference by a supreme being in our existence ever, not even in sporting events."

"What, not even sporting events?" Harold said with an exaggerated expression of shock.

"Okay, well maybe the Super Bowl, but nothing else. Oh yeah, and professional golf tournaments. The supreme being definitely decides all of those. I am not even sure why they bother playing them," Herman quipped.

Harold lay back on his blanket. He was tired, his headache had returned, and his ankle was aching.

"Will I remember this conversation tomorrow?" Harold asked the darkness.

"Yes, you will remember it for the rest of this life. But you will never be certain that it really happened, and you will have no recollection of this experience in your future physical lives."

The spirit's voice became quiet. "That is an awful lot of information all at once. You need your sleep, and we can talk again. Maybe tomorrow."

"Does that mean that I will still be here tomorrow night?"

"Spirits cannot read the future. Where you will be tomorrow will be influenced by many things, none of which we, as spirits, control. But whether or not you are here tomorrow, we will find a time to talk again."

"Soon?"

"I'm afraid that word means something very different to you than it does to me, but yes, soon."

"Can you tell me how Nancy is doing, and whether a search has started?" Harold asked.

"Nancy is terrified and, as so many humans do in situations like this, is alternately blaming herself and blaming you. The kids are doing their best to offer comfort, but they are almost as frightened as she is. The search has started, but unfortunately, with the lack of tracks, they have started in exactly the opposite direction." The spirit's tone seemed to consider how Harold would receive this news. "But the good news is that they have a good understanding of how far you would likely have travelled, so they already have a plan to switch to a new direction tomorrow."

"Is this new direction the right one?"

"Not exactly, but it is closer, and it will eliminate another option."

It was kind of the spirit to offer this bit of encouragement, but both the spirit and Harold knew the chances the search would be lucky enough to find Harold in the next couple of days were still almost non-existent. Without tracks, even if they began looking in the right direction, there was still only an infinitesimal chance they would find him.

Once Harold no longer felt the spirit's presence, he repeated his process of the night before, putting fresh hand warmers in each armpit and in his underwear. Right now, the cold was his biggest enemy, and he could not allow it to defeat him. He quickly faded off to sleep, which thankfully released him from his worry and concern about what his family was experiencing.

CHAPTER FIFTY-TWO

Waking up the Tuesday morning just as the light seeped into the hole, Harold immediately started thinking of Nancy and his children. By now, Nancy and the kids would be considering the real possibility that they would not find him alive and that if wolves or bears got to him first, they might never find him at all. He felt terrible that he was putting them through this. He thought having someone you love go missing was one of the worst things you could go through. You don't know what has happened to them, whether they are dead or alive, if they are in pain or being tortured, so your tendency is to make things up, and they are seldom good things.

Nancy and the children would all be strong for each other, and no matter what they really thought, they would all say that they knew Dad would be okay, that he would find a way to be okay. But when they were each alone, they would feel a pain Harold had hoped they would never feel. And knowing he was causing it made him rehash every decision he had made on Friday. What was wrong with him? What had he been thinking?

Finally, as the full force of the morning sun streamed into the hole, Harold decided it was time to stop beating himself up and get back to work on trying to get himself out of there and back to his family.

Using the butt end of his ski pole, he got up on his knees and began to drive the first pointed branch into the side of the hole about four feet above the hole's floor. The work was slow and tiring as each blow added almost imperceptibly to the penetration of the branch, and fatigue and the pain in his ankle required that he take frequent breaks. He didn't yet know how he would build the rest of his stairway to heaven, but he was sure that he would.

While he pounded on the branches, Harold began the ritual of shouting, screaming, and singing, hoping that someone would hear him.

He knew his ankle would not heal by tomorrow, but he hoped that if he was careful, it would be good enough to get him back to the highway. Having the physical ability to get back to the highway was one issue; finding his way back there was another problem. With the snowfall, Harold could not follow his tracks back to where his skis were secured on the tree. However, he was comfortable that if he could find the skis, he could find the highway. There would be a clear path through the trees. All he had to do was follow it due east. To make things even easier, he had made the decision to secure the skis on the east side of the tree to ensure that he would know where he was going, assuming that someone had not taken the skis. Who would take skis that were bungee-corded to a tree in the middle of a forest? Surely, no one is that mean or thoughtless.

Noises had startled Harold more than a few times during the day. He could not tell what was making the noise, but when he hollered and shouted, no one came to his rescue. It could have been birds or deer, maybe even a noisy rabbit. But even if it was a person, they were of no use to Harold if they did not respond to his shouting.

He drank some water and ate a little of his food at breakfast, lunch, and dinner. He was not worried about running out. Harold could not allow himself to stay in the hole that long. He was causing too much pain for his family, and he could not take the chance that the weather would change significantly. Right now, maintaining his strength was more important than having supplies for a week. One way or the other, he was crawling out of this hole tomorrow.

Once he had finished hammering in the first branch, he began on the second branch, about a foot and a half higher than the first and about two feet to the right. For this one, he had no option but to stand, which he did on one foot. This made the process even slower, but he could not stop. Using the ski pole was much more awkward at this height, so Harold dug around on the floor of the hole until he found a flat rock a little smaller than his hand. This became a much more effective hammer.

The next branch, and every branch after that, required Harold to sit on one of the branches that he had hammered in while he hammered in the next one. He knew that if one of those branches broke, the fall could eliminate any hope that he had of escaping the hole. But he had no other options. The risk had to be taken and right now, hope was his only strategy.

The piece of the branch protruding from the side of the hole's wall was only about six inches, which Harold believed would significantly reduce the chances of the branch breaking or dislodging from the wall. This made sitting on it extremely uncomfortable, but that was far from the greatest issue that Harold had to overcome. Climbing the branches to drive in the next branch without putting any weight on the broken ankle was far more difficult. To accomplish this, Harold had to keep the branches closer together than he had hoped and shift from his left butt cheek to his right butt cheek with each successive branch. This created two problems. First, hammering a branch in with his sprained wrist was incredibly painful but unavoidable. The second was that he ran out of branches before he was high enough to easily climb out of the hole.

Sitting at the bottom of the hole, looking up at the branches that he had driven into the wall of the hole, Harold looked at his surroundings. The remaining branches were too thin to provide reliable additional steps in his stairway, and he still had not figured out how he was going to get his foot up to the first step, four feet off the ground. Or, more importantly, how he was going to make it from the last step on the wall to actually exiting the hole.

CHAPTER FIFTY-THREE

It was Tuesday morning, and Nancy had decided that she needed to call Harold's office and let them know what was going on. She probably should have called on Monday because Harold seldom missed a day of work and never missed one without letting Ramesh or Alison know where he was. They would have been worried and had probably, like Nancy, called Harold's cell a half dozen times.

"Ramesh Kumar speaking," Ramesh said, answering his direct line.

"Hello, Ramesh. This is Nancy Bower calling."

"Hey, Nancy. How are you?"

"Good, thanks, Ramesh. I'm calling about Harold."

"We missed him yesterday. Not like Harold to be a no-show. I hope it's nothing serious," Ramesh commented in a fashion that suggested he was sure that it was not something serious.

Nancy had to take a moment to compose herself, which created an awkward pause that Ramesh could not help but notice.

"I'm afraid that it might be serious, Ramesh. Harold went missing in the mountains on Friday, and so far, the search and rescue team haven't been able to find any trace of him."

"Oh, my God. I'm so sorry. Are you okay, Nancy? Is there anything that we can do to help?"

"Thank you, Ramesh. Could you please let the staff know what's happening? Let them know that as soon as we know anything, we'll update them. But right now, all we know is that he's somewhere in the mountains."

"Is there anyone else you'd like us to contact?"

"The news is referring to Harold as a sixty-three-year-old man lost in the mountains. If they decide to use his name, we may ask you to connect with a few other people, but for now, just the staff."

"Would you like me to ask them to keep this information confidential?"

This one question seemed to exhaust Nancy. The need to consider it and provide Ramesh with a thoughtful answer seemed too much. "Do whatever you think is best, Ramesh. I need to go now. Thank you for your help."

Nancy, while getting ready to meet her children for breakfast, was reflecting on how close she had come to breaking down in tears talking to Ramesh. She knew Ramesh well. He and his wife had been guests in their home for dinners and parties many times. Somehow, the act of telling him what was happening made it so much more real. When she had said, "I'm calling about Harold," she could not help but wonder if Harold would ever be back at work again. And if he wasn't, what on earth would that mean?

Nancy was an incredibly strong person emotionally. She seldom got upset, never cried at weddings or funerals, and almost never thought much about the worst-case scenario. She was a born optimist. Things always seemed to work out. Harold, however, was suddenly making it extremely difficult for her to maintain her perspective.

She had always thought that she and Harold shared everything, but now she was beginning to wonder, and not just about Harold. She started questioning how open she really was with Harold. Were they two peas in a pod, sharing the sunshine and rainbows and keeping all the real issues to themselves? She had noticed the little blue pills in the drawer in the bathroom. The label was torn off, but she knew what they were. How many other secrets were there, and why weren't they talking? Was being the adult in the room that important to both of them?

She began to tear up. It seemed impossible to imagine living without Harold. From the day of his first proposal, he had always been no more than a phone call away. It was unimaginable she might never hear his voice again. In that moment, she wanted nothing more than to be in Harold's arms, to tell him everything that scared her in life, and to listen to everything that scared him.

Nancy quickly decided that wallowing in self-pity was not helping anyone, especially her children, so she pulled herself together and headed downstairs to have breakfast with them. As she walked down the stairs, it occurred to her that maybe that was the problem. Maybe neither of them ever made time to be vulnerable because they both thought they had to be the one who was there for everyone else.

CHAPTER FIFTY-FOUR

Harold took careful inventory of the items that he had with him and began planning a plausible way out of the hole. It would not be easy, especially with his injuries. The stairway to heaven was an important part of the puzzle, but it was not a complete solution. The hole he had created in the roof was about two and a half feet away from the closest wall. How would he get from the last step to the sturdy branches around the hole, and how would he pull himself out?

If Harold had been healthy and twenty years younger, he might have been able to swing over to the hole from branch to branch, like they were monkey bars. And then, maybe with a combination of chin-ups and gymnastics, he might have been able to wiggle out of the hole. But he was not healthy, and he was definitely not twenty years younger, and if he tried it and a branch broke . . . well, there was no point even considering it.

There had to be another solution. Something that required less strain and effort and provided a reasonably high level of safety. There was no point in getting out of the hole, only to collapse on the snow and freeze to death.

Harold began going through his pack carefully. What did he absolutely need once he was outside of the hole to get back to the highway? What could he get away with leaving behind?

He could snowshoe without poles if he had to, but he couldn't cross-country ski. Not a problem. It would take a little longer to snowshoe all the way, but if he needed to sacrifice the poles to get out of the giant hole in the ground, he would. The backpack was unnecessary, but he realized that he might need a few of the things in it, including the compass, the headlamp, and the hand and foot warmers. He saw no practical reason in taking the food and water, but decided he would anyway. *You never know when you may want to stop for a snack*, Harold thought with a smile.

So, the pack itself and the ski poles were expendable. That gave Harold an idea. Could he build some kind of ladder with a combination of the poles, the pack, and maybe the thermal blanket? All he would have to do would be to figure out how to secure it to the trees at the top of the hole. He could then use it to get from his stairway to the opening and easily climb out. This was all very doable; the only question was his ankle. Would he be able to walk?

That was tomorrow's concern. Today was about the escape route. Harold crawled over to the wall containing his staircase and immediately began to move dirt to build a platform that would get him close enough to the first branch that he could easily step up on it. To move the dirt, Harold tore the pack apart and used the hard compressed-board support piece from the pack as a shovel. The problem was not moving the dirt; it was packing it down so it would hold his weight. It was amazing how difficult it was to do things when you only had one good arm and one good leg.

As the sun began to set, the mound of dirt was high enough for Harold to easily step up on the first branch. So, he moved on to the next concern: building the ladder, the last piece of the escape route. Fortunately, he had brought his extendable poles, which easily pulled apart into two reasonably sturdy pieces, so he could build a four-step ladder, but with his bad leg, he wanted the steps to be as close together as possible.

Thinking it through, he figured that he would need about seven feet of ladder so he could sit on the top branch while he got his feet onto the ladder. And the last rung of the ladder could be about two feet from the opening, which would make crawling out easy. So, his four rungs only needed to cover five feet. A rung about every fifteen inches. That seemed workable.

The light from the hole was now completely gone, so Harold took out his headlamp, turned it on, and used its light to begin the work on the ladder. He used his Swiss Army knife to take apart the backpack. He had a limited amount of first-aid tape, so he would have to make sure that he did not waste even an inch of it securing the cloth of the pack in place around the poles. Crawling around the floor of the hole, Harold laid out the pieces and strips of the pack along with the ski poles in the shape of a ladder before he tried to put anything together. He had to make sure all the parts were in place and were going to work before he started assembling anything. He could not afford to waste a single piece of material.

Harold put the ladder together, carefully tying the pieces of the pack securely to the poles and then using the tape to secure the knot and the poles in position. When it was completed, he tested its strength the best he could; he was comfortable that the cloth and straps from the pack were strong enough. His concern was that the poles might buckle under his weight. To reduce the chances of that happening, he had made each rung only eight inches wide instead of the full width of the ski pole. The ladder felt very strong, but the only way he was going to know for sure would be to secure it to the trees above with the thermal blanket and step onto it with his full weight. He decided to leave that for tomorrow so that he could use the thermal blanket for his bed that night.

When he had completed the ladder, he had a few feet of first-aid tape left over, which Harold realized he was going to need to secure the tensor bandage he was planning to put on his ankle before he crawled out of the hole the next day. He had not removed his hiking boot since his fall; he had only loosened it long enough to feel the bone and then tightened it up again. Thanks to the boot, the ankle had not swollen, but the leg above it certainly had.

He was as ready as he was going to be, and he felt a strange combination of excitement and foreboding. Tomorrow, no matter what, Harold was leaving this hole. Once out, all he would have to worry about was finding his way back to his skis. Oh, yeah, and walking on a broken ankle. And, of course, dealing with that nasty little headache that kept coming back. Seriously, how hard could it be?

Oddly, and not dissimilar to the thought process that had put him into this situation, the real dangers he would face once he left his hole did not even cross his mind.

CHAPTER FIFTY-FIVE

The day had been an endless span of hearing periodic reports that basically said nothing, pacing back and forth at the RCMP detachment because everyone was too frightened to leave, and forcing down meals that no one wanted. Nancy did not want to admit it, but there were moments that day when she felt even the worst news would have been better than nothing at all.

Finally, at 8:00 p.m., Jack Holloway came into the conference room to give them an update on the result of the day's search activity and the plan for tomorrow. Jack had decided as the sun was setting that it was now time for the talk, the one he hated more than anything else about his job. He needed to tell them if they did not find Harold tomorrow, it was unlikely that they would find him alive. There was a cold front moving in, and nighttime temperatures would drop below −40 degrees Celsius. At that point, even with shelter, it would be nearly impossible for anyone to survive.

In Jack's opinion, it was easier to tell someone their loved one was dead than it was to tell them they should give up without knowing, but, in Jack's professional opinion, this was now a recovery mission, not a rescue mission, and it was time to let the family know. How the hell do you tell someone that they should give up on their husband, father, sister, brother, the person who they love more than anyone or anything else in their lives? Even worse, how do you tell them that you can no longer justify the resources to continue the search? How do you explain that these resources need to be reserved for someone who they are more likely going to be able to help?

It was a horrible responsibility, and almost no one received that information well. The Bower family was no exception.

By the time they all got back to the hotel, they were all cried out. They felt bad about how they had treated Jack when he told them it was time to consider that Harold was not going to be found alive, but they admired him for how well he handled their outbursts, and they knew none of this was his fault.

Despite doing nothing all day other than pacing and worrying, all of them said that they were exhausted and just wanted to get some sleep. In reality, they all just wanted to be alone with their thoughts, free to burst into tears or curse their father, brother, or husband without feeling guilty about it, or having someone hear them say something they would regret having said in the future.

CHAPTER FIFTY-SIX

As he sat in the almost complete darkness, Harold was thinking about how badly he and his hole in the ground must smell, though he personally could only catch whiffs of it. Something Harold truly appreciated. Between all the urine holes he had dug and the fact that he had not washed since his arrival, he was pretty sure the odour was well past tolerable.

As Harold contemplated what was likely to happen when he left the hole, there was at least one thing that he was reasonably sure of— once he left the hole, he would never hear from his friend Herman again. For the moment, he was past wondering if Herman was real or an illusion. It really didn't matter. The information Herman or the hallucination was providing was taking his mind off his situation, which was more than welcome. It was intriguing, and there was so much more that he wanted to know. He had not yet asked Herman if he was the presence he had felt so often in the weeks before. *Did any spirit lead even one life free of regrets? Could he give me even a hint about how to live the best possible life, one I could look back on with lots of joy and little regret?* Whatever or whoever was talking to him no longer mattered, he had made the decision to just go with it.

He looked at the preparations he had made for the planned escape from the hole that had imprisoned him. His work was solid. He had taken all the right steps. There was absolutely no question in his mind. He would definitely be leaving this hole tomorrow. The thought filled him with a sense of anticipation and anxiety, as well as pride in what he had already achieved and apprehension about the mountainous challenge that was ahead of him. It was a feeling he had experienced before, but never with this level of intensity, and certainly never with these types of stakes.

"You certainly have had a productive day," Herman stated without so much as a hello.

"Ah, there you are. I was hoping that you would join me today. Yes, I had a very productive day. I'm all ready for the big escape tomorrow," Harold responded, looking again at his handiwork, feeling confident that the makeshift ladder, the improvised mound of dirt, and the stairway to heaven would easily allow him to exit the hole.

"It all looks very impressive. How are you feeling?" Herman asked, even though he knew how Harold was feeling.

"It's my birthday tomorrow. I turn sixty-four years old. Hell of a thing to be doing on your sixty-fourth birthday, don't you think?" Harold said as he lay back on his blanket for the last time.

"To be honest, Harold, sixty-fourth birthdays do not really mean much to me. I have had more than I can count, and I do not remember any of them being of any note. At least you are about to have a sixty-fourth birthday worth remembering," Herman said, knowing full well what the sixty-fourth birthday meant to Harold but trying his best to keep the mood light for the moment.

Harold was staring off into the distance, which was odd given that, sitting in his hole in total darkness, there was no distance to stare off into.

"Your mind seems elsewhere, Harold."

"Did you know my father died at the age of sixty-four?"

"Yes, that is something that you seem to think about a lot," Herman replied.

"I'm sitting in a hole in the ground with a broken ankle that I probably can't walk on, I'm running out of food, freezing weather is going to show up eventually, and I turn sixty-four tomorrow." Harold paused. "Do you know how my father died?"

"You do remember that I can read your mind, right?"

"Yes, of course," Harold said, but he kept going because he really wanted to talk about it with someone. Talking seemed to make it less frightening. "He died from what they call the widowmaker, a sudden complete blockage of a left anterior descending artery, which is almost always fatal without immediate emergency care. Did you know it is often hereditary?"

"So, you have been thinking for months, maybe years, about dying at sixty-four, as your father did."

"I have not been thinking about dying. I have just been preparing to die so that I don't leave my family with the mess my father left for his family. After all there is a chance that I have a time bomb in my chest. You can't just ignore that."

"The operative words there are 'a chance,' and you certainly have not been ignoring it. Mark's and your father's deaths are pretty much all you have been able to think about lately, that and getting angry at anything that interferes with your plan for your family's future. Tell me, have you ever watched one of those movies about some poor guy who thinks everyone would be better off if he had never been born?"

"You mean like that Christmas movie with Jimmy Stewart?" Harold asked.

"Yeah, like that one."

"Are you going to show me what my family's lives would have been like if I had never been born? I suppose that would be interesting, but I wasn't even considering that."

"Ha, I do not have those types of powers, and I am pretty sure no one else does either, except Hollywood. But I was wondering if you have considered what your family's life would have been like if your father had been a different person, if he had not died, and if he had not left you with a mess."

"Sure, I've thought about it often. There would have been a lot fewer sleepless nights and a lot less stress for my mother, and I could've spent the time doing something a lot more interesting."

"What about your relationships with your mom, your brother, Shane, Fred, and a lot of other people, all of which you forged because of the mess that your father left behind?"

With an obvious tone of sarcasm, Harold responded, "Are you saying that I should be grateful to my dad because I developed some great relationships cleaning up his mess?"

"What I am saying is exactly what I have been saying all along. We exist to experience. Your father left you the opportunity to experience. Thanking him is not the point. The experience, and what you did with it, is the point. Would you give up all those wonderful relationships to not have had the experience of cleaning up your father's mess?"

"Of course not, but I'm sure as hell not going to thank my father."

"Boy, when you obsess, you really obsess. It is not about your father; it is about you. You will have a million fathers who will leave you in a million ways. What you will focus on, what will bring you joy and despair, for eternity, is not what they did; it is what you did."

Harold thought back to the experience of cleaning up after his father. Herman was right. It was an experience he felt good about, but it sure as hell was not something he would want to do to someone else.

"That is right, Harold. It is not something that you would want to do to someone else. So why are you?"

This comment shook Harold. "What are you talking about? I have taken care of everything for my family. My estate is in order. They will not have to worry about anything. If I don't make it, they will live a wonderful life. I've made sure of it."

Herman never lost his patience. In the spirit world, there is simply no need and no purpose. However, Harold did not need a calm, rational conversation. He needed a passionate demand that he remove his head from his ass and start thinking about what was really going to happen if he did not make it home alive. He had to understand the real reason he had been behaving the way he had. The actual driving force behind the nightmares, the will, and the outbursts. Herman decided it was time to show some significant impatience, even anger. These conversations were meant to help Harold and his spirit accomplish something; it was time to make sure Harold saw what it was.

Herman's voice became louder and more aggressive. "You have taken care of everything? Is that what you think? Have you not heard anything that I have said to you?"

Momentarily surprised by the change in Herman's tone of voice Harold responded. "What are you talking about? What have these discussions got to do with me taking care of my family?"

"You know, Harold, for an incredibly smart man, you can be an idiot at times, especially when it comes to your family." Herman lowered his voice to emphasize the difference in what he was about to say. "What did I tell you was the reason that you and your spirit and every intelligent life form and every spirit exists, why the universe exists?"

"So that we could experience the wonders of the universe," Harold responded, not having any idea where this was going.

"That is right, Harold. Your existence, my existence, everyone's existence is about experiencing life. That is how we grow. Tell me, do you believe that what you are leaving behind is actually going to provide your family with the best opportunity to experience life? Writing your will, talking Megan out of pursuing the business opportunity, telling Jessie not to adopt a child from another country, setting up your company so that it can never grow. I am not sure which is worse—your efforts to control your family's future with money or the continuous 'I don't trust you to make your own decisions' messages that you have been giving them for the last few months. And the most blaring statement of your lack of trust is this new will that you have created. You have not been encouraging them to experience life. You have been telling them to crawl into a hole to avoid life." The reference to the hole was intentional.

"That's completely unfair. I set the will up to make sure that they never have money concerns. And the only ideas I discouraged were the stupid ideas."

"Harold, who are you to say what is a stupid idea? How do you know that Megan's company will not be an amazing success? How do you know that the child that Jessie adopts will not give Jessie the same joy that Jessie has given you and Nancy?"

"Well, of course, I don't know for sure, but why take the risk?"

The volume of Herman's voice increased again, accompanied by a very modest bit of disdain to harden the point. "Why take the risk?

235

Because that is why we exist—to take risks, to create experiences, to feel the joy that can come from taking that risk, and when necessary, to deal with the pain that is caused when things go bad. Harold, after all that we have talked about, do you not see that the greatest gift you can leave for your family is to encourage them to live life to the fullest? To grab every bit of joy, even if it means taking the risk that they may experience pain? Do you think when your family and friends look back on their lives, they will find joy in avoiding risks at all costs? Or do you think they will find joy in what they created by taking a risk?"

The conditions of the will flashed through Harold's mind. Nancy and the children on a set monthly allowance, no ability to mortgage their homes without diminishing their monthly allowance, and no ability to leave their jobs without negatively affecting their monthly allowance. The trust would not even fund their children's education if the children did not maintain a certain GPA. And God forbid that one of the children wanted to go to trade school, which is not permissible under the trust conditions. Herman was right. He wasn't only trying to control his family and friends with his money, he was doing his best to stop them from taking any future risk.

"Jesus, Herman, you make it sound like I'm leaving my family destitute. There are lots of people who would be thrilled to have this much money, even with all the conditions," Harold stated defiantly, not fully understanding why he would continue to argue when he knew he was wrong.

"You are absolutely right, Harold. But to them, it would not matter that you did not trust them. They could not care less what you think of them. The money is not the issue. It is the complete lack of trust that accompanies the money. It is your obvious effort to control them. That is what will hurt. And it is not just your family."

"Consider how the people in your company, who have stood by you through the good times and the bad, are going to feel when they realize your will limits the activities of the company to the degree that they are caretakers reporting to a stranger at a trust company. Harold, you are about to tell the people that you love most in this world—Nancy, Jessie, Megan, the people who have run your company for decades—that you would rather trust someone who you have never met. That you are more comfortable with a face-less corporation."

"Shane will explain. He will make them understand—" Harold said before Herman interrupted him.

"Shane will explain. Are you kidding? You pulled the rug out from under your friend Shane when you lied to him about talking to Nancy and the kids about the will. How does Shane explain a will that he absolutely does not believe in? In one foul document, you stab your best friend in the back and tell everyone else that you do not trust them to live their own lives. Do you actually think all this is okay? Do you really believe that if you do not get out of this alive, you will look back and be happy about what you left behind?"

"You don't understand. My father left my mother nearly destitute. It took us years to dig our way out of the mess that he left behind."

"No, Harold, you do not seem to understand. It is not about what others did to you; it is all about what you did to others. You will not spend eternity feeling bad that Megan did not start her company. You will regret not encouraging her to take the chance, to chase the experience."

"They will do something else. They will have other experiences," Harold said, his confidence now completely gone.

"Harold, you are not listening or you do not want to hear. It is not about what they will do. It is about what you did. Are you really going to be happy with the legacy that you have left for them? Were your last words to them, 'life is worth living, take a chance'? Were they 'I trust you to make the best of whatever you choose to do'? What do you think Nancy, Jessie, Megan, and everyone else will think when they read your will? Are the words, the feelings that come from that will, really the last thing that you want to say to your family and friends?"

There was a long silence. Herman knew, sadly from experience, how Harold would come to feel if he left this world, this family, these friends with this will. With this message that he had so pains-takingly authored but had never really thought through.

"And what about your condition?" Herman asked.

"What condition?" Harold responded, wondering which of what at the moment seemed like many conditions Herman was refer-ring to.

"Your heart, your cholesterol levels, the chance that you may drop dead at the dinner table just like your father."

"I'm dealing with that."

"You have got to be kidding me," Herman said with an exagger-ated burst of frustration for Harold's benefit. "Harold, how do you think your family will feel if you drop dead from a condition that you did not trust them enough to share with them? I just do not understand why you do not get this stuff. Stop doing things that hurt the people you love."

Harold was exhausted. He was tired of defending the decisions that he knew were wrong. "Tell my family, let them help, or at least let them be prepared. Anything else?"

"The nightmares?" Herman said, trying to help Harold complete the thought process.

"Oh yeah, the nightmares. It is strange that I'm having them now. I never had them before." At that moment Harold was completely at a loss as to why he would have suddenly started having nightmares.

"So why do you think you would have them now?" Herman asked.

"Maybe there is a relationship. I have told no one other than you the truth about what happened. Maybe my spirit, or my subcon-scious, is trying to tell me I need to deal with the truth before it is too late."

"Is that what the nightmares are about?" Herman asked, even though he knew exactly what the nightmares were about.

Harold paused, trying to remember the details of the nightmares more clearly. "No, they were more about me doing something to stop what was happening."

Herman didn't respond. He let Harold consider the comment to figure it all out.

Harold's tone changed and each thought came out like a new and sudden revelation, "None of this is about Mark or my father. It's about me. My desire to be the hero, to handle everything myself. To step up, like I should have done for Mark. The nightmares, the will, the anger. It's all about me having control, making all the decisions. I wanted to make everything perfect. But not for their benefit, for mine."

Tears rolled down Harold's cheeks, then his head dropped into his hands and his entire body shuddered repeatedly. When it finally stopped, Harold said quietly, "I really thought that I was doing the right thing." He paused. "But all that I have done is screwed everything up. Haven't I?"

Herman did not respond; this piece of discovery was something Harold had to do on his own.

"I have spent a lifetime trying to run away from the guilt, and when I heard about Mark's suicide, I just wanted to fix everything."

Harold paused, considering his reaction to Megan, to Jessie, to Alison and Ramesh, and his need to write a new will.

"I was so consumed with being the hero, it never crossed my mind that I would be telling everyone else that they weren't good enough to be their own hero. It was all about me." He paused, contemplating the mess that he had created. "How do I fix it? Can you go to Shane and tell him to throw it away, to go back to the old will?"

"Harold, it doesn't work that way. Even if I could somehow connect with Shane, which is unlikely, would he act on the instructions of a voice? If this is important to you, really important to you, there is only one way to fix it."

Harold said nothing at first, processing where he was, the conditions that he had created, and why he had created them.

"I have to make it back alive," Harold said, more as an acknowledgement than a commitment.

"That is your only chance. If you do not make it home alive, your last will and testament will be the last statement you make to your family and friends."

"That and all the things that I told them not to do." Harold's head popped up from his hands as he added, "Shit, and if I die on the way back from a heart attack, they'll find out that I kept that from them, too. What a fucking disaster."

Herman knew what was going through Harold's mind. Death was something that was much easier to think about in the abstract. It was now a reality for Harold. A reality of which he was suddenly terrified. He knew he had not lived a perfect life. There were lots of things that he would regret. It was too late to change most of them, but he could change the will. Taking back all of the things he had told his family and friends to not do was impossible. But he could go back to being their greatest cheerleader. He could be honest with them. All he had to do was make it home alive.

"Herman, could I ask you a couple more questions?" Harold said in a quiet voice, knowing now what he had to do and why he had to do it.

"Of course."

"Were you the presence that I felt so often over the last few months?"

"No, it wasn't me," Herman responded.

"Was it another spirit?"

"Based on what has happened between us, I suppose that is possible, but unlikely. It could have been a feeling driven by something internal. You know, like your subconscious mind."

"Trying to tell me that I'm a fucking idiot," Harold butted in.

"Maybe." Herman laughed. "It could even be your own spirit, trying to communicate with you. As I told you, we still don't completely understand the evolution process. It is quite possible that what you were doing and who you really are were so disconnected that it felt like there was someone else entirely trying to influence you."

"When I think back to when I felt the presence, that makes a lot of sense," Harold said thoughtfully. "Do you think I will feel the presence again in the future?"

"If we are right about why it was there, I guess it would depend on your future actions," Herman responded.

"Do you think that when I get out of here, I should tell Mark's parents the truth?" Harold wondered out loud.

"Do you think that conversation would help Mark's parents or you?"

"Good point," Harold acknowledged.

"That is one of the tricky aspects of dealing with the mistakes we make. You want to atone for the mistakes, but you do not want to hurt others while you are doing it. As I said, the infinite universe was designed to be complex. Despite what people tell you, sometimes there simply is no completely right answer." Herman said.

Harold fell silent for a moment. He knew telling Mark's parents would probably take at least some of the guilt off his shoulders. But it was pretty clear it would be painful for them to hear, and it was just as clear that what he really wanted from confessing was their forgiveness. How could that possibly be fair to Mark's parents?

"I should leave you to get some rest. Is there anything else?" Herman said, interrupting Harold's thoughts.

Harold looked up as if someone had disturbed him from deep thought and said, "One other thing. Can you give me even the smallest hint about the right way to live a life? Does anyone live a life without regrets?"

"Harold, I am not aware of anyone living a perfect life, and I am not sure what a perfect life would look like. What I can tell you is that if you focus more on maximizing the joy and minimizing the pain that your actions create, you will have a lot better chance of enjoying the memories a million years from now. But remember sometimes there is no right answer, no matter what you do someone will get hurt."

"Seems like pretty good advice."

"But for now, I would focus on only one thing."

"Getting home," Harold remarked before Herman could complete the sentence. "Before you go, can you give me any update on Nancy and the kids? Are they doing okay? Do they still have hope?"

"Harold, you have an amazing family that loves you very much. They have not given up hope. The search and rescue team are doing the best that they can, but they are at the stage where they are trying to prepare your family for the worst."

"That they will not find me alive?"

"No, that they may never find you at all," the spirit responded in a quiet voice.

Tears again welled up in Harold's eyes as he contemplated how he would handle that news if it was about Nancy or one of his children. It would not just be the deep sorrow of never seeing them again. It would be the painful process of thinking through all the reasons no one ever found them. The horror of the last moments of a loved one's life, slowly freezing to death or being ripped apart alive by a hungry predator. And then dealing with the never-ending anguish of having the hope that somehow they had survived and that one day they would wander back into your life. *Not finding me would definitely be the worst.* Harold realized that no matter what, he could not let that happen.

"Harold, this may sound odd, given the circumstances, but as bad as this is, as much pain as you will experience tomorrow, this will not be the toughest or most painful experience you will have in a million lifetimes. Whatever you do tomorrow, do not leave yourself with the painful regret of knowing you could have done more."

There were no goodbyes, no human pleasantries. It was over, whatever or whomever the voice was that had been talking with Harold was gone, and Harold somehow knew that it was not coming back. He was on his own. Whatever was going to happen tomorrow would be entirely up to Harold.

CHAPTER FIFTY-SEVEN

When Harold opened his eyes, there was barely a glimmer of light, and he was cold. Too cold. Before he had fallen asleep, he had forgotten to put the hand warmers on. He decided he had better do that before he did anything else. Hypothermia was not something he could afford to be nonchalant about; there would be too many important decisions to make, and he had to be sharp.

The hand warmers helped immediately, so he began his preparation. The first thing that he did was to have something to eat and drink, not too much but enough to give him some energy. He then tested his wrist and ankle, still really sore but tolerable. When he climbed up his makeshift stairway to attach the ladder to the trees, he avoided putting any weight on his broken left ankle, which created much more inefficiency than he had expected, so securing the ladder took much longer. It was fortunate he had started so early.

To secure the ladder, Harold first tied the ladder around his neck, then stood on the top rung of his stairway with his right foot. Grabbing the largest of the branches that covered the hole, he inched his hands over to the opening. Once there, he untied the ladder and began tying it to the strongest branch he could find that was close enough to the opening to get him out. Tying the ladder with one hand was incredibly difficult, especially with the multiple knots Harold felt he needed to ensure the ladder would hold. A fall, once he was on the ladder, would be disastrous. He gave the ladder a hard tug; it held.

He climbed down the staircase to gather his meagre belongings and make his final preparations.

Harold was ready to go. He had no pack, no poles, only his snow-shoes to take with him. He had stuffed the remaining food into his pants pocket, his two full water bottles into the jacket that he was wearing, and his first-aid supplies into the pocket of the extra jacket, which had been in his backpack. He thought about pulling up the ladder once he got out and taking it apart so that he would have poles. It seemed like a waste of time, but then he reminded himself time would not be the issue. He needed as many tools as possible to give him the best chance of survival. Harold was also worried that if he could not find his way to the skis, he might have to come back and climb back into the hole for warmth and safety.

He reached into his pocket and pulled out the bottle of Aspirin. He had limited their use up to that point because of his concussion, but now pain control was essential. He put two tablets in his hand, added a third, and then finally added a fourth. As he swallowed them, he thought, *Fuck it. It won't be the pain or a heart attack that stops me.*

Using the second jacket, he strapped his snowshoes onto his back and made his way back up the stairway again, avoiding putting any weight on the left ankle. The first step onto the ladder was from kneeling on his left leg to his right foot on the lowest rung of the ladder. It went without a problem. But the next step required Harold to swing around to the other side of the ladder and he had no choice but to take the next step with his left foot.

"Holy Mother of God," Harold shouted as he put his weight onto his left leg and pushed himself up to the next rung of the ladder. To mitigate the pain while he waited for the Aspirin to kick in, he tried to use his arms as much as possible as he made his way up the last two rungs of the ladder. He took the next step and the next, his head was out of the hole for the first time in four days, and he hurt worse than he ever remembered hurting in his life. He took a deep breath and exhaled slowly, trying to release the pain at the same time.

As he pushed up on the final rung of the ladder, he grabbed for tree limbs to pull himself out of the hole. Another shot of pain streamed through his body as his ankle banged against the fallen trees as he dragged his body out of the hole and onto the snow. Lying there, he noticed the sun and the whiteness of the snow. After four days in the hole, it was almost blinding. He pulled his sunglasses from his coat pocket and put them on. They helped.

Harold decided he had to do something to make the ankle more stable. The idea of putting a tensor bandage on his ankle had been forgotten, and now Harold was afraid to take the boot off for any reason. He grabbed the tensor and the last of the tape out of the pocket of the spare coat and wrapped up his ankle on the outside of his boot as tight as he could. There would not be much movement, which Harold hoped would reduce the pain.

Sitting down to minimize the amount of extra strain he had to put on his ankle, he grabbed his snowshoes and put them on. It was a lot more difficult than he had expected, especially with the discomfort of the sprained wrist, but eventually, they were on and they were extra secure.

Harold decided that pulling the ladder out of the hole and reconstructing the poles was probably a good idea, but the last thing he wanted to do was fall back into the hole. So, he assumed the position of someone approaching a hole broken in the ice: lying flat on his belly and spreading his weight over the entire length and width of his body to ensure a weak spot in the trees covering the hole would not put him right back where he had come from.

Once he had untied the ladder from the tree and extracted it from the hole, reassembling the poles was easy. They had been designed to be disassembled and reassembled for easy storage. Harold realized that even holding the pole in the left hand would be painful, but he also knew that if he needed the left hand, it would instinctively react, regardless of the pain.

The next and most important step was to figure out what direction to go. A wrong first step could send him off in a direction he could never return from. He had to get it right from the start.

Come on, Harold. You have got to remember, he encouraged himself.

Even with all the new snow he recognized the fallen log he had stepped over, the one that had caused this entire problem. That was the first step back.

As Harold painfully placed himself at the beginning of his journey home, he looked at the forest ahead of him. Everything seemed the same at first, but the more he stared, the more he saw the differences. He recognized knots in the trees, small branches sticking out of the snow, dried-out leaves that had not yet fallen from the trees, and strands of moss that he remembered from his trip in. He even recognized slight indentations in the snow that were once his snow-shoe tracks. The more he looked, the more he remembered, and the clearer his path became.

Before following the path he could now see so clearly, Harold pulled out his cell phone and turned it on. He checked the time. It was important that he knew how long he walked in one direction. He turned the phone off.

It shocked Harold that he could be this confident he was walking in the right direction. He had always been impressed with the untapped power of the mind and its incredible ability to rise to the occasion in times of crises. It struck him that maybe it wasn't just his mind at work. Maybe his spirit was playing a role. His ankle continued to hurt, but it seemed to hurt a little less with each step. Harold was sure he was going to make it. He could see the path like it was a corridor in a building. There was no question in his mind.

Harold was making good time and was getting more and more comfortable that he would make it home, and then, as he walked slowly into a clearing, he saw something that caused his heart to leap. A smile creased his entire face, and for the first time in five days, he felt a true sense of unmitigated joy. This was the hill he had run down on his way in. He could still see the piles of snow he had created at the bottom of the hill when he had stopped, even though there was a significant blanket of new snow on them.

Harold was going home.

CHAPTER FIFTY-EIGHT

After a restless night for all of them, Nancy and the kids met in the hotel's lobby early, well before the sun rose and even before the hotel's restaurant opened. When the restaurant finally opened, they ate a quiet breakfast, having run out of things to say, and headed for the search staging site as soon as it was light.

The days were a little longer this time of year than they were in the dead of winter, but the sun still did not rise until around 8:30 a.m. and set by 5:00 p.m., which only allowed for about five hours of actual search time per day. Nancy wanted to see and be seen when the searchers left in the morning and when they gave up for the night.

She knew these were probably wonderful caring individuals that were fully committed to their job, and they probably wanted to do everything within reason to find Harold. But Nancy wanted to make it personal. She wanted them to see her and the kids, to make sure they saw and felt the anguish that the family was going through. It was probably completely unfair to the searchers, but she wanted to make a difference, even if that difference was only tiny.

The night before had been extremely tough on Nancy. Her phone had not stopped ringing. Everyone they knew had wanted an update. She knew everyone had simply been trying to be supportive, but every time she had to say, "They have not been able to find a trace of him yet," the emotions had welled up inside her, and she had wanted to throw her face in a pillow and cry herself to sleep. But she hadn't been able to because the phone had just kept ringing.

When the phone finally stopped, it was 10:00 p.m. and Nancy was now by herself, which was no better than being on the phone. She no longer wanted to cry herself to sleep. Now she was in the cycle of thinking through, in detail, all the worst possible outcomes. *What if we never find him? How do we explain stopping the search? What if our children want to continue searching? How do I tell them to give up? Jerry has been pretty quiet through this ordeal. What will he do if the search is called off? Will he insist on hiring a search team and extending the agony? Everyone says the chances of him still being alive even today are tiny. Will they get better tomorrow, next week?* And then she hated herself for even considering giving up.

Nancy thought of Harold freezing to death, being mauled by a bear, falling off a cliff, and lying at the bottom in pain, slowly losing hope that anyone would find him. The anger she had felt repeatedly toward Harold over this ordeal bubbled up again. She hated that she felt this way, but she could not help herself. *How stupid could he possibly be? If he wanted so badly to die, why hadn't he simply shot himself in the head and not put the family through such agony?*

Nancy then chastised herself; she knew Harold would never hurt his family on purpose, and if he was still alive, he would be doing everything he could to get back to them. Then her focus changed again in the whirlwind that was now her thought process, and she decided that if Harold was dead, she hoped that he had simply fallen asleep and had not woken up. The last thing that she wanted was to have Harold suffer, even for a moment. "If we can't have him back, please don't let him suffer," Nancy said out loud, not really knowing who she was expecting to grant such a wish.

Nancy slowly faded off into a restless sleep full of a tumbling nonsensical montage of dreams. In one moment, she and Harold were dancing at their wedding, then Harold was standing over her while she gave birth, but as the baby was placed in the nurse's arms, it turned into a bear that roared at them and Harold threw himself in front of her. The scene suddenly changed and her Maid of Honour Kate was telling her all the reasons she should not marry Harold. Nancy looked around and realized that she was standing in front of an altar. She was wearing a wedding gown, and the officiant was saying something that she could not understand. Harold was pulling at her veil, trying to get her attention, but Kate kept insisting that she could not marry Harold. Nancy was then standing at the top of a hill, looking down into the valley, where Harold was trying to run from four wolves who caught him and pulled him to the ground. Harold tried to push the wolves off and pull himself back to his feet. He made it halfway up and the wolves pulled him back down.

Nancy's eyes sprang open. She was lying in bed, shaking. She decided to not go back to sleep.

CHAPTER FIFTY-NINE

Harold had no intention of running down this slope this time. If the run down the hill didn't kill him, the climb back up would. But the knowledge that he was going in the right direction and that he had lots of time to get there did wonders for his energy level and his mood.

The euphoria that Harold felt might have been the reason that he picked up his pace, ever so slightly, and stopped focusing on each footstep as if it were his last. He was certain he knew exactly where to go from this ridge. His ankle hurt, but it was tolerable. Nothing was going to stop him.

He was deep in a daydream about what he was going to say to Nancy when his left foot stepped on the edge of a hidden rock and twisted his ankle. His immediate reaction was to collapse to save the ankle. Unfortunately, falling to the ground sent him tumbling down the hill, arms and legs flailing in every direction. As he fell, his mind pictured his broken ankle being completely twisted around to the point where his foot was pointing in the complete opposite direction.

When he came to rest near the bottom, his first instinct was to check the ankle. The foot was pointing in the right direction, but the pain had increased dramatically. Looking up the hill, it appeared significantly steeper than it had when he had climbed it the first time. He then made a decision that seemed reasonable at the time, and had things gone differently, would probably have been a good decision. He decided to crawl up the hill on all fours rather than add additional stress to his ankle. The decision he had actually made was that if he had to, he would crawl all the way back to the highway, no matter how long it took. He would test the ankle at the top of the ridge, but if he could not walk, he would crawl.

Climbing back up the hill was not technically difficult, especially on his hands and knees. It was just hard work, made harder by the snowshoes on his feet, and extremely slow. There was an added strain on his sprained wrist, but the cold and Harold's determination muffled the pain to the point he no longer noticed it.

The crawl back up the hill took much longer than he had anticipated. His hands and knees had very little grip, so he continually had his knees slip out from under him. Recovering into the crawling position was difficult and time-consuming, as it often took two or three tries to get in the right position. By the time Harold reached the top of the hill, he was soaking wet and exhausted. The ankle was throbbing with pain, and so far he had not even tried to stand up.

The fall had consumed too much time. He could not sit around wondering how the ankle was going to feel. He had to start walking, no matter how much it hurt. Standing up was painful, but the real pain came when he tried to take a step on his left foot. It was excruciating. Harold screamed in agony, but he took the next step and then the next. If he completely destroyed his ankle and never walked on it again, he didn't care as long as it got him home. In more pain than he could remember being in his entire life, he continued to walk. Given the pace at which he was moving, he was starting to worry about daylight. No daylight meant no searchers, which meant that he would have to find his way all the way back to his car on his own. He picked up his pace. It no longer mattered if he was walking or standing still—the pain in his ankle was constant and overwhelming.

But there were no other options available to Harold. He could not go back, and he could not stop there. He had to move forward no matter how much it hurt, no matter how much sun he had left. The only option was to find the strength to get to his car.

The path after the hill was as clear to Harold as it had been before the hill. He knew where he was going, and finding the hill had confirmed that it was not simply wishful thinking. He knew he could make it home to Nancy and the kids if he could just keep moving.

GREG ROYER

Everything depended on him doing no more than continuing to move forward, one step at a time.

Trying to put the pain and limited hours of sunlight out of his mind, Harold chanted quietly, *One more step, one more step. You can do this. One more step.* He might have heard it if he had not been so focused on putting one foot in front of the other. But it was doubtful that having heard it would have made any difference, and it was not like it was making a lot of noise.

He had been walking for about twenty minutes, repeating his chant, which helped him block out the pain and build the flow of adrenalin. He was starting to make some real progress. His pace was getting a little faster, his confidence a little stronger, when suddenly he noticed the smallest of movements to his right and turned his head and shoulders to see what it was.

The cat was in mid-air when Harold's right arm shot out and pushed the cat and himself just enough to avoid a direct hit. The force of the contact with the cat and the twisting of Harold's body were still enough to drive him to the ground. He rolled over as quickly as he could, barely in time to see the cougar leap at him again.

CHAPTER SIXTY

Nancy, Jerry, Megan, and Jessie had only been at the search site for a few minutes when Jack Holloway came over to talk with them. He wanted to make sure that the family knew exactly what was going to happen that day and what was in the forecast for that night.

This would be the hardest day for everyone, including Jack Holloway and his search and rescue team. They all knew this was it. There was little chance of them finding him alive today, and there would definitely be no chance tomorrow. Along with the cold front, that included temperatures as cold or colder than −40 degrees Celsius there would be high winds and more snow. Shelter or no shelter, there was no way anyone would survive in those conditions, especially after already being lost for five days.

Throughout the day, there was ongoing radio chatter, but all of it was negative, not in the tone but in the substance. It was all about where they looked and what they found, which was nothing. Not a track, not a trace, not a piece of clothing, not even a piece of cloth. Nothing that would even give them hope.

Nancy tried desperately to keep it together, to maintain faith, but with each passing hour, it was more and more difficult. More than once, she had to bury her face in her warm winter gloves to stop herself from crying. As she stared out into the forest that had swallowed her husband, she thought back to that night on the frozen lake, Harold on one knee, with a ring in his hand, trying as he always did to be the person who he so desperately wanted to be. The person he wanted to be for her, for both of them, for their kids.

Harold, Nancy said in her thoughts, *you were that man. For thirty-six wonderful years, you were that man. And no matter what happens today, that is what I will always remember.*

Saying that, even only to herself, somehow made it easier. No matter what, Harold and Nancy had thirty-six wonderful years and two beautiful children. Nancy would not allow anything to destroy that.

CHAPTER SIXTY-ONE

Harold instinctively threw his hands and arms in front of his face to stop the cougar from getting to his throat. Without even thinking, he knew that if the cougar got his teeth into his throat, it would all be over before he could do anything.

Luckily, on the cougar's first bite, it got a mouthful of the aluminum pole that was attached to the arm Harold had thrown in front of his face in a desperate effort to keep the cougar away from his neck. The cougar's second attempt got a piece of Harold's arm but only penetrated the Kevlar-covered sleeve of his jacket, and then, with one flick of the cougar's powerful neck, the material from the jacket was almost completely shredded.

Harold knew he could not beat the cougar. His only chance was to make it uncomfortable enough for the cougar that it would decide there were easier meals out there, which in the dead of winter might be a problem.

The cougar's third attack again found the aluminum pole, and this time Harold rammed the pole as hard as he could into the back of the cougar's mouth. The cougar squealed like a child, then bit down on the pole and tried with its mighty neck and jaws to tear it out of Harold's hands. Harold held on for dear life. The cougar pulled his head up and let go of the pole.

Waiting only seconds, the cougar attacked again, throwing his massive head at Harold's throat. He again threw up his arms in defence. This time the cougar's teeth sunk into Harold's bad arm. He felt the cougar's teeth puncture the skin, and he was sure he heard the bone break but oddly felt no pain.

As the warm blood from his arm dripped on his face, Harold reached with his good hand for anything that could help him. He felt what appeared to be a very pointed stick about three inches thick and about eighteen inches long. He grabbed it by what he was certain was the right end, and with all of his remaining strength, drove what he hoped was the very sharp end into the soft underbelly of the cougar, not stopping until he could feel the weight of the massive cat being removed from his body.

The elongated sound that came from the cougar as it leaped away from Harold was both frightening and shocking. It sounded like the high-pitched squeal of an incredibly unhappy baby. Harold did not know if the sound meant that he had injured the cougar and that it would wander away, looking for a more compliant lunch, or if he had simply pissed it off and the cougar would come back for more.

Harold sat up as quickly as he could, grabbed his ski pole, and repositioned it in his good hand. He pointed it at the cougar, who looked pissed, ears pinned back, baring its teeth, hissing and ready to rip Harold to shreds. His only defence was the pole, so he kept it between him and the cougar, switching positions as the cougar methodically circled him, looking for an attack point that did not include running through the sharp end of the pole.

It was a Mexican stand-off, and Harold knew the cougar would eventually win. It was only then that Harold was able to take a closer look at the cougar. It was smaller than he expected a cougar to be. He was certain that this was not a fully grown adult cougar, which was great if it was simply the runt of the litter, but really bad if Mom was somewhere nearby. The last thing Harold wanted to do was provoke another attack. Everything he did, every movement he made, was slow and deliberate, never taking his eyes off the cougar for even a moment. If Mom was nearby, Harold would not stand a chance anyway, so there was no point looking for her. This pint-sized cougar that had the strength to rip Harold in half had 100 percent of his attention.

After standing almost like statues, staring at each other for what seemed like forever, Harold realized darkness would definitely be in the cougar's favour, and his bleeding arm would make it impossible for him to outlast the cougar. His only option was to create a reason for the cougar to leave.

Standing up slowly without losing his defensive position with the cougar was difficult, especially when he had one working arm and one working leg, but Harold was experiencing so much adrenalin that pain was no longer a significant issue. Then he decided to try something that he knew could be suicidal, but doing nothing was almost assuredly suicidal.

"Run away you fucking piece of shit," Harold screamed as he poked the pole at the cougar. "I will rip your fucking heart right out of your chest, you four legged piece of garbage!"

The cougar swung its incredibly powerful paw at the pole, trying to knock it away so it would have an unobstructed path to its prey. Harold knew he needed to get at least one more good jab into the cougar, and it had to be somewhere soft or it would not hurt. But to get that jab in, he had to get closer. And the closer they were, the more advantage the cougar had.

As the cougar turned to get a better angle on his prey, Harold saw an opening and drove the pole again into the large cat's soft underbelly. The cougar leaped back and let out another loud squeal, but this time, when it landed, it immediately loped into the forest, not even looking back at Harold.

Giving himself only a moment to ensure the departure of the big cat, Harold then quickly turned back to the task of finding his skis and getting back to the car. Having been spun around trying to defend himself against the cougar, he was no longer as certain as he had been of where he was or where he was going. Knowing the cougar was there and could attack again at any moment made focusing difficult, but Harold had no choice. Time was running out for him. He had to keep moving and he couldn't make any more mistakes. He knew that wandering about in a forest in winter, not knowing where he was going, was not as frightening as encountering a cougar, but it was every bit as dangerous.

He was confident he had been headed in the right direction before the attack, so he looked carefully at the trees in front of him. Was there anything that looked familiar? Slowly it came back to him, the distance between the trees, the areas where there were no low-hanging branches, the ever so slight disturbance of the snow. The path again became obvious.

Harold looked down at his shredded left arm. It was bleeding, but not as bad as it would have been if the cougar had torn open one of the major veins. He was incredibly lucky. Harold did not have time or the medical supplies to wrap up the arm, so he packed it with snow and hoped that would stop or at least slow down the bleeding.

CHAPTER SIXTY-TWO

It was not an easy walk. The snow was deep, and Harold was creating a path, never knowing for sure what he was stepping down on. At this point, pain was no longer a factor. Harold felt nothing. He didn't even feel the cold. He pulled out his phone to see how long he had been walking. It had been over five hours, which struck him as impossible. He had taken five hours to cover less ground than he had covered in just over forty minutes on the way in. Even if there were no more falls or cougar encounters, at this pace, he would not even be close to his car when darkness fell. He had to find a way to move faster. He needed to see his skis soon if he was going to have a chance.

Refocusing his attention, seeing his path, Harold pushed harder. With each passing minute, he became more and more distracted. Between constantly looking around, trying to find his skis that were attached to a tree, and watching for the cougar, he began to doubt himself. Had he really seen the path, or was it nothing more than wishful thinking? Stopping, he looked around. Everything looked the same. He could be anywhere in the forest. His skis could be twenty feet or two miles from where he stood. Harold began to wish that he had never left the security of the hole. At least he would be safe, but for how long? For the first time since he had fallen through the trees, Harold could feel himself shivering. He had to calm down before he made any more decisions. He was not thinking rationally.

He took some deep calming breaths and looked again at his phone; only a few minutes had passed since he had last looked. He knew he had to focus to have any chance at all. If the cougar attacked

259

again, he knew he could not fight it off. The hole was no longer a possibility, so he decided to stop thinking of either the hole or the cougar and focus all of his attention on getting back to his car. At this point, nothing else mattered except taking another step.

He looked in the direction that he was certain he needed to go, and again, the path became clear. He started his chant, *one more step, one more step.*

Moments later, Harold felt a rush of adrenalin, as he was certain that he could see the path that he had skied in on. It was only thirty or forty feet ahead. His skis had to be close. The closer he got to the path, the more certain he was. And as he stepped into the opening, it was like stepping into his own backyard. This was his ski path, this was the route back to the road, and he only had to find his skis, which would confirm the right direction by how he had attached them to the tree.

His eyes searched the forest; carefully looking for the prize he was certain was here. It only took a moment. There they were. The skis that he had owned for twenty years had never looked as beautiful to him as they did at that moment. Harold was certain he heard the "Hallelujah Chorus" being sung in his head as he walked over to retrieve his skis from the tree.

Taking the skis down from the tree, Harold thought about his ankle and his arm. Skiing would be faster, but it was going to be far more difficult and much more painful than snowshoeing with his particular injuries. Pushing off with just one arm was not an option. He would have to use both arms no matter how much it hurt. The arm of his jacket was now covered with blood. The bare skin was visible where the cougar had torn away the jacket's fabric. The pain in the arm was no longer separate from all the other pain. Harold, hesitating for only a moment, lifted the skis, one in each hand, and threw them onto the snow, mumbling, "Fuck the pain, fuck the cougar, and fuck the fucking hole. I'm going home."

Switching from his snowshoes to his skis took a few minutes, but Harold was certain he would make the time up quickly. Once he started moving, it became immediately clear that his left leg was almost useless in the skiing motion, so he decided to depend almost entirely on pulling himself along with his arms and upper body. He no longer needed to concentrate on his path. He knew exactly where he was headed, so he focused on covering as much ground as possible with each pull. Going downhill was easy, but he depended entirely on his right leg to control his speed, leaving more weight on his left leg. Pulling himself uphill was exhausting, and too often, his inability to get himself in the right position to plant his poles and make the next pull left him sliding backward, forcing him to cover the same ground he had just covered.

With each setback, Harold's anxiety grew, but he was not stopping. No matter what, he was determined he would die of exhaustion before he would give up.

CHAPTER SIXTY-THREE

As the first of the search and rescue crew came out of the forest and back to the staging area, Jerry looked down at his watch and then signalled to Jessie with a nod of his head that Jessie should look at his. It was 4:00 p.m. and still no sign of Harold, no signals from the searchers. The wind had shifted about an hour ago and was now coming directly from the north. The temperature had dropped ten degrees in the last hour and would drop another ten degrees in the next hour.

There were still twenty to twenty-five search and rescue team members in the forest, but they would all be moving back toward the staging area. No one would be covering new ground.

Jessie pushed up against his uncle Jerry, standing close so that no one could hear. His eyes were moist, and his voice was filled with emotion. "There has to be more that they can do. We can't give up. I know he's alive. I can feel his presence."

Jerry put his arm around Jessie's shoulders and pulled him close.

"It's not over yet," he said, but even he no longer believed it.

Jack put his radio in its holster. There would be no more calls. Everyone was heading in. He looked over at Nancy and decided that this never got any easier. He started to walk toward them.

"Nancy," Jack said, making a point of using first names, "the searchers are all heading in. We've not been able to find any trace of Harold, and there is really nothing else we can do at this point. I need to wrap things up here, then I can meet with you and your family back at the RCMP detachment to discuss where we go from here."

Jack and Nancy both knew there was no place to go from there that either cared about, and that the conversation would be about why further efforts would be pointless. Once they had agreed on the futility of further effort, they would go on to when and how to declare someone dead when they had no body and no assurance that they, in fact, were dead.

CHAPTER SIXTY-FOUR

It had taken a while, maybe an hour and a half of slow and unsteady progress. Harold's strength was diminishing quickly. He was finding it more and more difficult to think coherently, and it was getting late. He started to feel lightheaded, like he had spun himself around in a circle for too long. His legs buckled, and he fell. Lying on the snow, lacking the strength to even lift his head, he began to softly sob. He had no more to give. He was exhausted. He wanted to stop. He wanted to sleep. Nancy would understand. She would know that he had tried.

Lying with his face in the snow, no longer feeling the cold, Herman's words suddenly rang in his head: *Don't stop feeling that you could have done more*. They repeated over and over.

Slowly, Harold lifted his head. He was not going to cause more pain because he hadn't given everything that he possibly could. He knew he could do more. *Get up!* his mind roared. *Just get the fuck up*.

He pushed himself up, first to his hands and knees and then slowly, painfully, back to his feet. Reaching out, he planted his poles, and with a roar that never really left his mouth, he pulled. Again he planted and pulled again and again, no longer even aware of where he was going other than forward. He stumbled again and again, but each time he fell, he heard Herman's words and his mind screamed at him to get back up, so he planted his poles, and he pulled.

As he slowly struggled to his feet after yet another fall, now almost completely blind to his surroundings, consumed by his exhaustion and his pain, his eyes caught a flicker of movement directly ahead of him. He looked again but saw nothing. He planted his poles and pulled. As he pulled forward, he looked again, but nothing. He planted and pulled and this time, as he lifted his head to look into the distance, he saw the movement again. At first, it was only specks of movement. Then he saw colours, bright colours.

He planted and pulled. He had to get closer. They had to see him. He tried to scream, but nothing came out. *Please turn around*, he begged. He planted and pulled. He stumbled again. He dragged himself up, planted and pulled. When he looked up again, he saw forms, human forms. He did not know who they were, but it made no difference. He screamed with all his might and fell to his knees. "Please turn around," he pleaded in a voice that no one could possibly hear.

Suddenly, the forms were running toward him. He could hear them shouting. They were calling his name. But Harold could not respond. He fell again and tried desperately to stand up, but he had no more strength. He was done. This had to be the end.

Harold had no idea who these people were, but he knew that it didn't matter. Whoever they were, they would make sure that he was safe, and they would take him back to Nancy and his children.

Harold allowed himself to collapse completely into the soft snow. The last thing he felt was a soft touch on his shoulder. Then everything went black.

As Nancy began to slowly turn away, completely broken and without hope, Jack's radio lit up with sound.

"Jack, I think I see someone," said one voice.

"Jack, I saw something falling in the snow about a hundred yards behind me. I'm going to take a look," said another.

Grabbing his radio, Jack quickly responded, "Are you sure it's not just an animal?"

"If it is," came the reply, "it's wearing a bright orange ski jacket."

Nancy screamed and started jumping up and down, finally wrapping her arms around Megan, who was not yet certain what was going on. "That beautiful, ugly orange jacket!" Nancy shouted.

"Just wait, just wait," Jack said calmly, not wanting himself or Nancy or anyone to get ahead of themselves. He waited anxiously for the next voice. It took a couple of minutes, which seemed to last forever, but finally, a voice came over the radio.

"It's him, Jack. It's Harold. He's okay, but we need a stretcher ASAP."

Instantly, everyone was jumping up and down and shouting. People were running to the ambulance, people were hugging, and people were smiling for the first time in days.

CHAPTER SIXTY-FIVE

Slowly, Harold recognized the activity surrounding him. The faces and bodies were distorted and impossible for Harold to focus on. It was like looking at people through a tube. People popped in and out of his field of vision so quickly he could not identify anyone. The cavalcade of voices, all talking at once, some shouting, some crying, some whispering things directly to him that he could not understand. He thought he saw Nancy for a second, but before he was certain, she was gone.

Harold felt himself being rolled over, first onto his face and then almost immediately onto his back. He could feel the hard round pole of the stretcher on his back, as they shifted him into position. Straps were tightened around his chest and hips, then suddenly, he was being lifted into the air. He could see bodies surrounding him, but he did not know who lifted him. He could feel the rough, bumpy motion, but he did not know where they were taking him.

The speed at which everything was happening frightened Harold, and his inability to recognize anyone or understand what they were saying scared him more.

Suddenly panic set in. *Where is Nancy? Where are they taking me? Who are these people? What are they doing with me?*

"Nancy! Nancy! Where is Nancy?" Harold was certain he had shouted these words, but no one reacted. Only being able to move his arms below his elbows, he desperately reached out and grabbed for the arms of the people carrying him, but their powerful hands pushed his hands away. In a fit of terror, he thrashed his arms and legs as much as possible, but the straps dramatically limited his mobility. Twisting his torso, he tried to dislodge himself from whatever he was being carried in, but the strong straps across his chest and his thighs made it impossible to escape. He shouted again, but again no one seemed to notice. They continued his bumpy ride toward an unknown destination. Harold continued to twist and thrash. Suddenly, the movement stopped.

"I think he's trying to say something," Harold heard an unidentified voice say.

This made Harold thrash harder. Something was wrong. Where was Nancy? He had to find her. She had to know that he was alright.

As he strained to free himself he felt a warm hand on his face and a calm voice saying his name over and over. Nancy's face came into view, she was crying. Reaching up he touched her face and wiped away a tear with his thumb. He tried desperately over and over to say "I love you," but nothing came out.

"Harold," Nancy said in a warm, loving voice. "We need to get you to a hospital. You're in pretty bad shape. I'll be with you every step of the way, so please lie still and let us take care of you."

A calmness overcame him, and reality slipped away.

CHAPTER SIXTY-SIX

A week had passed since members of the search and rescue team had found him on the path. They had been complete strangers to Harold, but just as he had expected, they had taken care of him, not leaving his side until he had been safely in the ambulance and on the way to the hospital.

Nancy rode with Harold in the ambulance, and Jerry, Jessie, and Megan followed the ambulance to the hospital in Jerry's SUV. One of them was at his bedside twenty-four hours a day as he slipped in and out of consciousness. The doctors said that he was in stable condition and that his inability to stay awake for more that a moment or two was only a response to total exhaustion. The cuts and scratches from his encounter with the cougar were much more than superficial, but they were not life-threatening. His survival and recovery were not in question. It was simply a matter of time.

When Harold finally regained a more normal level of consciousness, the joy of being with his family overwhelmed him. Not normally one for tears, he could not seem to stop them while he was hugging his family and telling them all how much he loved them.

The doctors and the hospital staff were terrific before and after the four-hour operation to repair his broken bones. The doctor told him he had a trimalleolar fracture in his ankle, and said it was a miracle he could stand on it, let alone walk out of the forest on it. The arm was a simple stable fracture. However, because the cougar had broken the skin, they wanted to wait until he was leaving the hospital before they put a cast on it to ensure there was no infection.

"And what about the heart attack?" Harold asked and then told them about what he had experienced when he had first fallen into his hole.

The doctor ran both an electrocardiogram and an MRI and told Harold there was no evidence of any damage to his heart. Routine blood work confirmed Dr. Wang's diagnosis of much higher-than-normal levels of cholesterol, and the doctors agreed with Dr. Wang's concerns about a potential problem, however, right now there was not only no damage to the heart, it looked very healthy. What he had experienced, the doctor told him, had more likely been an anxiety attack.

Surgery on the ankle had gone well. They had put in a couple of pins to hold the bones together, and they would have to be removed when everything healed.

The doctors and the nurses told Harold and Nancy the recovery and rehabilitation were going to be painful and lengthy. However, after what he had been through, Harold didn't think that rehabilitation with his family around him in the comfort of his own home sounded like something that he would find difficult to handle, and he was pretty sure pain would not be a problem.

As soon as the doctors left, Harold asked for his cell phone. Nancy was reluctant to give it to him, assuring him that whatever it was, it could wait, but he said that it couldn't. He smiled at Nancy, reached out, took her hand in his, and said, "Trust me, this is something that I need to take care of right away."

The phone only rang once. "Harold? Please tell me this is Harold," Shane said, recognizing the number.

"Yes, this is Harold."

"What the fuck? Were you trying to kill yourself? You scared the shit out of all of us." There was a clear tone of love in the words that Shane said. Harold heard them clearly.

"I've made a lot of mistakes in the last few weeks, and I need your help to correct some of them. I need to retract my last will and reinstate the old one. Could you make the appropriate arrangements for me as quickly as possible?"

"Harold, I can be there in thirty minutes with the documentation. Will that work for you?" Shane asked.

"Thanks, Shane. That would be perfect." Harold laughed as he got off the phone. He assumed Shane hated that will so much that he probably had drawn up the retraction document before Harold had even signed the will.

As Harold ended the call, Jerry, Jessie, and Megan joined Nancy at the end of his bed.

"Okay, we're all here. What is so urgent that it can't wait until you get home to talk about?" Jerry asked with a smile, thrilled that his big brother was safe but wondering why he had made such a fuss about them all having to be there together as soon as possible.

"Well, first, I want to tell you all that I love you and that you mean everything to me," Harold began.

"Yeah, yeah, you love us, and we love you. Now, what is so important?" Jerry's eyes began to tear up as he spoke.

Harold reached out and took Nancy's hand. "I also wanted to apologize for my recent behaviour."

"As you should. You have been absolutely horrible to all of us," Jerry said, feigning hurt.

"Uncle Jerry," Megan said, making it clear that it was time for Jerry to stop.

"You're right, Jerry. And while there are reasons for my behaviour, there are no excuses. Megan, I'm completely unqualified to advise you on your career or the value of the opportunity you are considering. What I am qualified to tell you is that your mom and I will always be there for you, no matter what you choose to do in your life.

"Jessie, you and Phillip having another child sounds like a wonderful idea. Your mom and I love having grandchildren. The more the merrier. If we can help facilitate you having additional children, I think I can speak for your mom when I say we'd be happy to do whatever we can."

Nancy smiled, nodded, and squeezed Harold's hand. At this point, everyone was dealing with their own tears, tissues were popping up everywhere, and the family had all huddled together on one side of Harold's bed.

"And Jerry, please move ahead with the growth plan for the foundation. Nancy and I have discussed it, and we are both very excited to be a part of the plan."

"You got it. Thanks, Nancy. I'm sure you had to browbeat Harold into agreeing," Jerry said. Turning to Harold and smiling, he continued, "Just giving you a bad time, big brother. I know you want this as much as the rest of us."

"I do, Jerry, but it is your passion and commitment that are going to make it happen, and I really appreciate it. All of it. It is wonderful having a brother who cares so much. I could learn a lot from you. Oh, and by the way, Ramesh and Alison have some great ideas about how to create some substantial growth at Bannister, so we may be able to contribute even more to the foundation in a few years. If that's okay with Nancy."

"That sounds great and you're right. You could learn a lot from me. Like being a good guy and finding some time to take your mom to church?" Jerry said, mostly joking.

Harold was silent for a moment. He had thought a lot about this issue while lying in his hole. Jerry deserved more than a flat refusal, and it was time to tell all of them the truth about what had really happened all those years ago. They loved him and he had to trust that the unforgivable mistake of a child would not change that.

"No, Jerry. I still won't take Mom to church. But if you all want to take a seat and get comfortable, I will explain why, and I will tell you about what has been going on with me for the last month or so."

Jerry and Jessie grabbed chairs for everyone, and they sat down to listen to the story of their husband, father, and brother's life. Harold told them about Mark, the horrible things that he had experienced, and how it destroyed Mark's life. He told them about the horrid mistakes he had made as a fourteen-year-old, not telling someone what he had seen Father Brown do to another young boy before the priest had molested his friend. He also explained how and why he had convinced his friend to not tell anyone about the priest molesting him. He admitted he had made both decisions because he had been afraid, and once he had made the decision, he felt that if people knew, this horrible mistake would define him.

He talked about how Mark's suicide had rekindled all the guilt. He described the nightmares as best as he could. He shared the information of his father's untimely death from a heart attack, and they all jokingly agreed that if this recent ordeal had not killed Harold, his heart was probably okay, at least for a few more decades.

The family was great. They said that he was only a child, and that children make mistakes. Jerry said that now they had a real problem because it would be really tough for him to go to the damn church anymore either, and that Mom was really going to be pissed. Harold and Jerry had a good laugh and agreed there was no point in telling their mom about this.

Then he gave them all the information about his condition, his cholesterol levels, why he couldn't take a statin, and what he did and could do to control his cholesterol. He promised he would get them all more information about what a widowmaker was and exactly what they should do if he ever had a heart attack. He did not want them to experience the helpless feeling he and Jerry had felt when their father had died.

Finally, Harold told them about the will. He did not cover every detail but gave them the biggest, most disturbing points. They were shocked, mostly because it was so out of character, and they asked Harold why he would create such a document.

"I'm not sure that I can fully explain. Part of it was fear of my own mortality, I guess. Part of it was my guilt about not taking action to protect Mark. I had convinced myself that I was doing the right thing. I even used the situation my dad left behind to justify it. Being in control seemed to suddenly become more important than everything. I never allowed it to cross my mind that I might be wrong."

Harold fell quiet for a moment. No one spoke, no one even looked at each other.

"When my dad died, the only thing that people talked about were the lies. Every good thing he had ever done was forgotten because he left behind a trail of misery. The dad I thought I knew was destroyed. Laying in that hole, day after day, I came to realize that I was about to do the same thing to my family. Not with the money, but with the trust in who their father, their husband, and their brother was. I was so intent on being in control, I completely lost track of what was right. I tried to use a legal document to ensure that I could always keep you safe, even if you didn't want to be. I thought being safe was the most important thing I could give you. It took a while, but finally, I came to realize that if I really loved you, I would not only let you take risks, I would encourage you to take those risks. In that hole, I realized that life is meant to be experienced, I mean truly experienced. Every life is an adventure and we should treat it like one."

"Life is just a big merry-go-round, and we should enjoy the ride," Jerry teased.

Harold laughed and responded, "Something like that. Now, if the three of you could leave us for a few minutes, I would like to have a few words with my wife."

When the others had left, Harold turned to Nancy and said, "I'm sorry, I'm so terribly sorry for having put you and the children through all of this."

Nancy leaned over and hugged her husband. "I know you are, and I'm sorry I wasn't there to listen to what you were going through."

"You were there. I just didn't talk."

"No, I mean really there, willing to accept that my big, strong husband may need some help. Willing to accept that, like you, I was too afraid to even consider that we don't have all the answers."

Harold reached out and took Nancy's hand. "Are we okay?"

Nancy squeezed Harold's hand. "We're better than okay."

CHAPTER SIXTY-SEVEN

One Year Later

The banner read "Grand Opening." They were all there to celebrate the opening of the new Margaret Mary Bower Foundation centre for career development. It was located right in the middle of the toughest part of the city, yet Jerry had convinced the city's biggest movers and shakers from business, politics, and charitable organizations to commit to supporting the centre. Jerry had made it clear that cheques alone would not cut it. They had to provide face time. They had to provide these children from underserved and often forgotten communities with the opportunity to build networks like the ones all of their children took for granted.

Megan and Edwin were busy making the rounds with their nephew Brennen and their daughter Layla, who, for a couple of toddlers, were uncommonly good ambassadors for the charity. Megan was starting a new job on Monday. The prototype had not worked despite their best efforts, but Megan had loved the experience and had been very clear that she did not intend this effort to be her last.

Jessie and Phillip were trying to calm their six-month-old twins. A girl, Nadiya, and a boy, Oleksiy. They had adopted them from the Ukraine when they had heard the twins had lost both their mother and father in the war with Russia. The adoption agency said it would be all right if Phillip and Jessie wanted to change the children's names, but both of them felt their names were their names and it should stay that way.

Ramesh, Alison, and the entire Bannister leadership team and their families were in attendance. As Harold and Nancy had supported their dreams and aspirations, the leadership team wanted to support Harold and Nancy's dreams. They were all great contributors of time and money to the work of the Margaret Mary Bower Foundation.

Nancy and Harold stood in the corner, watching the activity. They had spent a lot of time talking about just about everything over the last year. Nancy had talked with both Jeff and Shane; Harold had told them to tell her everything. Nancy had talked with Harold about why, in her mind, not allowing herself to get attached to her clients was so important. She had even admitted that she was afraid she couldn't handle it if she did get attached.

Harold continued to live a healthy life and have regular checkups, and the doctors continued to tell him he and his heart were in great shape. He did his best to stop worrying about it, but when he did, he talked with Nancy. They acknowledged that life was a bit of a crapshoot for everyone, and agreed to enjoy the time that they had no matter what. Nancy encouraged him to take advantage of his brother's offers, so Harold went on a ski trip and a golf trip with Jerry and really quite enjoyed himself.

He never heard from Herman again. As time went on, he was less and less certain that Herman had ever existed. Harold eventually told Nancy about Herman and repeated as much as he could remember about what Herman had told him. They never discussed whether Herman was real. It didn't seem to matter.

Harold never told anyone else about the voice that he heard in the hole, and never brought up the topic of what happened after death. If the subject was being discussed in his presence, he would be very clear about what he hoped would happen and what he hoped was really out there. Nancy asked him a few times if he truly believed what he heard from his friend Herman, and his consistent response was that he believed he didn't know, and he believed no other living creature really knew.

Maybe the infinite world of spirits really did exist, and maybe all of our spirits would live there someday. Or maybe it was just Harold trying to retain his sanity in an insane situation.

Whatever it was, it changed Harold's view of life and brought him home to his family, two things for which he would be eternally thankful. Although the thought of being eternally thankful now meant something very different to Harold.

The End

ACKNOWLEDGEMENTS

Thank you first and foremost to my wife and partner of over forty years, Cindy. Without her constant support and understanding, neither this book nor most of my other adventures in life would have occurred. To our four wonderful children—Chad, Bennett, Rhys, and Delaney—thank you for being our first, most important, and most successful adventure. Your encouragement and feedback on the book, especially in the final stages, made it better and much more fun.

A big thank you to my daughters-in-law, Kate Royer and Cathryn Royer, who have contributed so much joy to our family and have been so gracious about accepting us into their lives. And, of course, a special tribute to our four amazing grandchildren, Thomas, Willow, Sullivan, and Lilia, who are all just starting their journey.

A special thanks to my good friend, Dale Ens, who read a very early edition of the book. His ability to offer constructive criticism, which significantly improved the story, while congratulating me for what I had already accomplished, made that next major rewrite so much easier.

I owe a debt of gratitude to my friends Theresa Roessel, Adrian Hamfelt, and Susan Gilliland who waded through a mass of typos, grammatical errors, and poor spelling to provide me with incredibly helpful feedback on the underlying story.

To my two brothers Terry and Randy Royer and my sister-in-law Jane Royer, thank you so much for your feedback and encouragement.

Thank you to my wife, Cindy, and my good friend, Candace Dyer, who helped me with the time-consuming task of checking the proofreading, in an effort to eliminate every single error from the final book.

To my editor, Amelia Gilliland, who thankfully was the only person who read the very first draft of this book. Your encouragement and our amazing conversations kept this journey alive. Thank you so much for seeing past the many mistakes of a first-time writer.

Finally, a big thank you to the team at Friesen Press, especially Kayla Lang, James Stewart and Lorna Williamson who patiently walked me through the publishing and promotions process step by step.

Printed in Canada